"Give them...to me..."

ALUS THE STAR RUNNER

A wyvern champion who simultaneously wields legendary weapons and items he collected with his own strength.

WIELDER OF THREE-THOUSAND TREASURES

MACHINE CRAFTING AUTOMATON

REALM PIERCER

e mantle of True Hero.

INDESTRUCTIBLE

BEWITCHING INFECTION

VI

Glory Usurper

Keiso

ILLUSTRATION BY
Kureta

YEN
ON
New York

Keiso

ILLUSTRATION BY
Kureta

Translation by David Musto

This book is a work of fiction. Names, characters, places, and incidents are the product of the author's imagination or are used fictitiously. Any resemblance to actual events, locales, or persons, living or dead, is coincidental.

ISHURA Vol. 6 EIKOSANDATSUSHA
©Keiso 2022
First published in Japan in 2022 by KADOKAWA CORPORATION, Tokyo.
English translation rights arranged with KADOKAWA CORPORATION, Tokyo, through TUTTLE-MORI AGENCY, INC., Tokyo.

English translation © 2024 by Yen Press, LLC

Yen On
150 West 30th Street, 19th Floor
New York, NY 10001

Visit us at yenpress.com
facebook.com/yenpress
twitter.com/yenpress
yenpress.tumblr.com
instagram.com/yenpress

First Yen On Edition: March 2024
Edited by Yen On Editorial: Payton Campbell
Designed by Yen Press Design: Andy Swist

Yen On is an imprint of Yen Press, LLC.
The Yen On name and logo are trademarks of Yen Press, LLC.

The publisher is not responsible for websites (or their content) that are not owned by the publisher.

Library of Congress Cataloging-in-Publication Data
Names: Keiso (Manga author), author. | Kureta, illustrator. | Musto, David, translator.
Title: Ishura / Keiso ; illustration by Kureta ; translation by David Musto.
Other titles: Ishura. English
Description: First Yen On edition. | New York : Yen On, 2022.
Identifiers: LCCN 2021062849 | ISBN 9781975337865
    (v. 1 ; trade paperback) | ISBN 9781975337889
    (v. 2 ; trade paperback) | ISBN 9781975337902
    (v. 3 ; trade paperback) | ISBN 9781975337926
    (v. 4 ; trade paperback) | ISBN 9781975363079
    (v. 5 ; trade paperback) | ISBN 9781975369446
    (v. 6 ; trade paperback)
Subjects: LCGFT: Fantasy fiction. | Light novels.
Classification: LCC PL872.5.E57 I7413 2022 | DDC 895.63/6—dc23/
    eng/20220121
LC record available at https://lccn.loc.gov/2021062849

ISBNs: 978-1-9753-6944-6 (trade paperback)
       978-1-9753-6945-3 (ebook)

10 9 8 7 6 5 4 3 2 1

LSC-C

Printed in the United States of America

The identity of the one who defeated the True Demon King—the ultimate threat who gripped the world in terror—is shrouded in mystery.
Little is known about this hero.
The terror of the True Demon King abruptly came to an end.

Nevertheless, the champions born from the era of the Demon King still remain in this world.

Now, with the enemy of all life brought low,
these champions, wielding enough power to transform the world,
have begun to do as they please,
their untamed wills threatening a new era of war and strife.

To Aureatia, now the sole kingdom unifying the minian races,
the existence of these champions has become a threat.
No longer champions, they are now demons bringing ruin to all—
the shura.

To ensure peace in the new era,
it is necessary to eliminate any threat to the world's future,
and designate the True Hero to guide and protect the hopes of the people.

Thus, the Twenty-Nine Officials, the governing administrators of Aureatia, have gathered these shura and their miraculous abilities from across the land, regardless of race, and organized an imperial competition to crown the True Hero once and for all.

POWER RELATIONSHIPS

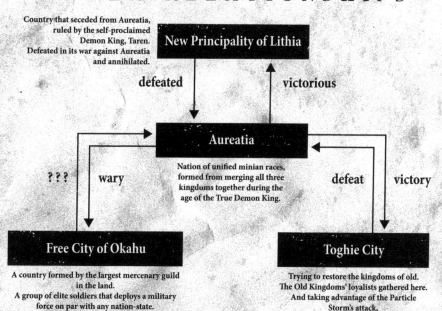

Country that seceded from Aureatia, ruled by the self-proclaimed Demon King, Taren. Defeated in its war against Aureatia and annihilated.

New Principality of Lithia

defeated ← → victorious

Aureatia

Nation of unified minian races, formed from merging all three kingdoms together during the age of the True Demon King.

??? wary

defeat victory

Free City of Okahu

A country formed by the largest mercenary guild in the land.
A group of elite soldiers that deploys a military force on par with any nation-state.
Completely independent of any outside authority.

Toghie City

Trying to restore the kingdoms of old.
The Old Kingdoms' loyalists gathered here.
And taking advantage of the Particle Storm's attack, declared war on Aureatia and were defeated.

ROSCLAY THE ABSOLUTE

Knight Minia

Sponsor
ELEA THE RED TAG

KIA THE WORLD WORD

Elven Word Arts Master

Sponsor
HARDY THE BULLET FLASHPOINT

SOUJIROU THE WILLOW-SWORD

Blade Minia

Sponsor
YUCA THE HALATION GAOL

OZONEZMA THE CAPRICIOUS

Medic Chimera

UHAK THE SILENT

Oracle Ogre

Sponsor
NOFELT THE SOMBER WIND

ZIGITA ZOGI THE THOUSANDTH

Tactician Goblin

Sponsor
DANT THE HEATH FURROW

SHALK THE SOUND SLICER

Spearhead Skeleton

Sponsor
HYAKKA THE HEAT HAZE

MELE THE HORIZON'S ROAR

Archer Gigant

Sponsor
CAYON THE THUNDERING

Sponsor
HARGHENT THE STILL

LUCNOCA THE WINTER

Silencer Dragon

Sponsor
HIDOW THE CLAMP

ALUS THE STAR RUNNER

Rogue Wyvern

Sponsor
MIZIAL THE IRON-PIERCING PLUMESHADE

TOROA THE AWFUL

Grim Reaper Dwarf

Sponsor
QWELL THE WAX FLOWER

PSIANOP THE INEXHAUSTIBLE STAGNATION

Grappler Ooze

SIXWAYS EXHIBITION

ZELJIRGA THE ABYSS WEB

Clown Zmeu

Sponsor
ENU THE DISTANT MIRROR

MESTELEXIL THE BOX OF DESPERATE KNOWLEDGE

Creator/Architect
Golem/Homunculus

Sponsor
KAETE THE ROUND TABLE

TU THE MAGIC

Juggernaut

Sponsor
FLINSUDA THE PORTENT

KUZE THE PASSING DISASTER

Paladin Minia

Sponsor
NOPHTOK THE CREPUSCULE BELL

GLOSSARY

❖ Word Arts

① Laws of the world that permit and establish phenomena and living creatures that physically shouldn't be able to exist, such as the construction of a gigant's body.
② Phenomenon that conveys the intentions of a speaker's words to the listener, regardless of the speaker's race or language.
③ Or the generic term for arts that utilize this phenomenon to distort natural phenomena via "requests" to a certain target.

Something much like what would be called magic. Force, Thermal, Craft, and Life Arts compose the four core groups, but there are some who can use arts outside of these four groups. While necessary to be familiarized with the target in order to utilize these arts, powerful Word Arts users are able to offset this requirement.

❖ Force Arts

Arts that inflict directed power and speed, what is known as momentum, on a target.

❖ Craft Arts

Arts that change a target's shape.

❖ Thermal Arts

Arts that inflict undirected energy, such as heat, electrical current, and light, on a target.

❖ Life Arts

Arts that change a target's nature.

❖ Visitors

Those who possess abilities that deviate greatly from all common knowledge, and thus were transported to this world from another one known as the Beyond. Visitors are unable to use Word Arts.

❖ Enchanted Sword • Magic Items

Swords and tools that possess potent abilities. Similar to visitors, due to their mighty power, there are some objects that were transported here from another world.

❖ Aureatia Twenty-Nine Officials

The highest functionaries who govern Aureatia. Ministers are civil servants, while Generals are military officers.
There is no hierarchy-based seniority or rank among the Twenty-Nine Officials.

❖ Self-Proclaimed Demon King

A generic term for "demonic monarch" not related to the One True King among the three kingdoms. There are some cases where even those who do not proclaim themselves as a monarch, but who wield great power to threaten Aureatia, are acknowledged as self-proclaimed demon kings by Aureatia and targeted for subjugation.

❖ Sixways Exhibition

A tournament to determine the True Hero. The person who wins each one-on-one match and advances all the way through to the end will be named the True Hero. Backing from a member of the Twenty-Nine Officials is required to enter the competition.

CONTENTS

◈ *EIGHTH VERSE:* **GLORY, IN ONE'S GRASP** ◈

AUREATIA TWENTY-NINE OFFICIALS

First Minister
GRASSE THE FOUNDATION MAP
A man nearing old age.
Tasked with being the chairperson who presides over Twenty-Nine Officials' meetings.
Not belonging to any of the factions in the Sixways Exhibition and maintaining neutrality.

Second General
ROSCLAY THE ABSOLUTE
A man who garners absolute trust as a champion.
Participates in the Sixways Exhibition, supporting himself. The leader of the largest faction within the Twenty-Nine Officials.

Third Minister
JELKY THE SWIFT INK
A bespectacled man with the air of a shrewd bureaucrat.
Planned the Sixways Exhibition.
Belongs to Rosclay's faction.

Fourth Minister
KAETE THE ROUND TABLE
A man with an extremely fierce temperament.
Sponsoring Mestelexil the Box of Desperate Knowledge.
Possesses preeminent military power and authority and is resisting Rosclay's faction.

Fifth Official
VACANT SEAT
Previously the seat of Iriolde the Atypical Tome. It is now vacant following his banishment.

Sixth General
HARGHENT THE STILL
A man who yearns for authority despite being ridiculed for being incompetent.
Sponsoring Lucnoca the Winter.
Has a deep connection with Alus the Star Runner.
Not part of any faction.

Seventh Minister
FLINSUDA THE PORTENT
Corpulent woman adorned in gold and silver accessories.
Leads the medical division.
A pragmatist who only believes in the power of money.
Sponsoring Tu the Magic.

Eighth Minister
SHEANEK THE WORD INTERMEDIARY
A man who can decipher and give accounts in a variety of different scripts.
Acts in practice as First Minister Grasse the Foundation Map's Secretary.
Maintains neutrality just like Grasse.

Ninth General
YANIEGIZ THE CHISEL
A sinewy man with a snaggletooth.
Belongs to Rosclay's Faction.

Tenth General
QWELL THE WAX FLOWER
A woman with long bangs that hide her eyes. Sponsor for Psianop the Inexhaustible Stagnation. Timid and always trembling in fright. For some unknown reason, even compared to the rest of the Twenty-Nine Officials, she possesses superlative physical strength.

Eleventh Minister
NOPHTOK THE CREPUSCULE BELL
An elderly man who gives a gentle, kindly impression.
Sponsor for Kuze the Passing Disaster.
Holds jurisdiction over the Order.

Twelfth General
SABFOM THE WHITE WEAVE
A man who covers his face with an iron mask.
Previously crossed swords with self-proclaimed demon king Morio and is currently recuperating.

Thirteenth Minister
ENU THE DISTANT MIRROR
An aristocratic man with slicked-back hair.
Sponsor for Zeljirga the Abyss Web.
Infected by Linaris the Obsidian and now under her control.

Fourteenth General
YUCA THE HALATION GAOL
A simple and honest man, round and plump. Doesn't have a shred of ambition. Head of Aureatia's Public Safety branch. Sponsoring Ozonezma the Capricious.

Fifteenth General
HAIZESTA THE GATHERING SPOT
A man in the prime of his life with a cynical smile.
Prominent for his misbehavior.

Twentieth Minister
HIDOW THE CLAMP
A haughty son of a noble family and at the same time a popular, quick-witted man.
Sponsor for Alus the Star Runner.
Sponsoring Alus to ensure he doesn't win.

Twenty-Fifth General
CAYON THE THUNDERING
A one-armed man with a feminine speaking manner.
Sponsor for Mele the Horizon's Roar.

Sixteenth General
NOFELT THE SOMBER WIND
An abnormally tall man.
Sponsor for Uhak the Silent.
Originated from the same Order almshouse as Kuze.
Killed by Kuze and Nastique.

Twenty-First General
TUTURI THE BLUE VIOLET FOAM
A woman with grizzled hair tied up behind her head.

Twenty-Sixth Minister
MEEKA THE WHISPERED
A stern woman who gives a rigid and rectangular impression.
Acting as the adjudicator of the Sixways Exhibition.

Seventeenth Minister
ELEA THE RED TAG
A young, beautiful woman who rose up from her prostitute ancestry. Supervised Aureatia's intelligence apparatus.
Put to the sword for her acts of foul play during Sixways Exhibition.

Twenty-Second General
MIZIAL THE IRON-PIERCING PLUMESHADE
A boy who became a member of the Twenty-Nine Officials at just sixteen years old.
Possesses a self-assured temperament.
Sponsoring Toroa the Awful.

Twenty-Seventh General
HAADE THE FLASHPOINT
A man who sincerely loves war. Sponsor for Soujirou the Willow-Sword. Prominent figure accompanied by the largest military faction.
Regarded as the largest rival to Rosclay's faction.

Eighteenth Minister
QUEWAI THE MOON FRAGMENT
A gloomy young man.

Twenty-Third Official
VACANT SEAT
Previously the seat of Taren the Punished.
However, it is currently vacant following her secession and defection.

Twenty-Eighth Minister
ANTEL THE ALIGNMENT
A tan-skinned man wearing dark-tinted glasses.

Nineteenth Minister
HYAKKA THE HEAT HAZE
A small-statured man who supervises the agricultural division. Straining himself to become worthy of his position in the Twenty-Nine Officials.
Sponsoring Shalk the Sound Slicer.

Twenty-Fourth General
DANT THE HEATH FURROW
An exceedingly serious man. Commands the northern front army, containing Old Kingdoms' loyalists' forces. Part of the Queen's faction—and harbors ill feelings toward Rosclay's faction.
Sponsoring Zigita Zogi the Thousandth.

Twenty-Ninth Official
VACANT SEAT

ISHURA

Keiso

ILLUSTRATION BY **Kureta**

Eighth Verse:
GLORY, IN ONE'S GRASP

Alus the Star Runner was alive.

A single wyvern, deep down in the blackness of the Mali Wastes, which had now frozen into rock-solid soil.

He's dead, Toroa thought.

Down in the crevice, there was no water, no food, no heat, and not the slightest strand of light. It was a veritable realm of death.

If there was anyone who had fallen down to those farthest depths and was still capable of speech and movement, they couldn't be anything other than dead, and they merely appeared to be living.

Alus the Star Runner tried to take flight with his wings, which had gone rigid from the subzero temperatures. His left wing was an inorganic metal one—an intermingling of flesh and machine.

So the Star Runner's practically become the living dead... Like me...

Faster than Toroa's mind could even register the motion, he had drawn his enchanted swords.

In his left hand, Mushain the Howling Blade. In his right, Wicked Sword Selfesk.

"Don't even try it," Alus murmured.

His similarly metallic arm grabbed the enchanted sword right in front of him—Hillensingen the Luminous Blade.

For Toroa, this was the blade that had started it all.

"You've stolen too much, Star Runner."

He needed to be defeated.

Similarly to how the mere existence of the True Demon King had become too great a threat, Alus the Star Runner had to be defeated at all costs.

When Toroa's father died, he forsook self-preservation and vowed to reclaim the Luminous Blade. For as long as he could remember, Toroa had been single-mindedly devoted to defeating the enemy before him. Now he would do exactly that.

"I—"

He saw the moment that Alus the Star Runner kicked off the ground and took to the sky.

Toroa twisted and thrust the Howling Blade skyward in an attempt to strike his aerial opponent. The violent wind sliced into the rock wall of the ravine. This was the enchanted sword's secret technique to deny the wyvern's flight and simultaneously crush him to death. It went by the name—

"Hrk!"

However, right when he attempted to use Mushain's technique, Migration, Toroa jerked his body and dodged a red light speeding toward him.

A gout of flame had been shot from the eye of the violent gale.

Though he had only been grazed by the fire attack, the edges of his black clothing had been scorched, and thin wisps of smoke now trailed from them.

The flames traveled along the cliff walls as if they had a mind of their own, swallowing up large amounts of oxygen as they went. They were headed for the spot where Toroa was standing.

Alus murmured a single phrase.

"...Ground Runner."

This was a magic item that Alus hadn't gotten a chance to show off during his battle with Lucnoca.

A superhot flame that raced along the terrain, autonomously pursuing its targets in accordance with its owner's will.

The violent tempest abated, allowing Alus to fly.

The musket had been trained on Toroa. The flames were quite literally in hot pursuit.

Alus the Star Runner... Back when you fought Dad, the Howling Blade was always the one you were the most cautious of. And now I see why...

Toroa the Awful widely swung the enchanted sword in his right hand.

It had no blade. To the untrained eye, it appeared to be nothing more than a hilt.

"Reverse Wing."

Alus was utterly shaken.

He collided with the soil as if being dragged down from the heavens.

Tiny metal shards became wedged in the gaps in the mechanical parts of the wyvern's body. This was the ability of the Wicked

Sword Selfesk, a weapon with a blade consisting of numerous metal shards controlled with magnetism.

The violent gale from Migration hadn't managed to hinder Alus's flight. However, by making use of his enchanted swords' techniques simultaneously, Toroa the Awful was able to manipulate the shards of Wicked Sword Selfesk like a scatter shot along the tempest winds to reach Alus.

It was a means of dragging the wyvern, rushing through the sky at ultrahigh speeds, into the range of Toroa's blades. Only Toroa the Awful, using the combined powers of his enchanted blades simultaneously, could devise a technique so perfectly suited to taking down the Star Runner.

"I see...," said Alus.

"You like that?! You're not getting away *this time!*" Toroa yelled.

"It was you, was it...?"

Facedown on the ground, Alus was next gripped by a force rapidly drawing him toward Toroa. Using one of the wedges he had sunk into the wyvern's flesh, Toroa was able to reel Alus in with magnetism.

In the very next moment, the Ground Runner's flame would engulf Toroa from behind.

However, the distance between the two of them would rapidly shrink. This was drawing Alus himself into its trajectory, too. As long as Toroa had the Howling Blade in his left hand, he didn't have to worry about gunfire, even at point-blank range. In which case—

You drew your sword, did you?

The short-bladed weapon Alus the Star Runner had unsheathed was a thrusting sword with a perpendicular cross guard. At that moment, robbed of his freedom of movement and hurtling toward Toroa at high speed, he sought to cross blades with the enchanted swordsman head-on.

Meanwhile Toroa the Awful had ropes, chains, hinge mechanisms, and more. He was ready for anything, and he had an enchanted sword to respond to any tactic an enemy employed.

No!

He couldn't switch to a different magic sword. With this snap judgment, Toroa used only the Howling Blade to smack down Alus's sword as it *swooped in* with a shriek.

It wasn't that Alus had resolved to fight at close range. This blade was an enchanted sword that could fly at will.

"Trembling Bird."

The distance between them had shrunk.

In that moment, when Toroa was forced to spare one hand for defense, Alus closed the gap.

"*Nhn...!*"

"Hillensingen the Luminous Blade—"

"Mi...gration!"

His movements to defend against Trembling Bird were themselves a secret technique. The violent gale raged as it was released from the Howling Blade's downward stroke. As he staved off the flaming pursuit of the Ground Runner, Toroa sent the hilt of Selfesk flying. Alus's flight trajectory was thrown off, and he collided into the rock wall along with the Luminous Blade. The destructive beam of light it released sliced through the dark abyss.

The magnetic blade drew its opponent in. A mysterious blade

cut unseen. The Luminous Blade delivered instant death. The special ability of the Howling Blade allowed the wielder to defend themselves, and then the magnetic blade drew the foe in once more.

This back-and-forth happened in the blink of an eye. And in an instant, the tables turned.

"It's…mine now."

Alus the Star Runner, embedded into the cliff face, had the enchanted sword's hilt gripped with his third arm.

The apex adventurer had overcome his perfect counter, the Wicked Sword Selfesk, which had so drastically hindered his flight.

"Not quite. I'm *lending* it to you. Just like the Luminous Blade."

Toroa brandished an enchanted sword in each of his hands.

On the left, Mushain the Howling Blade. On the right…

"I'm going to take everything back from you."

Trembling Bird.

In the blink of an eye, Toroa had similarly taken the enchanted sword that swooped down at him.

He was a monster of legend. Toroa the Awful could master the secret technique of every enchanted blade ever forged.

◆

On the surface of the Mali Wastes.

Alone in the vast, white expanse was an ooze, looking like a water droplet fallen from a colossal glacier, yet to freeze over.

Psianop the Inexhaustible Stagnation was quietly surveying the landscape before him.

This destruction, violently changing the very weather itself, had been engraved into the land by Psianop's round two opponent—a godlike dragon, Lucnoca the Winter, the living legend who had defeated the legend slayer, Alus the Star Runner.

A single breath was unleashed upon the valley. Lucnoca had built it up in midair.

The ravaged land spoke intricate details of her raw power, the trajectory of her attacks, her positioning, and more. Though Psianop hadn't been present to witness the battle himself, the scene before him painted a vivid picture.

Was it truly necessary for her to suspend her massive body in midair, all for her dragon breath, which barely needs a single word to release...? Impossible. There must've been a separate reason that Lucnoca stopped moving.

This stretch of earth was riddled with massive fissures. They were geographical evidence of the numerous, now-dry canals that once had nourished the land.

Here...Alus the Star Runner hid himself in this fissure, so Lucnoca's sights would've been pointing downward. Not only that, but with the way this crevice is positioned...

It had been said that Alus the Star Runner was the fastest flyer in the world, his aerial speed surpassing that of even dragons.

...he could've maneuvered behind Lucnoca.

In which case, he must have pulled off the extremely dangerous feat of flying freely through these deep, dark, labyrinthine fissures and used them to sneak around underground.

Alus's magic item restricted Lucnoca from behind. She launched her breath out in front of her, without looking back at it whatsoever. Everything froze. The extreme gap in atmospheric pressure dragged Alus into Lucnoca's range of attack. She swiped with her claws. He used a defensive magic item, or perhaps evaded it by coincidence… Whatever the case, it led to Alus being quite literally grounded.

Psianop the Inexhaustible Stagnation didn't possess any supernatural senses like Soujirou the Willow-Sword or Kuuro the Cautious. He merely speculated on the actions in the battle by using an extensive amount of battle theory, based on his knowledge and experiences.

By studying the end result, he could find the most logical course of events that led them to the battle's conclusion.

From there, the breath attack aimed straight downward.

Psianop looked down at the ground he stood upon. Likely owing to the abnormal condensation nearly bringing it to its physical limits, this spot on the ground had collapsed into a cone shape. It resembled the crater left behind by a meteor strike, about four kilometers in diameter.

Far too massive.

The battle continued even after this. The reactive capabilities of someone who had faced a great many legends…and had grown after each fight. Even after being ravaged by a violent tempest, Alus the Star Runner had survived.

◆

Currently, Alus the Star Runner's body was half machine.

A magic item of immortality, multiplying within the body, imitating an organism, and maintaining constant functionality without even requiring biological activity. It was called Chiklorakk the Eternity Machine.

However, even when its original owner, Vikeon the Smoldering, had been heavily wounded by Alus the Star Runner's assault, rendered unable to fight, the dragon hadn't made use of the magic item himself.

"It's mine. Mine... Mine..."

Alus's present state was the result of this item's influence.

It would replace lost sections of the physical body with machinery and maintain the same functionality as before these sections had been lost, but anyone who underwent this change was certainly not the same living creature they had once been. Though they lived, they would rapidly begin to lose their will. Before long, they would lose everything that made them an organic being and soon be reduced to a mindless machine.

This was true even for the strongest of all wyverns. Though the injuries he had sustained in the second match had been completely healed by the power of the magic item, Alus hadn't been able to budge deep in the abyss.

Before encountering Toroa, he had been unable to remember anything.

He was Alus the Star Runner, and yet he wasn't.

For Toroa, who had only ever dreamed of defeating him, this was a cruel sight.

Though he may be in this sorry state, one thing that hasn't changed.

A lot of space had opened up between himself and Alus. Their last clash had decimated the land itself. There had been a drastic shift in momentum, and the enchanted swordsman Toroa had no means of closing the gap.

Alus the Star Runner had a musket in one hand. In another, he held Hillensingen the Luminous Blade. Finally, in his third hand, he had Wicked Sword Selfesk, stolen from Toroa moments ago.

All of the wyvern's hands were occupied.

Alus never *lets go of any treasure he gets his hands on!*

Toroa took a giant step forward. He thrust Trembling Bird sharply out in front of him, far out of range for his attack to reach— he rotated his torso. Hinges worked together, traveling along the steel wires, and then—

Faster than Alus could swing Wicked Sword Selfesk, the base of his wing was completely run through—the attack had come from over twenty meters away.

"Peck!"

The enchanted sword in Toroa's right hand had been swapped out for a different sword. Deceiving Alus by feinting a thrust with Trembling Bird, he used the steel wire and hinges to exchange it for another.

The Divine Blade Ketelk. A secret technique that utilized the enchanted swords extending slashes to send out a long-range thrust at the opponent.

Since Alus the Star Runner was already familiar with this technique, Toroa had fired it at him without revealing his intentions.

Despite his wing being shot through, Alus sent the wedges of Wicked Sword Selfesk flying. Toroa saw several of them become embedded into the rock wall. What was terrifying was Alus's level of aptitude with the blade. There wasn't anyone else who could control an enchanted sword they had just held for the first time with such finesse—other than Toroa the Awful, that is.

"You were *testing* that brand-new enchanted sword, huh?"

"Wicked Sword Selfesk. M-my...my treasure..."

"Migration!"

Stepping forward and then turning, Toroa slashed wide. The Howling Blade swallowed the air and whipped the Ground Runner's flames into its violent gale. He then rerouted the attack, and the flames, destructive enough to burn down an entire nation, toward Alus.

"You can handle that much just fine, I bet... So have this, too."

If it was possible to control the wind, it was possible to control flames.

Mid-rotation, Toroa the Awful drew Nel Tseu the Burning Blade.

Ground Runner.

Rising heat. Tempest winds.

"Gathering Clouds."

An explosive flame erupted from the Mali Wastes fissure, high enough to reach the clouds.

The ice on the ground evaporated. Jet-black smoke formed a deathly domain that swallowed even the darkness of the earthen abyss.

The impact was intense enough to shatter bones and rupture organs.

This was the ultimate ability of Nel Tseu the Burning Blade, a technique he had held back during the first match out of worry for the town around him.

The furious updraft generated by the temperature difference between earth and sky cleared away the black smoke.

A wyvern silhouette. This adventurer possessed a magic item of absolute defense.

"Greatshield of the Dead..."

Alus brandished the Greatshield of the Dead and moved to counterattack.

The figure of the grim reaper was right before his eyes.

"Not good enough."

Just as he had done once before, in the eye of the Particle Storm...

...Toroa the Awful *plunged headfirst* into the hellish fireball.

But how could he grasp Alus's position while his vision was obscured by the black smoke?

The answer came when a blade, connected by a chain, was plunged into Alus's arm, the one that held Wicked Sword Selfesk.

It was an enchanted sword that would automatically respond to moving objects and then counterattack.

Toroa murmured its name.

"Lance of Faima."

The next slash rushed in from the opposite direction.

The arm holding the Greatshield of the Dead had been completely severed.

The instant Alus's attention had shifted to the Lance of Faima, Toroa the Awful slashed at him with the enchanted sword in his left hand. Vajgir the Frostvenom Blade infected its target with corrosive ice crystals.

In a close-quarters battle of enchanted swords, there was no warrior who could surpass Toroa the Awful.

"There is no shield that will protect you from Vajgir."

Toroa had constantly, even in his dreams, thought only of one day killing the strongest of all wyverns. He would need the perfect strategy to seize this impressive enemy, flying at ultrahigh speeds, wielding magic items innumerable, and capable of withstanding even the most lethal attack against him.

He sought out a means from the voices of the enchanted swords, to defeat a foe even his father hadn't been able to beat.

Unable to save his father, Toroa believed this was the last thing he had to do—his sovereign duty.

"Ahh... The Greatshield...of the Dead's..." murmured Alus.

"That's right. You've lost *that, too*," said Toroa.

This wasn't the first time Toroa the Awful had fought against Alus the Star Runner.

However, this was the first time Alus the Star Runner was fighting against *this* Toroa the Awful.

"You're going to die."

And then...

◆

Let's rewind the hands of time.

"Alus the Star Runner... I can't believe it. You're...still alive!"

Psianop the Inexhaustible Stagnation, having analyzed Lucnoca the Winter's fight up until moments prior, was genuinely flabbergasted.

The ooze's amorphous body didn't appear to contain any organs that allowed him movement, let alone swift movement, yet he flew over the complex terrain at terrifying speeds. He fluidly adjusted his center of gravity, his agility resembling a flow of water with a mind of its own.

A sound that the howling winds nearly drowned out. A rumbling from the very core of the world.

Even this was enough for Psianop to comprehend the tremendous abnormality.

There was a battle underway at the Mali Wastes. One between two of the most frightening monsters in the land.

There were still over ten kilometers between Psianop and his destination.

With his speed, it would take no time at all to cover that much ground. Nevertheless, given the combatants, the outcome would be decided far before Psianop could intervene.

"Toroa the Awful... This was your intention from the very beginning, wasn't it...?!"

From the slightest ground tremors and air currents transmitted across the still wastes, he could predict a fight to the death in the bowels of the planet.

Ground Runner raced along the rock wall. It reversed course to appear behind Toroa. Wind, huh? Must have blocked it with the enchanted wind sword. But that was to give Alus an opportunity to act. Toroa is...

The fire rushed, the wind deflected it, and even high above on the surface, there was a faint change in the air pressure.

This conflict... If this is all supposed to be for revenge, then it is a fruitless endeavor.

There came a concussive blast.

An explosion of flame erupted from an earthen fissure far out on the horizon, as if part of an active volcano.

It was the technique Psianop had witnessed on that day. The secret enchanted sword technique combining Nel Tseu the Burning Blade with Mushain the Howling Blade, Gathering Clouds.

When he had looked at Toroa the Awful during their carriage ride, Psianop hadn't seen any hint of rage or hatred on the dwarf's face.

He had believed the man had successfully managed to escape from the spiral of shura killing each other in battle.

"Toroa the Awful! You...aren't supposed to fight...!"

◆

I pierced his wing. I restrained one limb and severed another. I infected him with venomous ice crystals.

These weren't Toroa's thoughts. They were combat judgments that came in a flash, guided by his instincts.

I cut down the Greatshield of the Dead. He only has his musket and Wicked Sword Selfesk left. He can't use them at this range. He won't have the opportunity to change his equipment again.

Faster than his own instincts could process his next action, Toroa's moved to cut off Alus's head.

However, the Howling Blade's slash…

I missed…

…through the wyvern's skin severed his carotid artery and dug into the flesh beneath. He had felt the blow. Too shallow. It hadn't reached the bone.

Alus had moved—without using his wings, or his forelimbs—toward the upper rock wall.

The wyvern's mouth quietly muttered.

"Wicked Sword Selfesk…"

He applied magnetic force to the wedges embedded in the wall.

Toroa had understood he could evade attacks this way. More than that, it was a technique that Toroa the enchanted swordsman knew for himself. He had rejected the possibility because from that range, *it would've been far too late to dodge.*

"Why don't you die?" puzzled Toroa.

"……Good question…" Alus replied.

Cling, clank.

With an unpleasant creaking sound, his severed forelimbs, the nearly severed base of his wing, and his mostly severed neck had been replaced with microscopic machines, and they were slowly *healing him.*

Yet there was even more unbelievable development as well.

The crystals from the frostvenom blade, which had been eating at his body, had been burned away with fire, limb and all.

This was the reason he had sent Ground Runner ahead of him.

With the flames behind him, Alus murmured.

"…Consider the source; take countermeasures."

The apex rogue's combat judgment showed no signs of decline at all.

The farther he was pushed into a corner, the more he learned, and the more he surpassed every tactic his enemies brought against him.

"Consider the source; take countermeasures."

"...Ah, I get it now."

Alus the Star Runner was now *immortal*.

"I'm the same way... I'm trying to kill you even if I die in the process..."

Toroa was invoking the secret techniques of several enchanted swords with his entire body and soul.

He continued to battle in the depths of the frozen soil, hungrily clawing away at his opponent's life.

His enemy alone possessed a limitless life force.

"Wouldn't have been fair if you hadn't done the same, hm...?"

However, right now, Toroa the Awful was truly perfect.

He had never felt stronger. This newfound strength was derived from something greater than a sense of obligation or thirst for revenge.

He was blessed with a mightier body than his father's. Toroa had never once exhausted all his stamina. This was true even now.

"...This fight with you has been the most satisfying to date," Alus muttered.

Even his melted forelimb was regenerating.

High in the sky, from where enchanted swords couldn't reach, he aimed his musket.

Was there any means for Toroa's attack to reach him?

His past opponent Psianop had seen through absolutely all of his enigmatic enchanted sword techniques and had demonstrated he could run up through the air without any footing. If he was going to kill Alus the Star Runner, Toroa would have to do the same.

"...It's been a long time, Toroa the Awful..."

These words must have come from the remnants of Alus's hazy consciousness.

Was that truly how he felt?

If so, that would make Toroa happy.

From here on, he was going to fight in a way that didn't resemble his father in the slightest.

"With all my swords, I'll cut you down."

He took a long, deep breath.

Toroa the Awful stabbed into the ground with enchanted swords in both hands and both feet.

Like the limbs of an insect.

◆

While he was receiving medical treatment after the first match, Toroa had spoken a lot with Cuneigh the Wanderer and Kuuro the Cautious. While they both said they felt indebted to him, Toroa felt he was the one who truly owed them his life, with them and the currently absent Mizial being the first friends he had ever made.

"...Do you think that some inanimate objects can think and feel, Kuuro?"

"Where is this coming from?"

"That Clairvoyance of yours can perceive things ordinary folk like us can't even comprehend, right? I wondered, if that's how you perceive the world, maybe you could hear the voices of, like, a shoe, or a plate, or a sword."

"C'mon, you're talking crazy here."

Kuuro strained a smile, looking exasperated, and appeared to have interpreted Toroa's words as a joke.

"Objects are objects. Of course, every sort of material out there can give off some odd bit of sound or light, and my Clairvoyance will grant me information on an object, such as what it is or where it is... But you're asking if I can hear the *voices* of objects?"

"Well, actually...I've heard a voice before."

"...Oh?"

"It's true."

Could the idea of enchanted swords possessing wills of their own have been nothing more than a myth?

Toroa would be lying if he said he had never doubted it before.

In the middle of the first match, Toro the Awful had practically become possessed by his blades.

He surrendered his body to the influence flowing into him, becoming a mythical beast of slaughter.

However, if this was a concept that even Kuuro the Cautious couldn't comprehend, perhaps enchanted swords had never possessed wills of their own, and all of it had simply been the impulses Toroa himself contained from the very start.

They discussed it all with each other.

"That's totally not right!" Cuneigh objected, leaning her body forward from where she sat on the edge of the bed.

"I mean, you saved Kuuro back then, right?! There's no way that someone who saved someone else, when they were in the most danger of all, could be a bad person!"

"…That's not true. I'm a murderer."

He had killed the bandits who'd come to steal his enchanted swords. They were opponents he should have been able to incapacitate without killing. But the next time similar adversaries came along, he couldn't stop himself from taking their lives.

Above all, during his match, Toroa had fought with the intention of killing Psianop. The reason he was able to end the match without killing his opponent was because he hadn't known that Psianop was capable of using Life Arts that completely regenerated his body.

Psianop must have felt Toroa's bloodlust for himself, too. Even then, he had been able to settle the match without taking Toroa's life. It had been a total defeat for Toroa.

"Alus the Star Runner's dead, too. From here on, I won't need to fight in any battles with my enchanted blades… But I'm afraid that if a day comes when I need to wield them again, I may be overcome with the desire."

"Toroa, I've learned a great many things about the brain and its perceptions. I've investigated every avenue at my disposal for the sake of learning about my own power of Clairvoyance," Kuuro began. "There's apparently a nerve in the brain that serves as a *behavioral mirror*."

"A behavioral mirror?"

"This function allows one to understand the actions of another as if they were carrying out the actions themselves. Animal offspring will acquire their own patterns of behavior by imitating the actions of other members of their group. If one were to develop this nerve to an extreme degree...they might be able to intuit a first-time opponent's thought patterns as if they were their own, even faster than their mind could process, or grant one the ability to perfectly replicate a technique they'd seen only once before."

"Imitation. You're saying that's what's truly happening in those instances?"

He recalled his battles against Mestelexil and Psianop.

They were powerful foes he had been unable to kill even after drawing out the near-limited potential of his enchanted blades.

Still, it was because of such opponents that Toroa had finally been able to experience a *lengthy battle*. He had been able to watch his opponent's fighting style from up close and imagine what their next move might be.

"...Hmm. It might be fine to express it as a kind of 'notion' or 'idea.' The basis for sympathy lies in imitation, after all. By constantly imagining what your opponent's thinking, you can understand what they're thinking and where their thoughts are going to lead them next."

"If that's your explanation, then what about the enchanted swords' voices? Nerves can't explain that."

"I wonder. When it comes to sympathizing with magic items... there's a lot of uncertainty. For example, there are some that can be manipulated through the thoughts of the user alone. If these items had wills of their own, you'd definitely be able to pick up on that; that's for sure."

"..."

"Even putting that aside, you're able to read how you need to handle a sword, whether it's from its shape, or its center of gravity, to unleash its absolute maximum power. You might be subconsciously perceiving how the previous owners of the enchanted swords used them from the slightest frays of the sheath or placement of the nicks on the blade. Maybe you're using that information to better understand the one who forged the blade and the ones who wielded it?"

"I'm not sure I'm even capable of something like that..."

"Or maybe, in a more direct way, you saw *someone using the secret techniques* of your enchanted swords before."

"......"

He wasn't Toroa the Awful.

Ultimately, he had been able to tell this truth to Mizial and Mizial only.

"Toroa, kindness stems from having a great amount of empathy for beings other than yourself. There's even the chance that an excessive amount of it will end up overwriting your own will. It's certainly a risky power to have, but..."

He could take the empathy that he'd been gifted for the sake of saving others and use it to kill them instead.

"Even my Clairvoyance can't see through the realm of the heart."

◆

The enchanted sword mountain was moving.

Alus the Star Runner looked down on it with vague thoughts. *Treasure.*

It was either an enemy protecting the treasure, or perhaps the treasure itself, and he would need to defeat his enemy to obtain this mountain of enchanted swords for himself. As he had always done.

"Wicked Sword...Selfesk."

He murmured the name of the enchanted sword in his hand. In response to Alus's thoughts, the countless shards began stabbing into the rock wall in a line. Come to think of it, there was once a time when he had hunted this enchanted sword.

He couldn't recall just how long ago it had been, but even back then, the enemy before him had gotten to it first.

"...Toroa the Awful."

He had mumbled the name several times at that point, but Alus wasn't aware of the fact.

Each time he traced his memories of enchanted swords, he would remember that this enemy of his was Toroa the Awful.

Whenever he traveled the skies in pursuit of treasure, Alus would try to take an enchanted sword for himself, yet the shadow of this man was always there.

The enchanted swords Alus the Star Runner managed to keep for himself numbered only two, Trembling Bird and Hillensingen the Luminous Blade.

And now...

"...Toroa."

...he would have them all.

Without really knowing where he was, or even what he was doing, Alus had that alone as the only certainty in his mind.

Alus loaded his lightning bullet.

"Give them....to me... Now..."

Like a drill from the heavens piercing the earth, lightning crashed down from the sky.

Light. Sound. Destruction.

The terrain crumbled and broke.

The phenomenon the magic bullet wrought was truly like lightning itself.

"Gngh, lrngh."

Alus heard the growl coming from above him.

His eyes beheld...the limbs of an insect? Mushain the Howling Blade. Vajgir the Frostvenom Blade. Nel Tseu the Burning Blade. Inrate the Sickle of Repose.

Spreading out the abnormal number of enchanted swords in a radial pattern, Toroa the Awful instantly reached his current position.

...An updraft...

Even through hazy thoughts, Alus the Star Runner's staggering amount of combat experience allowed him to understand the situation.

A tremendous air current was generated from the massive explosion that came in their last clash, erupting from the superheated depths to the frozen surface above. Riding that turbulent wind...and adjusting his trajectory with the Howling Blade, had he *changed the topography of the land*?

On top of it, the updraft continued to throw Alus the Star Runner's greatest asset, his flying ability, into disarray.

"Graaawl!"

Toroa's entire body twisted in midair, and he brought the explosive heat hurtling downward. The Burning Blade was out of control.

Explosion. Explosion. Explosion. Explosion.

The terrain was hollowed out. The sky burned. Destruction rained over the land like a meteor shower.

Alus's body contorted as he evaded the lethal heat wave.

The magnetic force of the Wicked Sword Selfesk could instantly pull Alus's own body to the points where the metallic wedges were embedded in the cliff face. He had accounted for this.

Clinging to the wall, Alus was now able to line up a shot at Toroa from a stable position. After Toroa had jumped into the air, what came next was his descent. It was only natural.

"Ngh!"

A shock hit Alus's body. Wailsever. There was interference coming from the vibrations of the crystal blade.

His musket's aim strayed ever so slightly. Toroa continued his descent…

"…………"

…and the trajectory of his fall changed in midair.

As if bounding through the air with some invisible force, occasionally kicking off the rock wall, he came for Alus like a flying insect of nightmare.

"Gwarrrrrrrrngh!"

Counteraction.

Alus the Star Runner would have found it difficult to believe his eyes even if he had been fully lucid.

A long-range thrust and lunging slash with Divine Blade Ketelk.

Toroa, using the counteraction from the long-range attack, was *kicking the stone wall* while in midair. His bizarre emergence from moments ago similarly couldn't be explained merely by propelling himself up the wall with his kicks. Toroa had used this technique at the same time and gotten above Alus the Star Runner.

The enchanted swordsman was fighting a midair battle.

It was abnormal.

Propelled by a beast-like instinct, he made rapid and simultaneous use of his magic swords' secret techniques.

"*Gwar, hraaah!*"

"Rotting Soil Su—"

Before he could make use of the magic item resembling a lump of mud, the Howling Blade's gale slammed Alus into the cliff. His bones shattered. Alus activated Wicked Sword Selfesk's magnetic force. He didn't move.

The arm gripping the sword's hilt was entangled by a chain.

This was Toroa the Awful's enchanted sword that autonomously pursued its target—Lance of Faima. It possessed the ability to release incredibly fast vibrations. With its chain wrapped around Alus's arm, the vibrations caused the metal to shred Alus's flesh away.

"*Ha, ha-ha, gwa-ha ha-ha-ha-ha-ha-ha!*"

Not unlike the wings of an insect, this was known as *flapping*.

While Alus held the Wicked Sword Selfesk in a mechanical arm, this enchanted sword's technique was more than enough to sever its structure and completely destroy it.

"Gwaaaarllll!"

As they descended together, Toroa bound Alus's neck with his chain, crushing it with a sneer.

Though it was only a second until they crashed to the ground, he managed to stab Alus at least four times with the Frostvenom Blade.

Even then, the blades of mud coming from behind them repeatedly stabbed into Toroa's upper arm and back, running him through until they pierced his stomach. As Toroa laughed, he coughed up an immense amount of blood. The binds on Alus loosened.

Rotting Soil Sun, which molded and shot bullets of hardened mud, was the magic item Alus had deployed with the intention of raining down death on Toroa as they fell together. Using his enemy's massive frame as a shield, Alus narrowly avoided the blindly fired metal blades.

"...Consider the source; take countermeasures."

Riding the air current, he ascended once more.

Toroa the Awful continued to descend alone, spraying fresh blood as he went.

"There have been many others...who've risen over me before."

◆

His consciousness was fading.

Perhaps that wasn't it, and it was returning to him.

Toroa the Awful was laid out on his back, with both his hands thrown up into the air.

His entire body had been impaled. He had slammed violently against the ground.

His limbs had been singed in the aftermath of the Burning Blade's rampage, and his extraordinary rapid-fire usage of Divine Blade Ketelk had pushed it so hard that the sword itself was close to disintegrating.

If this had been an official match, he would have been judged the loser. Alus the Star Runner likely believed that he had killed Toroa.

Indeed, the wounds he had suffered were near fatal.

After all, these are just techniques borrowed from another.

He recalled what Psianop had said to him before.

The skills of a beast who abandoned himself and succumbed to the will of the blades hadn't been enough to claim true victory.

"I knew all that, though…"

This was different from back then. *He knew, and he had pushed them to the limit anyway.*

He opened and closed a hand.

Toroa's body could still move.

He was strong. He was still alive. He could still fight.

Though his fighting style forced him to abandon everything but his killing instinct, he had a personal reason for getting his enchanted sword back.

"Wicked Sword Selfesk."

The first wedge he had fired toward Alus the Star Runner was still lodged inside Alus's mechanical body. Now that he was part machine, the wyvern likely hadn't felt the sort of pain or discomfort an organic body would. Toroa, using his excessive stamina to maintain a nonstop onslaught, hadn't given the world's strongest rogue the slightest opening to take it out.

With his right hand, he activated Wicked Sword Selfesk's magnetic force.

"...!"

The magnetism took hold of Alus the Star Runner's body, and he plummeted to the ground below.

Gunshot retribution. A thunderous magic bullet that winds couldn't deflect.

However, it didn't directly hit him.

A wedge from Wicked Sword Selfesk, under Toroa's control, acted as a lightning rod and guided it away.

"...So, you're still alive..."

"That's right. However many times it takes...and however many more after that...I'm dragging you down to the depths of hell with me...Alus the Star Runner!"

From the skies above, more of Rotting Soil Sun's earthen blades fell toward him. Toroa had barely managed to raise his upper body off the ground, but the wedges of Wicked Sword Selfesk flew about at high speeds and repelled all the mud.

Just as he'd calculated, Rotting Soil Sun's position couldn't be changed. Toroa could easily deal with attacks coming at him from the front.

Nevertheless, Alus the Star Runner was a rogue wielding a limitless supply of magical items.

The flame's coming.

Ground Runner. Alus had devoted his extra limb to dealing with this flame running along the ground. Thus, Toroa aimed for the chance to deliver the fatal blow.

The glint of light was rapidly closing in. The heat encroached on Toroa's face.

However, the flame, seemingly about to consume Toroa as he sat unable to stand, suddenly spread out on either side and stopped.

As if the terrain had been a cliff face, unconnected to what was ahead of it.

"...Karmic Castigation."

A single-edged sword with a curved blade. A very delicate subspace sword, not suited for combat.

It left behind spatial fissures along the surface of any material it sliced.

He had experienced Ground Runner's attack several times by now. It was a magic item that sent flames racing along terrain. Taking this into consideration, Toroa then understood that it couldn't traverse *over gaps in terrain.*

Strangely enough, much like how Mele the Horizon's Roar tried to stop Shalk the Sound Slicer in the seventh match by destroying the terrain itself, Tora the Awful had stopped the Ground Runner's flames with the slightest spatial severance.

Alus the Star Runner descended.

Toroa the Awful watched him from the ground below.

Both fighters were rapidly approaching each other.

"Venom shot."

"Migration."

The attacks were simultaneous.

The deadly bullet Alus fired, aimed with precision at Toroa's body, even as he was drawn in and unable to move freely, ultimately had its path thrown off by the enchanted wind sword's secret technique, deployed with a twist of Toroa's upper body, and landed on the earth.

The violent gust threw off Alus's flight position even more. Twisting into a tailspin, the wyvern ended up with his back to Toroa. Toroa could see one of his three arms attempting to reach for the Luminous Blade.

"*Kylse ko khnmy.*" (From Alus to Nimi gravel.)

Word Arts.

What was his aim in a situation like that? Even if he did unsheathe the Luminous Blade from his current position, buffeted by wind and magnetic force, he would never outpace Toroa's sword skills. What was he doing?

Alus's body was closing in. Toroa could cut him down.

Toroa had no time to spare.

"*Konaue ko.*" (Trickling water.)

"......"

Toroa swung Karmic Castigation.

It wasn't at Alus. He swung down to his right. Aiming at the ground.

"*Kastgraim.*" (Pierce.)

The needle, instantly formed from the poison bullet, was stopped by the blade of Karmic Castigation.

Craft Arts. If there was any focal point with a reliable position that Alus could confidently use for his Word Arts in this situation, the only option was the very bullet he had just fired.

The single second when the needle was blocked gave Alus the Star Runner more than enough time to readjust and right his positioning.

The strongest enchanted sword of all, prohibiting any sort of defenses when inside its reach...

"Hillensingen..."

"Inrate..."

The same moment he intercepted the needle, Toroa swung the halberd in his right hand.

The longest enchanted sword, shaped like a poleax, even then was too slow to stop the Luminous Blade.

"...the Luminous..."

"...the Sickle of..."

"...Bla—"

There was the sound of fire.

The ultimate enchanted sword, piercing and severing all defenses in its path the moment it was unsheathed, was sent flying faster than it could be drawn by some invisible force.

"...Repose *and*—"

Inrate the Sickle of Repose. Hanging on the tip of its scythe blade was yet another enchanted sword.

"Divine Blade Ketelk."

This wasn't a secret technique of any kind. It was the Divine Blade Ketelk's most basic ability—*elongated slashes.*

There were *two* enchanted swords that Toroa had unsheathed in that moment. Using the tip of Inrate the Sickle of Repose with its long hilt, he handled Divine Blade Ketelk with even more acrobatic movements. Using the elongated slash and extending it even farther, he had knocked down the Luminous Blade before Alus could draw it. Could even Soujirou the Willow-Sword possibly perform such a feat?

Against the mightiest enchanted sword that rendered defense impossible, he simply needed to cut down his foe before they drew it.

"Don't think you'll be able to best an enchanted swordsman with an enchanted sword of your own."

As the Luminous Blade was swung, Alus and Toroa passed by each other. The Lance of Faima was reacting.

His father's life, taken from him that day. Retrieving the enchanted sword of light had been his earnest wish.

Toroa reached out his hand. In order to reclaim the enchanted sword, he had needed to take his hand off another.

I'm not letting anyone else take this from me.

The enchanted sword that would let Toroa the Awful stop being Toroa.

Please let me finish this.

At last, he grabbed the falling Hillensingen, the enchanted sword of light.

At the same moment, there was a sharp pain from his shoulder down his back. Metal claws.

His muscles were deeply rent, his veins torn away, and his red-hot vitality was slowly being taken away from him.

No price was too steep for the recovery of the Luminous Blade.

Ahh.

The mud blades from Rotting Soil Sun, now free to find their mark, once again gained momentum and swooped down on Toroa. He slashed with the enchanted wind sword to clear them away, but even with it, there were blades that pierced into his flesh. Swapping out Wicked Sword Selfesk, he couldn't control Alus's movements.

He had thought he could fully handle all of the wyverns' limitless magic items. In truth, Toroa had just done that.

However, there was still one more weapon left over in his enemy's arsenal.

The rogue's bare hands.

What would his next move be? How much longer could he continue to fight?

The majority of his insides were eviscerated. Even his extraordinary physical stamina was reaching its limit. His consciousness was fading, and the cold of the earthen depths seeped into the bottom of his lungs.

"*Hmph.*"

He laughed with a sigh.

"Alus…Alus the Star Runner. I always have nightmares. Nightmares where I fight you, and I'm killed."

He knew his voice might not reach his opponent.

Even then, Toroa continued to speak.

"In my desperate fight to the death, I tried to live on. I… Toroa the Awful was searching for the possibility of surviving and going back home. I was always fighting, even in my dreams... I've continued to think solely of ways to kill you."

The fissure in the frozen soil of the Mali Wastes had now been etched with ruptures and destruction on par with the terrain on the surface.

A storm, just like the Particle Storm that day—or perhaps even more intense—continued to rage between the two shura.

"But I wonder why...?"

Vengeance for the father he thought had died—or perhaps vengeance for himself—still lived within him.

His father's nemesis, thought to be long dead... Though perhaps Alus was *his* nemesis now.

Toroa had believed that a fiercer, uncontrollable darkness had taken root in his soul. To take revenge for his father. To reclaim his own life. To be stirred by the impulses of the enchanted swords.

"Alus the Star Runner. I feel that...I have a different reason for wanting to kill you."

Was there anyone who could kill Alus the Star Runner as he was now?

He had a magic item that would regenerate his body, even after his neck had been almost completely sliced through. Even against Vajgir the Frostvenom Blade, which extinguished lives slowly over time, Alus was able to freely move the portions of his body that sprouted deadly crystals.

There may have been a critical point that served as the magic item's core, but Toroa the Awful didn't have the sort of sixth sense that would let him see through to it. There didn't appear to be anything like it, either, judging from Alus the Star Runner's behavior.

Nevertheless.

...I can kill him for good.

As was true for the other enchanted swords, Karmic Castigation had a secret technique of its own.

It was an enchanted sword that made minute, incorporeal cracks across the surface of whatever it slashed, spatially rupturing it.

It then pried open those minute spatial ruptures and created a trench that expelled it from this very world—it was called "Beak."

Anything that fell into one of the tiny spatial rifts would never be able to return from whence it came.

"All right. This is where it really kicks off."

Though the moment was long enough for a only few deep breaths, it was enough rest for both of Toroa's legs. He could stand again.

Stepping firmly on the ground, he could use the enchanted sword's secret technique.

He had been blessed with incredible tenacity from birth, the ultimate sword skills from the parent who had raised him.

It's not over yet. These wounds are nothing. I'm still fully conscious. My organs are only a bit injured, my bones aren't broken, and all my tendons are still intact. I'm only just getting warmed up.

Hillensingen the Luminous Blade.

The ultimate enchanted sword, which he had long searched for, was finally in Toroa's hand.

This had been the sovereign duty that Toroa, the enchanted blade beast, could not die without completing.

Now that he had recovered it...

"Time to go all out."

"......"

For that brief interval, Alus the Star Runner made no move to attack Toroa.

He was staring up at the sky beyond the edge of the cliffs.

"...There was something..." Alus murmured.

The one who had possessed more than anyone else now had lost absolutely everything.

At the edge of an isolated, frozen hell, he faced off against the monstrous Toroa.

"...I needed to do. I collected everything...for that purpose."

"I gleaned as much."

Karmic Castigation was stabbed into the earth. A crevice, threatening to swallow Toroa's opponent whole, yawned wide.

The deep black crevice seemed almost like a path through the underworld connecting Alus and Toroa.

"Alus the Star Runner, you don't have *anything like that* anymore."

"...I do."

"You no longer need to take from others. You could even head back to your homeland and live out your remaining days in peace and quiet. This..."

Toroa wondered just how strong the influence of a magic item could be.

Treasures that had consumed an innumerable number of lives and hearts.

They each possessed too many such treasures.

"...This ends here. It ends with us."

"It's my treasure."

Ground Runner's flame had returned to Alus and settled into the small pot that was meant to contain it. It appeared he had already collected Rotting Soil Sun as well. The metallic wedges which were stuck into his body must have fallen out during the previous clash.

Toroa could sense that another flurry of magical item attacks was fast approaching. Alus would send both Ground Runner and Rotting Soil Sun to hit him directly this time, without driving them across the terrain. Or like when he battled against Toroa's father, he could use the flash of the flame to momentarily blind him.

Toroa was confident. This next clash of theirs would be the last.

"Come, Alus the Star Runner! This ends now!"

Alus kicked off the ground and flew into the air.

Though Karmic Castigation carved a deep fissure into the earth, it didn't hinder Alus the Star Runner's fighting ability in the slightest.

This rogue's strengths had been his magic items and his rifle attacks from the skies. His one-sided barrage had left no room for counterattack.

Toroa needed it to be this way.

Just as Alus took off from the ground, the area right above his head became a true blind spot. Without a sound, a short sword fell.

"...Trembling Bird!"

Skewering Alus's torso, it pinned him to the surface. This was Trembling Bird's true secret technique.

"Harrier!"

If the wielder of the blade knew nothing of its unique characteristics, its hidden potential, the sword would remain silent. But in the hands of Toroa, it sliced through the air with a shriek.

C'mon move! Kuuro the Cautious protected these legs, didn't he?!

Even with blood gushing from his wounds, Toroa ran, tracing the spatial fissure carved into the surface. Trembling Bird's secret technique was a surprise attack he could use only once. In the brief moment he was able to stop Alus's flight, he needed to close the distance and cut him down.

Merely knocking him down into the fissure would never be enough to kill Alus. If the magic item really did make him immortal, he wouldn't have needed to dodge and defend.

Nel Tseu the Burning Blade. Mushain the Howling Blade.

"Gathering Clouds! Migra—"

Yet Toroa stopped just before launching the attacks, using the combined incinerating techniques of wind and explosive flame. The moment he touched the Howling Blade's hilt, he could tell the sword's center of gravity had shifted ever so slightly.

Mud.

In that midair clash, Alus had deployed Rotting Soil Sun at point-blank range against the Howling Blade. Right after reclaiming the Luminous Blade, Toroa had defended against the barrage of mud shards with the Howling Blade. And just before that, he had used it to deflect the magic poison bullet in order to throw Alus's stance off.

Alus had made the mud adhere to the sword in order to delay the release of its ability by a fraction of a second—quicker than a flash of light.

All of this was premeditated in order to ensure that Toroa grabbed a different sword.

"Wicked Sword—"

As he scorched Alus with the Burning Blade's heat wave, his other arm held Wicked Sword Selfesk.

The maneuver to effectively utilize the wedges was *simultaneous assembly*. The wedges that had been fired into the stone crag to provide Alus with footing peppered the Star Runner from all directions.

The metallic shards became embedded in Alus's spread wings, and the magnetism dragged him in along with them. This was how Toroa was trying to close the distance.

Toroa couldn't stop his forward momentum. If he stopped his legs now, they would never move again.

"You're…different. You're not Toroa the Awful."

"No, I'm *still* Toroa the Awful!"

Alus had deployed the mud blades and Ground Runner's flames. He lost a finger and an eye as he persisted. With his body wreathed in flames, he pushed forward. His prioritization of autonomous magic items was proof that he didn't have any reprieve to aim his musket.

If Alus was prepared to take any attack thrown at him, Toroa had to be ready for the very same. If he took a moment to defend himself, his legs would stop entirely. He already had the enchanted sword prepped for his attack.

Don't stop.

The enchanted sword with the farthest reach, bringing absolute death, as well as the fated start of it all.

If Dad hadn't been a leprechaun... If his arms had been just a little bit longer and he'd been able to get to the Luminous Blade first...

"*Kylse ko kyakowak.*" (From Alus to the Hillensingen blade.)

An attack that needed no stance.

He had to laugh. Given that Alus the Star Runner had been in possession of the Luminous Blade all that time, of course this would be the case. He could even use it as a focus for his Word Arts.

If Dad had just had the power to shoulder several enchanted swords at once!

"*Kestlek kogbakyau. Kaameksa. Koikasyaknoken. Kairokraino.*" (Hail to heaven and earth. Axis is the left ear. Changing ring. Rotate.)

This wyvern was a jack of all trades, possessing an aptitude for everything. At almost the exact same moment Toroa took his next step forward, the wyvern had finished invoking his Word Arts on the Luminous Blade.

Hillensingen the Luminous Blade was moved by Alus's Force Arts...

"The one who lost that day, Alus..."

And even then, it yielded to the skill of its wielder, Toroa.

He stepped forward.

Drawing the sword. Light. The range.

"...was you!"

The light from the sword's slash severed Alus the Star Runner in two, vertically.

At the same time, Toroa coughed and spat up an immense amount of blood.

It was an unmatched sword stroke, completely catching the midline of his enemy.

"*Koff...gahak.*"

Toroa was spitting up blood. He felt a heat in his gut, as if something was invading his very nerves.

He heard a voice.

"...Magic poison bullet."

"Ahh."

Whatever the extent of his immortality, if he was completely cleaved in two from his head through his torso, it shouldn't have been possible for him to speak and aim his musket to shoot Toroa.

"...I get it. Right from the start."

The strength in his knees gave out, and he nearly collapsed.

This was the spot where Alus had let the Greatshield of the Dead fall during their first clash, when Toroa had showered the wyvern with his combined secret technique of explosive flame.

He had understood that in this position, where he could extend the arm holding the Greatshield of the Dead, he would enter the Luminous Blade's area of effect.

Even as Toroa broke through the attacks from Rotting Soil Sun and Ground Runner, and drew the wyvern toward him, Alus never adjusted his stance to launch another attack. That was because his only aim was for Toroa to touch the magic bullet, fallen on the ground where he stood.

While Toroa tried to make Alus wary of the ground with the secret technique of Karmic Castigation, Alus did the exact opposite.

Even the successive attacks from Rotting Soil Sun and Ground Runner had merely been to turn Toroa's attention away from the ground below and to cloud his vision.

"I get it..."

Hillensingen the Luminous Blade possessed the ultimate cutting ability. Even the Greatshield of the Dead, a tool of absolute defense, couldn't fully guard against it. However, what Toroa had cut through after slightly piercing through this defense was the mechanical half of Alus's body, converted by Chiklorakk the Eternity Machine.

Even now, with Chiklorakk the Eternity Machine cut from him, Alus hadn't withered in the slightest. His judgment, his thinking, and the fighting prowess he had accumulated from repeatedly coming up with counterplans for these prolonged battles, and the growth that followed, remained truly all-powerful.

The mangled visage before Toroa was all that remained of Alus the Star Runner.

"I'll live. I'm...I'm going to live," Toroa murmured.

Toroa didn't hesitate in the slightest. Using Vajgir the Frost-venom Blade, he sliced open his own stomach. The cells infected by the poison began to crystallize. Thanks to this, he gained the briefest possible moment of respite.

Now missing a finger on his right hand and unable to move it properly, he slashed.

Defeating Alus the Star Runner was all that mattered to him.

"...I know," Alus murmured.

His whip bent, and Toroa's right arm was severed at the elbow. This was Kio's Hand, previously torn apart by Lucnoca. It was torn to shreds, so it could barely still be called a whip, but it was more than powerful enough to kill Toroa in his current state.

"*Koff...* I want...to live my life..."

He restrained Alus against the rock wall with his right shoulder, pressing all of his weight into him.

He brandished Inrate the Sickle of Repose. A silent sword. The one his father had been the most skilled with.

Alus drearily replied, "You're not even...Toroa the Awful."

The gunshots echoed in rapid succession. Though they were nothing but normal bullets, Toroa's left thigh and knee were shot through.

Even then, Toroa continued slashing at Alus's body. When he cut him open from his stomach to his hips with the sickle, the wyvern's fleshy organs slithered out.

He lashed with the whip—Alus was trying to sever Toroa's left arm. This was a fair trade. He thrust the crystal sword hanging from his arm, Wailsever, into Alus's abdominal cavity.

He used this sword, with its shocks and rapid vibrations, at maximum output.

"Incubation!"

Alus the Star Runner would be blasted apart from the shock waves within his body, along with Wailsever itself.

...However, it didn't happen.

Alus the Star Runner had three arms. With his body recovering over time, he touched the Greatshield of the Dead lying on the ground. No matter how many times Toroa put his life and body on the line to attack him, nothing would come of it. Even he understood for himself that there was no longer anything he could do.

"It's over…and it's the end…for you, too."

"Not yet… It's not over yet. My life…my life still hasn't begun!"

Alus lashed the whip.

His right leg had been severed, but he wasn't done yet. A leg was a small price to pay for the sake of living another second. He would keep fighting for as long as it took, even if it meant gripping an enchanted sword in his teeth.

He could no longer unleash their secret techniques, but he still had the spatial fissure he had opened up with Karmic Castigation. He just needed to grab Alus with his remaining left arm and drag him down into it.

He would be the beast of legend that dragged the villain into the abyss with him.

One more step. This will be the end of it. If I can just…kill Alus with this…

He didn't need any glory. This wasn't for revenge.

Toroa took pity on Alus the Star Runner.

Stuck at the bottom of an abyss without ever dying, it was as if Toroa was looking into a mirror.

He had thought that killing Alus would be the end of his days as Toroa the Awful.

He had wanted to save the wyvern, but that was out of the question now.

Toroa could fight to the bitter end. As long as he didn't give up, he could keep fighting like a rampaging demon.

However, if they were both to become monsters and descend into the pits of hell…

Could that really be considered salvation?

I…I wanted to live out my life in the Wyte Mountains. I could've kept on living exactly as Dad had wanted, without harming anyone. I…the whole time.

His tears spilled over.

He had no idea when they had begun.

He was supposed to have been the monster from a horror story that brought tears to children's eyes.

"Enchanted swords…aren't yours…"

"…………"

Not taking from anyone, while not letting them take from him.

He knew how to break the cycle.

It was something that he was sure his father had known from the very start.

"They're not mine, either."

He stretched out his hand with the last of his strength, and Trembling Bird flew back into it as if it had a will of its own.

Birds. The names of the sword skills his father loved.

The young man had a gift allowing him to listen to the voices of his enchanted swords.

"You're coming with me, huh?"

The rogue didn't even try to take this one from him.

The colossal body of this nameless dwarf staggered and fell.

Into the abyss—together with the reclaimed Luminous Blade and all the other enchanted swords he had collected.

...Dad. I'm coming...to join you...

Into a darker, and deeper, hell than the bottom of this frozen wasteland.

This was, after all, a fitting resting place for a monster.

◆

Twentieth Minister Hidow the Clamp, on standby in the central assembly hall, received an emergency report from the Fifth South Communications Tower.

This tower had been reserved by Hidow even before the start of the second match just in case—and to prepare for the truly worst-case scenario—and provided observation reports of the Mali Wastes region.

"I'm issuing an anti-dragon alert," said Hidow to his attendant, the very first words out of his mouth after exiting the communications room.

"The location is the Mali Wastes. Gather every single soldier that can be deployed. They might immediately get sent out to fight, but don't let anyone move on their own until they get the order from us. Did you prepare the line?"

"While you were receiving your report, we opened up radzio lines in the second switch room to all the rooms in the assembly hall, Master Hidow! Would you like to head there immediately?!"

"Good job. In that case, I'll inform everyone in this building directly about the current situation! For the other Twenty-Nine in outside ministries, you're to split up and get in contact with them. The order of priority goes Haade, Jelky, Rosclay, Flinsuda! That's still not going to be enough for this. Reach out to Dant, Sabfom, and Cayon, too! You got that?!"

They were currently preparing themselves.

One part of the rules for this Sixways Exhibition had been decided after Hidow had introduced the idea.

Anyone who deliberately wrought destruction unrelated to the sanctioned matches and anyone who opposed Aureatia as a self-proclaimed demon king...

...was to be crushed by the remaining Hero candidates.

Before the beginning of the Sixways Exhibition, Hidow had steered the assembly meeting to decide these rules.

The "process we discussed" that Hidow had relayed during the second match referred to Rosclay the Absolute's scheme to use these rules to dispose of threats outside of any match.

...*I didn't expect we'd be using it on* this guy *instead of Lucnoca the Winter.*

Drawing his arms through the sleeves of his Twenty-Nine Officials overcoat, Hidow quickened his pace. A bead of cold sweat ran down his cheek.

This matter didn't only affect him. If this enemy couldn't be defeated, everyone would die.

Aureatia had a long, long day ahead of it.

"Alus the Star Runner is approaching from the Mali Wastes! Send an word to all hero candidates! I repeat!"

Alus the Star Runner versus Aureatia.

"Gather all the hero candidates! There's only one enemy! *Self-proclaimed demon king* Alus!"

Ever since the day the eighth match concluded and an alarm rang out across Aureatia, many of the people who would soon find themselves in a life-or-death struggle with Alus the Star Runner had spent their time unaware of their fate.

Tu the Magic, for example, hadn't left Flinsuda's mansion since she forfeited the fifth match against Kuze.

Of course, there was no beastfolk cage in existence that could keep Tu imprisoned. The reason behind her continued good behavior largely lay in her inferiority complex toward Flinsuda the Portent and the presence of the one surveilling her.

"Food time, Tu."

A somewhat pallid-faced servant entered the room. They had no hair, and their eyes had been replaced with pearls.

It was a revenant under the control of Krafnir the Hatch of Truth.

"...Thanks, Krafnir. But I really don't need to eat anything."

"Still, I can't leave you alone without giving you anything. I'd be the one held accountable."

"Yeah..."

Tu was sitting on a chair, curled up, with her knees to her chest. Before her was a dish cooked by Flinsuda's personal chef, extravagant and luxurious.

When she thought about Kuze the Passing Disaster, and what he was trying to protect, it was hard to keep anything down, especially something so rich.

"...Why do I...think that something tastes good? Why do I think baths feel good? When I was protecting the Land of the End, I didn't really eat anything at all."

"I DON'T...HAVE A VERY GOOD ANSWER. REGARDING IZIK THE CHROMATIC'S CREATIVE ENDEAVORS, THEY ARE NOTHING BUT CONVENIENT FUNCTIONS TO HIM HELP FIT INTO MINIAN SOCIETY. THERE ARE VERY FEW OF THE MINIAN RACES WHO WOULD LET THEIR GUARD DOWN AROUND SOMEONE THAT CAN'T FEEL ANY POSITIVE SENSATIONS. IN SHORT, IT'S A FUNCTION TO *MAKE OTHERS GET ALONG WITH YOU*."

"...Like you and Rique do?"

"...I CAN'T HAVE YOU SEE ME AS A FRIEND...PUTTING RIQUE ASIDE."

After attempting a sneak attack on Kuze the Passing Disaster, Rique the Misfortune had died.

Given that Tu the Magic had been knocked out of the Sixways Exhibition, a man like Krafnir should have similarly lost any need to associate with Tu like this; however, he must have had something on his mind to continue his job of keeping watch over her.

Tu wanted to believe so.

"I...couldn't stand to see someone end up unhappy. So back when I was in the Land of the End, I was always angry. I thought of how much the people there suffered... I wondered why no one ever thought of them or offered them any help... But I ended up being just as bad."

The world was far bigger than she had realized. There was far more pain and sadness than she had the ability to affect. An invincible organism like Tu hadn't been able to save either the children of the Order or Kuze the Passing Disaster.

"I...find food tasty, as other people do. But unlike other people, pain and agony are unknown to me. I was created without the ability to feel that stuff. I'm only pretending to be a minia... Izick was the one who made me, after all."

Izick, the Life Arts user who created Tu the Magic and Ozonezma the Capricious.

However, before Izick the Chromic became famous as a member of the First Party, he was a damnable demon king who destroyed cities on a whim, killing simply for the fun of it. Everywhere he went, he left a sea of blood in his wake.

"Izick told me that I was a weapon. I think I told him that I didn't want to be one. But as long as I'm alive, I can't do anything about the nature of this body, so...I wonder what I gotta do to be able to understand everyone's feelings..."

Her long triple braid swayed in the night breeze that blew into the room.

She couldn't help thinking that she should have talked more about that stuff with Rique while he was still alive. In truth, she had sat through countless lectures of his on the things that set her apart from the average person.

"Your troubles make no sense to me. Just possessing a minia's senses, well... There are still heterodoxic examples like Izick. In fact, there are even examples of the opposite, I think. The incident with Kuze the Passing Disaster...that was something Flinsuda and I set up, and you don't need to feel responsible for it."

The pupilless revenant matched Tu's gaze.

"...So don't give in to despair. Don't do anything rash. Flinsuda says that she won't force any combat on you for now. Just keep being well behaved and let her look after you, even just for a little while. While you do, you can slowly begin searching for a way to accomplish your own goals...whether it's to meet the queen or something else."

"...You're a good guy, Krafnir."

"I've just been hired to be here. My Mind Arts research needs funding."

Tu's current inability to move about this mansion wasn't because she was stricken with grief over Rique's death.

She still didn't understand—what did she have to do? What was needed for her to be able to save another?

Tu had come all the way to Aureatia to meet Queen Sephite. But shouldn't she have been using her strength for some greater purpose?

"...Hey, Krafnir. Why are you so interested in Mind Arts?"

"I get that you're bored, but... You really want to hear about that?"

"Yeah."

She had never seen Krafnir's face before, as he was always controlling a revenant instead.

However, he was far more involved with the behavior of others than Tu and making use of his own talents. Just as it was for everyone else Tu encountered, he must have lived a life that led him to be this way.

"......"

Revenants didn't breathe, but perhaps because of Krafnir's connection with it, its gesture resembled a sigh.

"...Well, if it'll distract you a bit, then fine. I...was originally born in the Northern Kingdom. I had studied Word Arts at the National Institute, but partway through, I aspired to study on my own. Though, well... that was because no one around me could really follow along with my theories."

"So even back then you were really brilliant, huh, Krafnir?! That's amazing."

"No, um...brilliant is a bit... Hmph, I suppose...you could see it that way, depending on how you look at it. Anyway, after I was expelled from school, I met a reclusive self-proclaimed demon king. She was afflicted with a serious illness and couldn't fully lift herself out of bed, but she tried to teach me her skills...though, it appeared that she just really enjoyed teaching. Honestly, at the time, I was fed up with studying Word Arts. I was so naturally talented that I found studying them boring."

"But you still studied them as much as you could, huh?"

"Well, yes, I suppose…"

"You were a prodigy from the very beginning, but you didn't want to disappoint that teacher of yours. You're kind to a fault."

Tu rocked her body with a beaming smile. The revenant's gaze darted to and fro, looking embarrassed.

"…Anyway! That was when I learned the fundamentals of construct creation theory. As I deepened my understanding, I began thinking I was ready to continue on past just theory and learn more. It was there…I asked my master. After she was dead, who was the person I was supposed to learn construct creation from?"

"Who was it?"

"Izick the Chromatic."

"……"

"The illness my master was afflicted with…had been a bacteriological weapon Izick had created. He had successfully applied the cellular modification done through Life Arts on microorganisms. My master lost all of her pupils to this weapon, and she had been continuously tormented with half-paralysis herself. However, as a fellow construct researcher, she couldn't help acknowledging the fact he had an outstanding knack for it, if nothing else… It must have been humiliating."

Izick the Chromatic. The First Party, the seven legends who were the first in the land to challenge the True Demon King. The other six names had been passed down with honor and respect, but Izick's name was the only one that was always accompanied by hatred and rancor.

While the terror of the True Demon King may have overwritten everything that came before it, the misfortune he brought upon the world in the previous age was all too great. Even Krafnir the Hatch of Truth sat at the end of a chain of misfortune wrought by the man.

"...Krafnir, I'm sorry."

"DON'T GET THE WRONG IDEA. WHILE IT'S TRUE YOU'RE ONE OF HIS CREATIONS, I'M NOT SO PETTY AS TO DIRECT MY GRUDGE AT YOU. BUT, WELL...AFTER MY MASTER DIED...I WASN'T ABLE TO ASK IZICK TO TEACH ME... IT HAD BEEN MY MASTER'S WISH THAT I COMPLETE MY THEORY."

"But it's a good thing you didn't involve yourself with a guy like Izick! I wonder what your master was thinking. You were one of their precious apprentices, too, weren't you?"

"HMPH... THAT'S YOUR WAY OF LOOKING AT IT. IT WASN'T ABOUT FRIENDS OR FOES, DANGER OR SAFETY. TO US, PROVING THE THEORY BEHIND MIND ARTS AND STANDARDIZING WAS EVERYTHING... I WANTED TO STUDY ON MY OWN AGAIN AND HAVE OUR IDEAS BEAR FRUIT. THIS WAS BEFORE THE APPEARANCE OF THE TRUE DEMON KING. IZICK RAMPAGED ABOUT AS HE SAW FIT, WITH HIS INSECT CONSTRUCTS, VERMIN CONSTRUCTS, PLAGUE CONSTRUCTS...MENACING THE NORTHERN KINGDOM WITH ALL MANNERS OF GRUESOME DEATH. BUT IF WE COULD COMPLETE OUR THEORY, WE WOULD HAVE BEEN ABLE TO WIPE OUT THE BAD reputation Izick had created regarding constructs and demonstrate their utility. Establish construct creation theory not as a source of calamity but as technology for people to make use of. That was what our research was about."

"Wow, really? I knew it… You really are amazing, Krafnir."

Tu smiled. Born strong and unable to feel pain or agony, for Tu, the acts of "hard work" and "effort" proved far too difficult. Spending all that time, the past several decades behind him growing fainter…Krafnir had put in more and more hard work. And now his name was known as the one who discovered the fifth system of Word Arts.

"…You made your master's dream come true. Having constructs now be beneficial for everyone…"

"No. There's more to this story."

The revenant slowly shook his head. His voice seemed to be laughing, but his words were spoken with a self-deprecating tone.

"For a long time, my research stagnated…but then one day, in a ruined city, I found a single construct corpse. A very small, wormlike revenant. However, the Word Arts that built it were extremely advanced yet simple…and structured. This single specimen was able to completely fill in the gap in my research."

"…………"

"It was one of Izick's constructs."

Izick the Chromatic was a genius without peer.

"My master had spent her life unsuccessfully trying

TO ACHIEVE THE SYSTEMIZATION OF MIND ARTS, AND IZICK HAD ALREADY GOTTEN THERE A LONG, LONG TIME AGO."

"Krafnir..."

"DON'T LOOK AT ME LIKE THAT! LISTEN. WHAT I'M GETTING AT IS...EVEN THOUGH HE HAD THESE AMAZING SKILLS, WHY HASN'T ANY OF IZICK'S RESEARCH BEEN LEFT BEHIND? IT'S BECAUSE ALTHOUGH HE HAD SUCH IMMENSE POWER, HE NEVER ONCE TRIED TO USE IT FOR THE SAKE OF SOMEONE ELSE. HIS NAME'S PASSED DOWN NOT AS A GREAT HERO, BUT AS THE MOST TERRIBLE SELF-PROCLAIMED DEMON KING OF THEM ALL. THAT'S WHY YOU'RE DIFFERENT FROM HIM!"

Izick the Chromatic had been a genius. A solitary genius.

Never in his life had he shared his successes with anyone else, nor did he use them to do anything but satisfy his own desires.

"WHAT I'M TRYING TO SAY IS... TU, YOU HAVE A MIND OF YOUR OWN, DIFFERENT FROM IZICK'S. MORE THAN JUST THE STRENGTH TO SAVE SOMEONE ELSE, YOU HAVE THE *DESIRE* TO USE THAT POWER FOR THE SAKE OF ANOTHER. SO YOU DON'T NEED TO BELIEVE YOU'RE POWERLESS. THERE WILL COME A DAY WHEN YOU'LL BE ABLE TO SAVE SOMEONE. THAT'S THE END OF THIS CONVERSATION."

"...Okay."

Even Tu could tell Krafnir's past wasn't something he spoke about easily.

Yet in this moment, he was an open book, as if they were engaging in idle chitchat. He was trying to soothe her feeling of helplessness at having been unable to save Kuze or Rique.

She understood that was what he was doing for her.

Krafnir…really is kind, after all. I want to become kind, too…

Still hugging her knees to her chest, Tu gazed out at the jeweled city lights before looking up into the dark sky.

◆

Right before the end of the sixth match. In a corner of the new town, filled with the light of the night, there was a secret conversation going on.

A slightly rotund man with a camera hanging from his neck, Yukiharu the Twilight Diver, entered the abandoned restaurant. He beamed an amiable smile unfit for the ruins he stood in and raised his hand.

"Hello there. Forgive me for calling you out of the blue."

"I might double-cross you," declared the silhouette right after he spotted Yukiharu. The shadow's name was Kuze the Passing Disaster.

"I've already told this to Hiroto and Zigita Zogi, but I should let you know, too. If anything happens to the Order children who were sent to Okafu, then there won't be meaning to any of this… Yukiharu the Twilight Diver, I want you to keep watch on Okafu, too."

"*Ha-ha-ha.* And if I don't, will you end up stabbing me, too?"

"…*Ha-ha.*" Kuze merely replied with a dry laugh.

"Ah, well… You don't need to worry, I've set things up so all Okafu information will automatically get sent my way. As a reporter, it's best to find material for my articles on my own, but to get my feet going, I need connections to create a foundation to walk on. Still, Hiroto and Zigita Zogi are keeping the children close at hand to try to ensure you won't double-cross them, right? If the kids were all killed because you betrayed them, I mean, you'd have your priorities all backward, wouldn't you?"

"*Bweh-heh-heh.* You may be right. So don't read too deeply into this, but...lately, the thoughts come to me."

Since winning the sixth match by default, something had changed within Kuze.

Everything looked the same as it had up until now, but there were signs of some sort of strife. A sense that something was off, like the small parts of a watch beginning to slip out of sync.

"Perhaps, maybe I might..."

Kuze paused.

"...kill the children. I might end up doing that to protect everything else within the Order. When I think about all the sacrifices I've made thus far, maybe I shouldn't be swayed by someone using my love and attachments anymore."

The man had abandoned himself and had done absolute everything for the Order. He had sacrificed so much. His mentor, his friends, the things that he loved—he had thrown them all away for the sake of the Order.

Would such a man truly be able to discard the things he was supposed to protect?

"*Ha-ha-ha.* I hope that doesn't happen. Fortunately, Hiroto's interests align with yours. I, myself, don't really think he'd have any motive take those children hostage in order to compel you into doing something."

"Hiroto said the same thing to me. I just want him to take protecting the kids seriously to ensure *nothing happens* to them."

"…Well, there's no guarantee that another foe willing to use the same methods as Nophtok won't appear again, unfortunately."

Kuze the Passing Disaster was nigh invincible, but his weakness was all too clear. It didn't only extend to the children, either. Any and every follower of the Order in Aureatia could be used as a hostage against him.

Yukiharu thought, however, that it was already becoming impossible to say this with one hundred percent certainty. Would it truly be possible to control this ultimate assassin right up to the end, even for the aberrant politician Hiroto the Paradox?

"You guys protected Nophtok the Crepuscle Bell, too, didn't you?"

"Yes. While he is a fiend who's totally worthless alive or dead, if we kept him here in Aureatia, it's likely he'd just be assassinated and eliminate you from the tournament. We're having him stay hidden until your next match. It's a simple plan but quite effective, wouldn't you say?"

"…Yeah, it sure is."

For some reason, there was a self-deprecating slant to Kuze's smile.

"An almost laughably effective plan."

"Well then, about the business I called you out here to discuss. On the day of the eighth match, we'd like you to head to the castle garden theater."

"Is this on Zigita Zogi's orders? I can go as a spectator, but I can't kill anyone while they're fighting against someone else, and wasn't the whole idea that you had to let Uhak survive and get him to join your side for everything to work out?"

"About that, you see, they've estimated that it's highly likely another force will take advantage of the eighth match to make a move. They're calling this force the 'invisible army.' They're a spy collective consisting of several vampires. They've already planted their agents into most of the other organizations, and they've already been successful at masking many casualties as rebellion or suicide. I have several photos as proof. Want to see?"

"...Suicide?" Kuze murmured, as if to himself.

At the almshouse where the children, now in Okafu, used to live, a priest-in-training named Naiji the Rhombus Knot had committed suicide. Yukiharu knew this and purposely chose to include the word *suicide* in his briefing.

"The most likely timing for them to make a move is while Zigita Zogi is fighting in the eighth match. We want you to act as a commando in the spectator seats and keep an eye on anyone you suspect belongs to the invisible army. There's nothing unnatural about having another hero candidate spectate the other matches, right?"

"Right. Sure... It'd be best if nothing happened, after all."

With an affable smile, Yukiharu rubbed his hands together.

"Oh thank goodness. Speaking of betrayal, I was rather on edge thinking that you might refuse. In any case, let's hash out the steps to take for after you arrive on the scene."

◆

The nighttime city was overflowing with eye-catching lights and colors; there was no one who took deliberate notice of the black-clad man walking through the crowds.

Just by covering up everything below his eyes with his black scarf, there would be few who could point him out to be the hero candidate Kuze.

...*Now, there's nothing left I have to worry about.*

The children were in the Free City of Okafu, affiliated with Hiroto the Paradox.

All he could do about the Order's future, after Kuze's sins were eventually brought to light, was entrust it to Hiroto. For the children, it just meant their inevitable fates would come a bit sooner than expected.

I'll kill the Queen, and we'll be the only ones who'll take on the persecution of the Order. That's all I had to do. Just like Nastique... I only have to become a blade with a singular purpose.

Compared to his battles up until now, where he struggled to save everything and everyone only to lose it all, this battle was much, much easier, knowing he'd lose everything from the very start.

He purchased some of the day's leftover mead and barley bread from a store that was open late.

Among the countless lights in Aureatia, could the light of the faith Kuze had protected be found?

Or perhaps...was it only the believers in the Wordmaker who had fallen into darkness in between the gaps in light—just as people had criticized—and were now beyond salvation?

At the very least, the children in the Western Outer Ward Church hadn't been able to live among Aureatia's light.

"......"

Walking along as he ate his bread, Kuze came to a stop in front of a narrow alley that stretched out beside him.

In the center of the darkness, he thought he saw the image of a seated child.

"Taking a bit of a break, are we?"

"......"

Kuze had been right on the mark. He heard her breathing change in response to his voice.

The shadow stirred, and strands of her blond hair faintly reflected the light from the main road.

"I've done the same plenty of times. But if you sleep sitting up, it'll come back to bite you when you get older. Should I call for someone? Or perhaps not?"

"...Leave me alone."

The child wasn't all that young. A prim young elf girl, about thirteen or fourteen years old.

Based on the state of her, she didn't seem to be a vagabond or a starveling. Kuze figured she must have run away from home.

"Or maybe you've been ordered to capture me, is that it?"

"Oh, heavens no." He humorously lifted up both hands. "You don't know who I am? And here I thought I'd gotten a little bit of fame for myself..."

"Nope, no clue. Who are you?"

"Seriously..." Kuze awkwardly scratched his head.

It wasn't strange for someone not to know the faces of the hero candidates. Kuze himself hadn't actually seen beneath Toroa the Awful's hood, and when it came to Ozonezma the Capricious or the young girl named Kia who appeared in the fourth match, he knew nothing of their appearance beyond the rumors.

"Hmm, so...who's trying to capture you, then? Are you running from somebody?"

"If I tell you that—" The girl's large aquamarine eyes narrowed. "You're gonna sell me out to them, aren't you?"

"Whaaaat? No, fine, I get it. If that's how it is, you don't have to tell me anything. I just thought if you were having a rough time, maybe I could split some of my bread with you."

"Huh?"

The girl took out her own bread. It was much larger, whiter, and softer than what Kuze had just purchased for himself—a truly high-quality loaf.

"I—I guess you didn't need any of my help at all... That's great. Real happy for you."

"I don't need *anyone's* help. There's nothing I can't do."

The young girl may have been speaking the truth. Her appearance was much neater and tidier than other stray children Kuze had seen. She showed no signs of fear, and she wasn't even hurting for food, either.

"All right, then, why are you hiding in the shadows, *avoiding the eyes of others* like that?"

"......"

This girl was running from someone. If she hadn't had some

personal circumstances weighing on her conscience, then she could've just sought out help. While they had exchanged only a few words, she didn't seem like the type who was incapable of asking for help.

She was burdened by some large sin she'd committed. Kuze might've felt it in his gut.

"...What's that got to do with anything?"

"I'm with the Order, you see. I teach everyone that all lives stand to benefit from the Wordmaker's salvation."

"The Wordmaker. Oh, right, I remember. You people on the outside believe in that stuff, don't you...? You believe that the Wordmaker is the God who made this whole world, and they can do anything. Tee-hee. Hee-hee-hee-hee." The young girl's shoulders trembled as she laughed. "...That's so stupid. If that's true, then that means the Wordmaker is *just like me*."

"Whoa, whoa now, what's that supp—"

"Blind him."

Without warning, there was a blinding flash from the alleyway. The source of the light was utterly ambiguous, and it gave off neither sound nor heat.

With the reflexive movements of a warrior, Kuze braced himself, preparing for a fight.

"...What was that just now?"

When his vision finally recovered enough to see the dark alley, the young girl was already gone.

Kuze turned around, and on a building's roof, right under the moon, there was a small, white figure. Had the angel Nastique been able to see who exactly that girl was?

...That means the Wordmaker is just like me.

The Wordmaker is everywhere.

It was what Kuze had been taught, and what he had taught others. The conscience in one's heart was itself the Wordmaker's salvation to all, and the Wordmaker was present in the eyes of every living creature with a soul.

I'm sure they'll be watching the whole time, even on the day I commit my sin.

◆

After finishing his clandestine meeting with Kuze, Yukiharu the Twilight Diver headed off in a new direction. His destination could be described as a blind spot in the vast Aureatia, an abandoned shipyard.

He was now carrying a wooden box on his back.

"I never would've expected we'd bump up against someone else while covering the National Defense Institute. Ended up making a weird connection through it all, too!"

"I agree."

The wooden box was far smaller than a person's whole body. Although there wasn't enough capacity to fit any of the minian races, an eloquent voice resonated from within.

"Think we can trust what Haizesta talked about? That if we looked into Enu the Distant Mirror's conduct, it'd link back to the National Defense Research Institute."

"I wonder. But if Enu's in charge of city development, then I don't think it would be that hard for him to secretly provide a base of operations inside the Institute without the Aureatia government catching on."

The Fifteenth General, Haizesta the Gathering Spot. He had belonged to the third faction in Aureatia, Kaete's camp. However, Kaete the Round Table fell from power after his defeat in the sixth match. In the process of investigating Kaete's opponent, Enu the Distant Mirror, Haizesta had learned about the existence of the National Defense Research Institute and had secretly made contact with Yukiharu the Twilight Diver, who was also investigating the Institute.

Haizesta's movements afterward were unknown.

"Is it true that the charges of foul play laid on Kaete and Kiyazuna were all part of Obsidian Eyes' machinations? The garden theater bombing, using airships for acts of sabotage, Mestelexil's rampage... With how many witnesses there were, Aureatia concluded that Kaete's camp were the perpetrators. I still think it's a bit too much of a stretch to say it was all a conspiracy."

"Even within the Aureatia Assembly, Kaete's camp was seen as an unwelcome player by the most powerful factions, Rosclay's and Haade's. The suspicions of foul play may have all been a setup, but on the Aureatia side of things, it had to be something they *wanted to go along with* anyway. Since they could use the charges to cleanly snuff out a threat."

"But there's no evidence of any conspiracy, right? It's already dubious whether Obsidian Eyes actually exists or not."

"If Enu's guilty, just like Haizesta claimed, then it's highly likely that Zeljirga has a contact within Obsidian Eyes. That would mean that the invisible army's true identity was Obsidian Eyes, just as Zigita Zogi hypothesized. The now-missing Kaete and Kiyazuna might've been killed or captured by them. Why don't we act just as Haizesta requested…? We can search for the two of them and rescue them if they're still alive."

"True, asking the two of them directly would probably be the fastest way to go about it, but…if Obsidian Eyes really are the opponents here, how are we supposed to save them? Heck, if we went out to help then, we'd definitely end up dead instead."

"Whoa, whoa, we're not doing this ourselves here. The Old Kingdoms' loyalists are."

The shipyard Yukiharu was heading toward was a secretly hidden basepoint for the Old Kingdoms' loyalists inside Aureatia. Knowing this country from its days as the Central Kingdom, the Old Kingdoms' loyalists had secured a great number of basepoints just like it.

Furthermore, Yukiharu's employer, Hiroto the Paradox, was the mastermind who had previously given economic support to the Old Kingdoms' loyalists' occupation of Gimeena City and had spurred them into their uprising.

Even now, after the loyalists lost their war with Aureatia, Yukiharu always maintained a direct connection with them.

"Right now, the Old Kingdoms' loyalists are in desperate need of someone formidable and powerful to mobilize their camp. They keep getting themselves caught in battles of attrition, which is the problem. Given that they were driven out of the Aureatia government, Kaete and Kiyazuna should be capable individuals who they'd definitely want to have on their side...which is how Zigita Zogi explained it all."

"You didn't think that all up yourself, then, Yukiharu?"

"*Aha-ha*. The story I'm after is still just the National Defensive Research Institute, after all. It's the same for you, too, though, right?"

"...Yeah."

There were hardly any people who knew about the contents of the wooden box Yukiharu carried on his back.

However, its objective was an exceedingly simple one.

"I'm going to make sure you keep your promise—I might be able to see *Mother*."

CHAPTER 3 ◆ Romog Joint Military Hospital

It was early in the morning on the day of the eighth match.

Since claiming victory over Ozonezma the Capricious in the third match, Soujirou the Willow-Sword had received extensive medical treatment in this army hospital.

"…I'm bored."

It wasn't only the losers who were wounded in the Sixways Exhibition. If anything, it was the winners who needed the most medical attention of all, and they performed under strict security to prevent other camps from setting up a *win by default*.

Romog Joint Military Hospital was a major hospital that had existed in Aureatia since the days of the Central Kingdom, possessing the facilities to meet these requirements.

"When're they gonna hurry up and announce my next match…?"

His right leg had been lost—the price he had paid for his victory. There was no hope of regenerating it with Life Arts, and for the average person, the injury was severe enough to deem him unfit for battle.

"You've got guts, Soujirou the Willow-Sword!"

As Soujirou casually mumbled to himself, there came a booming voice, nearly ten times as loud. It was the sickbed right beside him, separated with a curtain.

"Though you've lost your leg, you haven't lost your fighting spirit! And seeking to return to the battlefield yourself, to boot! What pluck! Visitors really are something! I wish my men would follow your example!"

"Jeez, you were awake?"

The sun still hadn't risen. The chirping of songbirds could be heard in the distance.

"Sabfom, aren't they always tellin' you to keep yer voice down?" Soujirou said with a yawn. The booming voice had dissolved any drowsiness he had left.

"Ahh! Good heavens! I can't have myself disturbing the other patients' sleep. With only two of us in this room, I'm always quick to forget that! *Fwa-ha-ha-ha!*"

"Seriously, pipe down."

Sabfom the White Weaver was Aureatia's Twelfth General. Possessing the perfected muscular physique befitting a military officer, the man seemed to be completely unfamiliar with the inside of a hospital room; however, his face was covered in what seemed like a mask of smooth iron.

Previously, he was a general fighting on the front lines during a brief dispute with the Free City of Okafu.

Despite pressing forward until he was right in front of Okafu's ringleader, Morio the Sentinel, the skin on his face was flayed from his left cheek to his right eyelid, and as result, he now required long-term medical treatment. This was why his mask was smooth to the point that it didn't even have an indent to cover his nose.

"Visitors are grand. Morio the Sentinel is a Visitor himself! I, myself, think people like you and him—those who laugh in the face of death—they're the truest of warriors! If I could, I'd love to head over to the Beyond and battle other monsters like Morio to the death!"

"I told ya, the Beyond ain't that fun of a place, believe me. So how did that duel with Morio end anyway? You got your face messed up, right?"

"*Fwa-ha-ha-ha!* Right you are. As I mentioned last night, I was able to dodge Morio's short sword by a hairsbreadth. But at the time, I dodged by too fine a line. Since I gauged the dodge with my eyes, *everything past my eyes* got sliced off. Skin. Nose. My right eyelid! It was a clean cut; in fact, I didn't feel any pain at all. The thing is, Soujirou, I was still in the midst of a duel to the death against *the* Morio the Sentinel."

Sabfom rapped against the metal plate covering his face.

"Having all of that stuff dangling down around my neck would've cost me my life. I immediately tore off a chunk of my own face. I even felt happy to do so. I was so focused on the battle, I made the decision without a second thought."

"You got guts; I'll give ya that."

Soujirou smirked.

"Until you're face-to-face with life-threatening peril, it's impossible to know how your heart'll react in that situation. So I view this wound with honor, not shame. It's my proof that I really do love battle after all."

The stories Sabfom told Soujirou were all lurid and gruesome tales on par with the battles he had experienced in the Beyond, but unlike most others, Sabfom never mixed in any negative feelings toward his life-threatening experiences.

In this world where, even after the True Demon King's demise, most of the populace looked to be at war with terror and madness in their hearts, it was fair to say Sabfom's temperament was a rare gift.

"Here I thought all these Twenty-Nine Officials types or who-ever were all busy with some overblown pretentious stuff. But I guess there are all sorts of types among 'em. Even got guys like that old dude Harghent, too," said Soujirou.

"Oh, you've met Harghent?!"

"Yup. But wait, you been in here longer than me, right? You're sayin' *you* haven't seen him?"

"Hrmm… I guess Harghent doesn't know I've been admitted here, then! This was all back when I still had a face, but I actually helped Harghent out a lot and looked after him."

"Huh. What sorta help?"

"Well, in regard to this work, Harghent's, well…not a totally incompetent man, but he's got a tendency to let things build up inside himself. On our days off, I'd always take him out for drinks and give him all sorts of advice from my own experiences on how to do his job right. Sometimes I'd gather up the young and talented among my men to have him enjoy their stimulating conversations!"

"Whoa…that's a lot. Anything else?"

"I've also invited him many times to join me on my snowy mountain climbs! Soujirou, let me tell you, mountain climbing is a wonderful hobby. You can have plenty of time for a conversation while also getting some exercise. It's great for cultivating the body and the mind. Plus, the scenery's nothing to sneeze at! I believe that there's no better atmosphere for two military officers to have a chat."

"That's wild."

Soujirou determined that he wasn't supposed to say anything here. Even Soujirou the Willow-Sword, an audacious shura who longed only for battle, still possessed the barest minimum social skills.

"I can't be relaxing here like this. Harghent and I have to get back on our feet as soon as we can. We must show the public that Aureatia's defenses are strong and that there's nothing to fear!"

"...What d'ya mean, defenses? We went and crushed Lithia, and I heard that those something-something loyalist guys got put down, too. Who's there to fight at this point?"

"Oh, is that how you see it? There are definitely still opponents out there! For example..."

Aureatia's Twenty-Nine Officials was a wartime regime that had persisted from the age of the True Demon King. The military officials who made up close to half the seats still demonstrated a focused mind toward the wars Aureatia fought. Toward the might of hypothetical enemies.

"The hero candidates."

"......"

"...Oops, I guess it's hard to laugh at a joke like that, huh? Still, it's not entirely impossible, either!"

The fact that Sabfom here was in the same room as Soujirou wasn't a simple coincidence. Behind the scenes of the Sixways Exhibition, there were many powers plotting the defeats and victories of the various hero candidates. Enough that even one of the Twenty-Nine Officials themselves, while bedridden in the hospital, needed to keep watch to ensure there was no foul play.

Sabfom the White Weave was also an expert military official, who had experience crossing swords with a visitor from his battle with Morio.

"...My next opponent's this guy named Rosclay. He's one of the Twenty-Nine guys, same as you. He didn't put you in here, did he?"

"*Fwa-ha-ha-ha!* No, of course not. That young lad wouldn't make a move that's so cheap and unlikely to succeed. But it's not just him—others must be thinking the same as well. Your very existences themselves are antithetical to peace. So long as individuals who wield power rivaling that of entire nations are left to their own devices, the world could be destroyed *on a whim*. Me, you, Morio the Sentinel—all our spirits crave conflict, without a doubt. However, your strength is the one thing that differs."

"What a pain in the ass... None of that is my responsibility or anything."

"Oh? So even with all that strength you have, you're still against getting targeted, are you?!"

"I'm sick of it. Fighting off weaklings is boring."

The Sixways Exhibition was a deceptive ploy to entice the

strongest beings in the land to crush each other. A majority of the hero candidates must have already understood this fact, as well.

"...If that's how it's gonna be, I'd rather just get my next match started already."

However, this truly ingenious stratagem had been devised to ensure that these players would want to continue with it *even after seeing through to the truth underneath.*

◆

Just like the greater part of Aureatia's medical institutions, jurisdiction over Romog Joint Military Hospital fell to the medical division led by the Seventh Minister, Flinsuda the Portent. Therefore, there weren't any of the other Twenty-Nine Officials with the authority to interfere with what went on inside them, no matter who she may invite inside their walls.

At the moment, Flinsuda was sitting in a chair, her flesh sinking into it, inside the reception room.

Her corpulent body was decorated with countless pieces of jewelry, as if to deliberately flaunt her wealth. However, she certainly wasn't dressed in a crude or gaudy manner—if anything, they afforded her an air of elegance.

Flinsuda lit her cigarette full of fragrant herbs and then spoke as if remembering something.

"...I forget, do you dislike smoke?"

"No, it's fine... No need to show consideration for these old bones."

The man sitting opposite her was elderly with thick wrinkles. He almost looked like a corpse propped up in a chair.

However, behind the chair were four elven slaves, even though slavery was forbidden under the current laws. They were there as his bodyguards and vaunted the hidden authority this old man possessed.

"Originally, I planned on finishing up my work this morning and showing my dear Tu a bit of fun. If you've come here yourself instead of a messenger...you must have quite a serious matter to discuss with me."

"*Kweh-heh*... No need to be so guarded; this request isn't nearly as big as you think it is... Flinsuda, there's a patient I'd like you to treat in absolute secrecy," the elderly man continued.

"You know about the clinic that was burned to the ground last night? There is someone with severe burns that was miraculously rescued from the blaze. We've done everything we possibly can but... Unfortunately, their life is currently in danger. I would ask you to use your most cutting-edge medical technology to save this precious life..."

"My, my, that *is* quite a predicament. I wonder if you were aware, though. Matters that involved the lives of others are *quite serious topics of discussion*, Minister Iriolde."

Despite the jocular smile coming to her face, Flinsuda never took her eyes off the old man in front of her.

She and the rest of the Twenty-Nine Officials were the highest authority currently controlling Aureatia. However, there was a phantom who continued to exert a mighty influence from outside their ranks.

An authority of the aristocracy, from the era of the Central Kingdom. The only one of the Twenty-Nine Officials to be expelled from their ranks, charged with three counts of corruption. The first suspect behind the invisible army—former Fifth Minister, Iriolde the Atypical Tome.

"You see, for me...I haven't the slightest interest in this factional power struggle you, Rosclay, and Haade are all wrapped up in. Money alone is more than enough for me. So once this treatment's over, whatever your group does with this patient of yours has absolutely nothing to do with me. At the very least, I hope you'd promise me that."

"You do not need to worry... That is precisely why I am asking you for the utmost secrecy. As long as you don't mention it to anyone, our involvement will never come to light. After all, there's no reason at all to reproach a doctor for saving a patient's life... now is there?"

"*Ho-ho-ho-ho-ho-ho!* But of course! I don't intend to tell a soul. What I'm concerned about is you, Minister Iriolde. Whether *you'll* talk about it or not."

This secret bargain implied that Flinsuda belonged to Iriolde's camp. However, if she gave this impression to the other powers at play, she would have no choice but to join Iriolde in earnest.

It was an all-too-likely course of events, when she thought about how the man had done things in the past.

"*Kweh-heh...* You're not going to trust me?"

"Oh no, I certainly trust you. About as much as I did when you were part of the Twenty-Nine Officials."

"In that case…would you like to spend more time here talking with your old acquaintance then, Flinsuda?"

"……"

A syrupy smile formed between Iriolde's wrinkles.

"…No. I'll dispatch a doctor at once. If the patient is indeed racing the clock, then we can discuss compensation later."

On Flinsuda's side of the room, she was no longer making herself smile. He could use the life of this patient he asked her to save as a shield. That was the type of man Iriolde was.

"Thank you. I was right… You are indeed a friend worthy of my trust."

"What's the patient's name?"

In contrast to Flinsuda standing to leave the room, Iriolde remained solemnly seated as he replied.

Perhaps it was because he was indifferent as to whether this patient lived or died.

Or maybe…it was because he was convinced that they would survive.

"Kuuro the Cautious."

There was an extra Official sponsoring a shura who existed outside the playing field.

"I'm sure he, too…will become a great friend of mine."

◆

After he'd finished forcing down his bland breakfast, he went up to the hospital roof without speaking to anyone else. Listening to the far sounds of the market abuzz with the Sixways Exhibition, he absentmindedly stared out at the balloons swaying in the city air.

This was how Aureatia's Sixth General, Harghent the Still, spent his days.

"......"

Left alone in the Mali Wastes after Lucnoca the Winter had won the second match, he was diagnosed with a severe case of mania and was ordered by the assembly to undergo a long-term recuperation period.

This manner of disposing of him, in the midst of the Sixways Exhibition, effectively stripped him of his rights as a sponsor, but no one among the Twenty-Nine Officials had appeared to plead against this unfair treatment—including Harghent himself.

A lunatic who had sponsored Lucnoca the Winter and summoned danger to Aureatia. That was exactly right, Harghent thought. He had committed such a heinous crime, and even then, he hadn't been able to obtain a single thing someone might wish for.

Either way, together with the death of Alus the Star Runner's legend, his life had ended as well.

"...Alus..."

What was he thinking, staring up at the sky?

He might have believed that from far beyond the sky, his friend would come home.

Or perhaps he simply pretended to believe that, trying to evade the guilt he felt for consigning Alus to his death.

"You up here *again*, old man?" came the exasperated young voice from behind him.

He wore a red track jacket draped over his shoulders. He held a crutch beneath each arm, and his right leg was missing from the thigh down.

A transcendent master swordsman from another world—Soujirou the Willow-Sword.

"Stop wandering around on the roof—enough already. Yer just wasting your time."

"W-wasting my time...?! What do you know?! Aren't I free to do whatever I please, or go wh-wherever I want?! That's what makes visitors like you so evil! Unable to do anything but force your sense of values—"

"Mhm, sorry, but I got no clue what you're talkin' about. I mean 's not like you actually *wanna* do this anyway, right?"

"That's not true!"

"It was pouring like hell the other day, and you still came out here."

He was right. On that day, Harghent was sure that the hospital would have locked up to make sure none of the wind and rain had blown in, but he had been able to get outside, so he did.

"...and you poked your head out for a bit and then came right back in, didn't ya? Completely soaked, and everything. The hell was that about?"

"*Hngh...*"

In the end, Harghent the Still wasn't even capable of becoming the madman he was diagnosed to be.

He wasn't an empty husk. He only needed the reality set before him in order to live another day.

"What're you gonna do from here on out? That Sabfom guy was worried about you."

"*Gah*, Sabfom...?! You haven't told him about this place, have you?!"

"Should I?"

"No! I beg you—anything but that."

Soujirou sat down on the small step in front of the building.

He had lost a leg, and yet even then he seemed far mightier and far more alert than Harghent, who had all his limbs still intact.

"Seriously, though, you're totally healthy, ain'tcha? You gotta get yourself outta here; it's a waste being cooped up in this place."

"No! I'll stay here for the rest of my life! I...I'm a fool who let his worthless feelings get the better of him and exposed Aureatia to danger. I'm sure that none of the other Twenty-Nine Officials wish to see me return."

"Yer a real pain in the ass, aren't ya, old man?"

"B-besides...why's a visitor like you going out of your way to worry about me anyway? I'm not involved in the Sixways Exhibition anymore. They'll remove me from my seat on the Twenty-Nine Officials eventually, too. You're the one wasting your time, aren't you?"

"...Huh? Uh, I'm not really worrying about ya or anything; I'm just talking to you like I talk to all the other patients in here. Got nothing better to do."

"*Mrrn.*"

"I mean, I got my own stuff going on, too. This is a military hospital and all, so I can hear all sorts of battle stories and stuff.

There's even a soldier that was fightin' in Lithia while I was over there. That dude's got nothing left of his arms, though."

"I see... Right, you participated in that operation, didn't you?"

Although he had forced himself to be a part of it, Harghent was one of the Twenty-Nine Officials who'd participated on one end of the operation to assassinate Taren. While there hadn't been any chance for them to meet directly, the freshly verified visitor at the time, Soujirou the Willow-Sword, had been used over and over by Aureatia. When Harghent thought about it, the connection between them began back then.

"Did you know...that Alus the Star Runner was there at the time, too?"

"Oh, that so? I mean, makes sense he might've. There were wyverns flying all over the damn place."

"You didn't know after all, then... To ensure Alus could be sponsored as a hero candidate, Aureatia hid the truth behind the Lithia conflagration. Alus the Star Runner was the one who destroyed Lithia's air defense web and burned down the city."

"Oh yeah...?"

Soujirou's eyes narrowed. It made him resemble a snake or some other type of reptile.

"Alus...was a true champion. But at the same time, he was a living disaster capable of toppling entire nations. While all of you, and Lithia's own monsters, were fighting as two opposing sides in a conflict...he accomplished much all by himself."

There was no point in telling all of this to Soujirou now.

Despite the countless legends Alus had been a part of, there were far more that came to an end without ever being spoken of.

Alus the Star Runner only ever took pride in the treasures he collected, and there was no one who had recorded the magnificent journey he had taken to acquire them all, with Harghent himself knowing only a tiny portion of his truth.

"That Lucnoca the Winter... She has to be one hell of a fighter herself if she took down a monster like that."

"Y-yeah... She sure is..."

The memory made his breath catch in his throat.

Even the soldiers admitted here in this hospital were the lucky ones. There were countless numbers of innocent citizens who had met their demise in the flames of the Lithia War. There were minia among the souls that had been snuffed out Alus. These were the people Harghent was supposed to protect.

He knew this.

"An individual capable of destroying a nation cannot be allowed to exist in this world... That's why...while my methods may have been incorrect...I still believe that Star Runner needed to be killed by someone eventually."

"...Sabfom said something pretty close to that. He said just knowing there are super-powerful guys living and breathing out there in the world is terrifying."

Soujirou cast his eyes upward and looked at the light coming in between the gaps in the cloudy sky.

"Say. What's 'scary' anyway?"

"…What?"

"When I fought with Ozonezma, it was the first time I ever got like that. Fighting to the death…and feeling scared. Sabfom said he felt happy that he didn't get scared at all, even as he was about to die, y'know? But me, seems like I was the exact opposite."

Soujirou the Willow-Sword had experienced fear.

Was it even possible for this visitor swordsman, who had no qualms against running roughshod over this world with his violence, for one of the shura gathered here to the Sixways Exhibition, to feel an emotion like that at all? Harghent hadn't even imagined such a possibility.

They were all powerful beings who lived in a completely different world from Harghent and his ilk.

"That's because…until you fought with Ozonezma, you'd never fought against someone stronger than you, right?"

In which case, what had Alus the Star Runner felt when faced against Lucnoca the Winter?

Had the fearless rogue finally felt fear?

"…I'm always scared. I may have climbed all the way up to the Twenty-Nine Officials, but there are plenty more powerful than I out there. People with wits and talent. People with unwavering spirits. People with righteousness. Those people terrify me, and I know I'll only ever lose to them. That's why people like you will never understand how it feels."

"Hey, you *did it*, didn't ya?"

"……"

"I don't know that much about Lucnoca the Winter or anything.

But the reason you're here is 'cause you did something stupid, even knowing the whole time how scary it was, yeah? How'd you fight against that? Me...I'm satisfied that I got to have a go with Ozonezma, but that's one thing I still have regrets about. Next time someone else like that comes along, I really want to kill them. Though I've never thought too hard about killing someone before I did it, I don't think..."

Soujirou had a serious look in his eyes.

"Someday, I'll become able to cut 'em down."

"No... Wait, is that why you're going around the hospital, listening to the patients' stories? To hear what they felt when they were locked in battle, or about what type of emotion 'terror' is?"

"Yup."

Consider the source; take countermeasures.

Was it possible even to defeat tremendous foes such as fear or regret?

Harghent couldn't come up with a single thing that an incompetent man like him was able to do, that a man powerful enough to transcend worlds themselves like Soujirou couldn't.

"I..."

He covered his face with a hand to shield his own eyes from the sky.

"...I just decided...I wouldn't betray myself. I can't even tell... if I've truly been able to do it or not."

If he hadn't betrayed himself, then he wouldn't have lost his only friend, Harghent thought.

The eighth match of the Sixways Exhibition was over.

The war underneath the surface that unfolded between Zigita Zogi the Thousandth and Obsidian Eyes concluded, and the brain that Hiroto the Paradox had relied on more than any other, Zigita Zogi the Thousandth, had perished.

However, there were still battles being fought. Toroa the Awful left Aureatia and headed for the Mali Wastes...

"Toroa the Awful!"

Psianop the Inexhaustible Stagnation was rushing along the frozen surface of the Mali Wastes. He now understood the finer details of the magnificent battle that had unfolded far below the surface, down to the precise coordinates where it was located.

Psianop's keen senses told him more than that—he understood that this battle had *already been decided* as well.

"You were supposed to live on... Why didn't you understand that?"

Without a moment's hesitation, he jumped down into the Mali Wastes fissure, several meters deep.

It was a swift descent.

As he felt gravity and wind, he could detect a presence ascending from the depths of darkened abyss.

He could tell. Its speed vastly outstripped that of Psianop's descent.

Was it just a coincidence? Or was he waiting for me to jump down, knowing full well I was nearby?

He fell.

They were going to cross paths.

Midair. He couldn't dodge.

Star...

Two wings and three arms then—

A gunshot.

Alus the Star Runner, flying at terrifying speeds up from the abyss, fired two magic bullets of lethal poison with precision at Psianop mid-descent.

There was an abnormal scraping sound of the bullets' impact.

...Runner.

A stone fragment that Psianop gripped, enveloping it with his gelatinous body, bent in a bizarre shape, likely from the strength he used to parry the bullet's impact.

Psianop spun around. He flipped the stone fragment at the shadow now above him.

The target of this flicked projectile, revolving at high speeds, wasn't Alus the Star Runner's body itself.

It was his item bag.

Alus, with a flash of his magic whip, reflected the projectile, ascending from directly below his blind spot, as if he had been able to see it the entire time.

"......"

All of it had occurred in a single moment.

Psianop the Inexhaustible Stagnation fell to the deepest pits of the silent frozen earth.

◆

The fastest wyvern carried a tremendous selection of magical tools, far more than one person could typically possess, and displayed an aptitude with every single one of them, as well as being equipped with intellect and the experience of felling countless legends.

Alus the Star Runner had survived after forcing the world's strongest dragon, whom the word *calamity* failed to properly describe, to use her breath attack three times, and even brought low the beast of enchanted blades.

The horrifying wings flew off into the distant sky and were soon out of sight.

"...Toroa the Awful," Psianop simply mumbled, landing at the bottom of the frozen abyss.

A circular track had been etched into his landing point, like a geometrical wave shape, making it clear that he had been able to completely disperse the impact of his fall, despite the length of his descent.

There was nothing left behind but the vestiges of destruction.

There were none of Alus the Star Runner's magic items, nor Toroa the Awful's enchanted swords.

The remnants of the spatial fissure carved by Karmic Castigation were just barely visible, but they, too, disappeared shortly after.

"So you died, huh?"

Had Toroa the Awful managed to settle one of his grudges?

Psianop the Inexhaustible Stagnation had no reason to feel sentimental.

Almost all the people he was supposed to mourn had met their demise.

Tora and Alus faced off at this position. Star Runner went to take off.

He looked at the scars of the battle, carved into the earth and the rock wall.

Toroa used the flame sword's secret technique...and to stop his flight, he must've fired those magnetic wedges.

There were places all along the wall where it seemed like wedges had been driven in.

A chilling sensation.

None of the heat of the flames that were exchanged in the recent battle remained in this glacial hellscape, born of Lucnoca's breath.

The fiery magical item scorched all in its path. With magnetic force, he threw off Star Runner's rifle aim...

He had matured.

Toroa the Awful appeared to have gotten even stronger compared to when they had fought in the first match.

Alus...used something to blind him for a moment. He got in range of the Luminous Blade.

Perhaps Toroa had had an encounter of some kind that dispelled his hesitation. Or perhaps it was because he had several techniques to guarantee his victory, honed precisely for this one moment, that made it seem like he had grown stronger.

But Toroa saw through the feint. Well done. He had stepped forward to use the Howling Blade's secret technique...

There was no longer any heat left here. Still, Psianop knew.

Toroa had grown.

A long-range stab. Wind defense. There were still another few dozen moves after that. Toroa...

Psianop didn't feel any sentimentality.

He simply understood.

...Toroa didn't lose.

Right up to the last moments, even if his life came to an end.

CHAPTER
5

Central Assembly Hall
Second Communications Room
(Provisional Self-Proclaimed
Demon King Response
Headquarters)

After he'd announced the alert for Alus the Star Runner's attack, Hidow's feet carried him toward the Central Assembly Hall's second communications room, and he immediately established it as the headquarters for their response.

The radzios installed in this room could connect to the government buildings throughout Aureatia's domain. He had already decided on the ones he needed to reach out to first for this emergency radzio conference.

The head of the military. Twenty-Seventh General, Haade the Flashpoint.

The keystone of domestic affairs. Third Minister, Jelky the Swift Ink.

After he had finished sharing several of the known facts of the situation, Hidow brought out the topic they needed to decide on first in order to confront this disaster. In short, their defensive priorities.

"The reports from the observation station say that Alus the Star Runner is approaching from the southeast. If we let him in close from that direction, there'll be damage at the great bridge and in the commercial quarter. Personally, I want to avoid that. What do you think, Jel?"

<*Agreed. If we intercepted Alus the Star Runner in the commercial quarter, even assuming no civilian casualties, it'll cause considerable economic loss. In addition to necessitating the cancellation of the rest of the Sixways Exhibition, it will be impossible to support our population with reduced production capabilities.*>

<*Hmph! Well, what then? Intercepting an enemy that fast and powerful before he gets to Aureatia will be impossible. If fighting on Aureatia soil is inevitable...then the question is which one of the city's sections are we fine with getting torn apart.*>

"This is an emergency; it's unavoidable. You have any requests, Haade?"

<*Nope. That said, for military action against an enemy like Alus, I can't let my troops fight nice and clean, either. Once we've gotten the go-ahead to destroy the city itself if we want, we'll be able to fight without holding anything back. You're the one who's better at making the decisions here, right?*>

"...I feel bad for the people living there, but our only choice'll be to have Alus attack the Eastern Outer Ward, somewhere in between the third and sixth boroughs. The only cultural asset there is the Summit Sword Spire from the time of King Rekut. Haade, tell me how feasible that sounds."

<*If that's the course we're taking, then a squad deployed around the Thirty-Eighth Fortress can try launching an all-out cannon barrage at him to make him go off course. Even if we can't kill him, it'll be enough to make it divert him. As long as we can get him to move*>

east, there's nothing there but the Eastern Outer Ward anyway. The buildings aren't tall and definitely weren't built to protect from an aerial attack, but that might make it all the easier.>

The sound of him puffing out smoke mixed into the radzio's static.

<Thinking from Alus's perspective, if we block his path forward, he should want to head to where there's less stuff in the way of his flight path. Records show that there have been forty percent more wyvern raids coming from the Eastern Outer Ward side, as well. Also, it's easier to aim at targets from the ground when you're on terrain that gives you a good view of the sky. I definitely would've opposed the idea if my troops were going to be the only ones handling it, but this time the main fighting force'll be the hero candidates anyway.>

"All right, Eastern Outer Ward it is, then. Deploy your troops immediately. I'd like to know how many candidates we've been able to get together. How many of them can fight, Jel?"

<Two are absent. Psianop the Inexhaustible Stagnation and Toroa the Awful. We have witnesses saying they departed for the Mali Wastes early this morning. We have confirmed locations for two of them. Mele the Horizon's Roar, Shalk the Sound Slicer. However, Mele is wounded from the seventh match. There are three we still don't have definitive locations for. Ozonezma the Capricious, Kuze the Passing Disaster, and Zeljirga the Abyss Web. These three are definitely still inside the city. After they've been summoned by the alert, we'll instruct them to act. Kia and Mestelexil the Box of Desperate Knowledge are still on the run. Zigita Zogi the Thousandth

and Uhak the Silent are in the middle of their match. Meanwhile, Flinsuda has said she wishes to negotiate with us regarding the use of Tu the Magic. I'll scrape together the funds for this on my end. Tu should absolutely be added to our defense forces.>

"What the hell is that hag going off about while Aureatia's on the brink of destruction?! She planning on dying with fists full of cash or something? Jel, listen, if that woman is gonna be difficult, then I'll—"

<It's not your job to get angry. The most guaranteed way to get her to act is money, and I can swiftly arrange that for her. Do you have a problem with that, Hidow?>

"That's not what I was getting at! What about Soujirou, Haade?!"

<Ah, well...honestly, I don't really want to send him out there in that state, but he can definitely move. He'll do it if he wants to either way, in any case. Still, though, a one-legged swordsman ain't going to be able to kill Alus from down on the ground.>

"Dammit... So basically, Mele and Kuze are the only ones up to it? Given Mele's wounds, the best idea is to get Alus to target Kuze and attack him for us. Not really someone I want to owe anything to, but with Kuze, I can act as the go-between for the negotiations. We're acquainted at least."

<Bwah! If we really don't have any chance against anyone else, you want to head to Igania right now and call Lucnoca the Winter back for help?>

"Uh, Haade? That's a terrible joke. You already deploy your troops?"

<You underestimating my staff? By the time this conversation's over, all the cannons at the Thirty-Eighth Fortress'll be fully locked and loaded. Don't talk about changing the plan now, 'cause it's too late.>

<...Haade, let me say one thing. You shouldn't preemptively fire at Alus the Star Runner.>

"Yeah. I was going to say the same thing. One of the comms towers got knocked out on his way here, but if we can avoid engaging him entirely, obviously that'll be the best possible outcome. I want to check to see if Star Runner has *any intention of attacking us or not.* I'm working out the details on how."

Currently preparing for hostilities, Aureatia was deploying most of its fighting force.

However, if it all proved to be nothing to worry about, and Alus disappeared off somewhere without heading toward Aureatia, that would still be the best development of all. Even if he did make for Aureatia, there was the possibility that he didn't have any will to fight.

If they took Alus's attack without any resistance, the troops at the fortress would inevitably die; however, if Aureatia's side was the first to open fire, avoiding conflict would instantly become impossible.

It was necessary for them to obtain conclusive proof that Alus the Star Runner was a self-proclaimed demon king, intending to attack Aureatia, without anyone falling victim to him. It was a quandary they needed to solve as soon as possible.

Haade needed only a short time to come up with an idea.

<If I remember correctly, there's an abandoned district south of the Thirty-Eighth Stronghold. The place that had the textile mills. They're officially ruins and not a part of Aureatia city, but we can make it Aureatia. Mobilize two or three squads of sappers, leave some carriages behind, light the lamps, and we can make it look like people are living there. If that gets destroyed, we can consider him intent on bringing harm to civilian facilities. In that case, we immediately intercept 'im. If he approaches without attacking the abandoned district, the Thirty-Eighth Stronghold can try to hide their plans to intercept him as much as possible and warn him to stop. Prepare for his preemptive attack.>

"So the plan is to have the story say that we counterattacked due to his attack on the abandoned district?"

<Afterward, I can rewrite the records to say some number of the soldiers killed in all of this were assigned on patrol duty through the abandoned area. While we're at it, there was the clinic that burned to nothing yesterday morning. We could make that into Alus the Star Runner's handiwork, too. No matter how much proof we get that shows Alus is out of control, if we don't make sure to have it look like he picked this fight first, the guys below will make a real big stink about it.>

"Sacrifice some number of carriages, and we can see what Alus is up to. Not bad. What do you say, Jel?"

<I support it. I'll work as best I can on controlling the flow of information. However, I'm thinking that if we concentrate all of Haade's soldiers on opposing Alus, that will in turn delay the evacuation of citizens from the Eastern Outer Ward. As a contingency,

I'd like some personnel that we can deploy as specialists to lead the evacuation. Dant is mid-match, but could we adjust things according to when we expect his support to arrive?>

<Why don't I take care of that?>

A cool voice interrupted the meeting through the wireless radzio.

Hidow immediately knew who the voice belonged to, as well. The Second General, Rosclay the Absolute.

"Rosclay! Do you know the situation?!"

<I only just connected to this call, but please tell me if I'm mistaken. Alus the Star Runner is being guided to the Eastern Outer Ward. This is just my guess, but the area will cover the fourth to the sixth borough, given the negligible economic losses. General Haade's troops will have to spare some of their numbers to lure him there, and the current conversation topic is how to compensate for that loss to guide the residents' evacuation.>

"That's right. *Heh-heh…!* Saw through it all, huh? Impressive."

<I'll appeal to the citizens myself. I'll negotiate with Yaniegiz and secure as many personnel as I can who can be deployed as needed. Is there any problem with that plan, including my forces and having Haade act as support?>

<Heh…! I'm grateful, believe me, but is that leg of yours all right after it got trashed in your match? Work too hard and it'll work against ya in the next round.>

If the Sixways Exhibition was to continue, Rosclay the Absolute, in the second round, was already set to battle against Haade's hero candidate, Soujirou the Willow-Sword.

<I appreciate your concern. That said, you don't need to worry.>

"Sorry, but we don't have any time for this. I'll go over the whole operation with Rosclay myself, but Haade, command your troops, Jel, internal coordination. Time to move. Any other things to worry about?"

<If there is, I'm handling it how I want. Leave it to me.>

<I also can't afford to waste time. I'll get started right away.>

"We're counting on you."

With their decision, Aureatia was plunged into a state of high alert.

The alert declaring the state of emergency was first rung to guide the residents of the Eastern Outer Ward in their evacuation... Owing to the attack of self-proclaimed demon king Alus on the abandoned district, it would reverberate throughout the entire city.

They all began to act as if they were one single organism.

Aureatia's Twenty-Nine Officials were a wartime regime organized specifically to fight against demon kings of the past.

◆

Along the spacious avenue, large carriages stopped one after another and filled with citizens before driving off.

Following the resolution reached by the emergency response meeting Hidow called, the evacuation had begun within the residential district of Aureatia's Eastern Outer Ward ahead of the emergency alert.

Haade had mobilized two of the Twenty-Nine Officials under his command and charged them with supervising the area.

Eighteenth Minister, Quewai the Moon Fragment. As well as Twenty-First General, Tuturi the Blue Violet Foam.

"All right, all right now, first ones to board should be the children, the elderly, as well as the injured and infirmed, okay now? We'll split you all up, so no huddling together with your families! As long as you remember your carriage number, you'll be able to meet up again at the evacuation point, no problem."

Tuturi the Blue Violet Foam was a woman with graying hair tied behind her head. Even within this pressing situation, her casual disposition didn't waver in the slightest, and she eloquently called out to the citizens while directing her subordinates.

Conversely, the gloomy young man lingering being her, as if trying to hide himself, didn't look to be doing any such work at all. Standing upright like a machine, he merely controlled the calcurite in his hand.

"Tuturi, this isn't going to be enough carriages, is it?"

"Oh, fell down, did you, miss? It's fine, it's fine, just remain calm, okay? Did you say something, Quewai?"

"I apologize if you couldn't hear me. I said that I think that the transportation capabilities of the carriages you've arranged for may not be adequate."

"...*Pfft*, I know all that. I sorta need you to be shouting with me, Quewai. I'm the only one working here."

"I avoid doing things inefficiently like you do, Tuturi."

Eighteenth Minister, Quewai the Moon Fragment, spoke in a fast mumble, without ever looking Tuturi in the eye.

"I used the civilian statistical survey from Enu to estimate the ratio of old, young, and infirm. To get straight to the point, in order to transport everyone while preserving a twenty percent margin to spare, before Alus the Star Runner's estimated time of arrival, it would require the support of thirty-six or more ten-person carriages. Perhaps it would be best to petition Master Haade to spare us some military tanks to use for the evacuation."

"Thirty-six carriages, ten passengers each, is...how many people? Hmmm, what're we gonna do then?"

"Why can't you manage such a simple calculation, Tuturi?"

Tuturi leaned up against a nearby iron fence and stretched out her back like a cat.

"I mean, even if we work our butts off and protect all these citizens, don't you think Rosclay's just going to end up with all the credit anyway? If that's the case, it might be a lot more interesting to have this whole area go *kaboom*."

"Master Haade is the person responsible here, so I don't believe that will deal Rosclay a serious blow."

"*Tee-hee!* Just kidding, c'mon. There's gotta be some that think like that, right? Even right as Aureatia's on the brink of ruin like this, it's still money and power struggles... Actually, wait, maybe that's all the more reason, huh? If everyone's all focused on the threat, then that means they can outwit all the others and make their move."

"Am I safe to assume that in regard to the citizens unable to escape in time, your policy is to not rescue them?"

Quewai looked idly at Tuturi, without showing any noticeable emotion.

"Well, I didn't say that."

There were the sounds of a new group of carriages. They were giving off the locomotive sounds of a steam-powered vehicle.

However, these weren't automobiles or carriages.

Unmanned machines with iron plating and wheels, constructed from abnormal technology. They had neither horse nor driver.

"There they are! An extra forty-three transports. What d'ya think?"

"What are these things?"

"Golems. We requisitioned them from Kaete."

It was a variety of golem created by Kiyazuna the Axle called a Chariot Golem. During the Particle Storm interception operation, they had identified a weapon believed to be a prototype of this golem variety.

Autonomous vehicles combining armor and mobility—if they had been introduced in the large-scale political upheaval that Kaete's camp had planned, they would've certainly become a menace that upturned this world's current practical war wisdom.

"They can only comprehend simple commands, but we're able to control them to go back and forth between here and the set evacuation point. No way they'll be useful in combat against someone like Alus anyway, so way better to use them for the evacuation, right?"

"You're always astute when it comes to things like that, Tuturi."

"Well, usually I'm so inefficient and all, right? Anyway, think we'll make it in time?"

The outskirts of southeast Aureatia. The Thirty-Eighth Stronghold was located outside the city.

The number of personnel called into action here by the emergency was on par with their wartime numbers, and they were preparing their cannon barrage.

The flak battery towers, coupled together in a series like a wall, had been loaded with antiair cannons in expectation of a wyvern assault, and the ones handling them were Haade's elite troops who had fought through and survived the era of the True Demon King.

"If there's any change in wind speed, reporting protocol says…"

"Got the firing table drilling into those heads of yours?! You better be able to hit 'im with your eyes closed!"

"I'll let them know. Now, moving to the sharing of artillery ammunition between towers…"

…It feels like I really shouldn't be here.

Amid the mania recalling past wars, Cheena the Wind-Wrought Pattern's emotions were colder and subdued.

She was a new dwarf recruit.

As she wasn't trained fully on operating cannons, she was

tasked with observing and keeping close guard in the direction of the abandoned district. It wasn't official spotter work and more akin to being a reserve battle recorder.

She understood that her mission was important. If necessary, she'd move her body exactly as her strict training had drilled into her, and she wasn't scared or fearful for her life.

Cheena's mental state was the opposite, if anything.

Is all this really happening? Is Alus the Star Runner really alive and rampaging across Aureatia?

It must have been.

People far more brilliant than her—the Twenty-Nine Officials, high enough above her to be up in the clouds—had determined it to be so.

There were sure to be much more certain predictions than any of the arbitrary preconceptions of Cheena or any other of the citizens in Aureatia.

That said, this was *the* Alus the Star Runner that even Cheena had heard several legends about. And he was attacking the most prosperous basepoint for all of miniankind, Aureatia.

...It's a possibility. If that actually did happen, it would be a huge disaster, and that's why everyone's in such a frenzy, desperately preparing themselves... Which is why making sure it doesn't *happen* is my job.

Peering through the binoculars, she carefully observed if the silhouette of their foe was around the abandoned district or not.

Nothing. She even felt it looked tranquil.

She didn't pick out a three-armed wyvern or anything in particular—

"Enemy attack! The abandoned district's up in flames!"

"Alus the Star Runner's here!"

"...Huh?!"

Before she could see the sight for herself, the shout of another observation scout made Cheena cognizant of the situation.

The abandoned district had been lit aflame. Not just one specific building or a certain section—*all of it* had.

"No way."

She didn't understand why, or how exactly, something like it had occurred in the span of a single second.

A shadow. She could see a silhouette of wings backlit among the flames.

"E-e-enemy attack! A wyvern...A-Alus the Star Runner is attacking! Located...between observation points sixty-six and sixty-seven! The abandoned district...i-is completely up in flames!"

She shouted out her observation report as much as she could, but it was probably all meaningless.

The soldiers around her were already getting into battle positions following the report from the regular observation scouts, and the sounds of the heavy antiair cannons in motion echoed in untold numbers, practically splitting open the ground with the noise.

Alus the Star Runner did all of this?

She hadn't ever thought that such a thing would really happen.

The reason being that, for an ordinary person like Cheena, fighting against Alus the Star Runner meant *death*.

Yet for some reason, he had the will to attack Aureatia's city, her comrades, and her superiors, and their superiors farther up were all planning on fighting against him.

Are we really—

The ear-splitting sounds of cannon fire drowned out Cheena's thoughts.

Single-shot cannons weren't used against flocks of wyverns flying at high speeds; those weapons were intended for personnel and matériel. Anti-wyvern cannons used shrapnel shells. Artillery shells were aimed above the target's head to burst, annihilating everything in a wide conical area below the bursting point with a scatter shot.

As the rulers of the skies, wyverns had a difficult time evading scatter shots that would rain down over them from positions even farther above their lines of sight in the sky.

In addition, the deployed cannon corps fired countless artillery rounds one after another, without even a moment's breath in between. They not only shot where Alus was located, but also, they unleashed a barrage that seemed to completely blanket the sky ahead of him.

I get it. Even the world's strongest rogue can't dodge this.

Since scatter shots *had no will of their own.*

Of course, it was the artillery soldiers' skilled precision that aimed for the shot to burst above where Alus was in the sky. However, from that point on, the trajectory of the scatter shot itself, subject to randomness, was impossible to fully read, no matter how maneuverable or how precise one's senses were. On top of that, he couldn't discern the individual aim and intentions for each of the innumerable number of cannoneers in the Thirty-Eighth Stronghold and deal with them all in simultaneous parallel.

By utilizing the latest weapons with a strength of numbers, even killing an outstanding champion was possible.

Was this the reality of war in this new era?

"............"

Cheena continued her observation. She needed to verify that Alus had been brought down.

She was immediately able to confirm the results of the barrage.

"......! R-report..."

While he was within cannon range, Alus was still far off in the distance. Even when she looked through the binoculars, the silhouette was little more than a speck in the sky.

Nevertheless, the distance was what made her understand. This individual, more than any other wyvern, was simply *too fast*.

"The barrage...missed the target! Impossible... H-his stance...!"

"Record spotter, what the hell're you doing?! Give your report, now!"

"Sorry! His stance... He's...he's flying *upside down*!"

Wyverns were vulnerable to attacks from above.

This was because normal wyverns didn't fly while watching above them.

Yet did this mean Alus the Star Runner was capable of inverse flight? Not only that, but he was racing in their direction without dropping his speed whatsoever, flying through this onslaught of iron, through the lethal storm that still continued to rain down on him.

"H-he's...looking at the scatter shots...! Directly watching their trajectory *after they burst*! He's continuing his flight in this position and evading the scatter shots the whole time, too...!"

A monster.

How was it possible to believe such a thing was happening in the world she knew?

Myriad questions flew across Cheena's mind.

Wasn't anyone else as perplexed as she was? Or perhaps no one had the capacity for questions given the absurdity of the present situation?

Why had the abandoned district been *reduced to ash in a second*?

Alus the Star Runner apparently used a flame magic item—or so Cheena had heard. Even then, was it actually possible to burn an entire town to ash in an instant?

"Load the next round!"

"Keep firing! We just have to make him hesitate!"

"If he breaches the cannon's minimum range, he'll kill us all! Everyone! Put your lives on the line!"

...Everyone will die. Even with so many soldiers here. Why? How?

When Alus flapped his wings, what appeared to be a ring-shaped afterimage flashed, and the path of his flight grew blurred. He brandished a magic whip known as Kio's Hand seemingly to knock down the scatter shots with the smallest movements possible, but Cheena's eyes, keeping a visual on him from far away through binoculars, couldn't perceive his transcendental speed.

No one's ever been trained on how to take down wyverns that're immune to scatter shots. Even the armaments of the Thirty-Eighth Fortress can't handle it, because no one ever predicted such a scenario. If we can't deal with this somehow, we'll die.

He was closing in. This was surely not mere recklessness or some hostile intentions toward the soldiers here.

Alus knew that the antiair cannons' greatest weakness was getting in close enough to render cannon fire impossible.

This was why among the hail of cannon fire, he immediately set his aim on the Thirty-Eighth Fortress.

He was close.

Even then, musket sniper fire still should have been impossible at this range. He was still well inside the cannons' range—

"Alus the Star Runner's readied his gun!" Cheena shouted before coming to her conclusion.

The next moment, the flak tower next to her exploded.

"Huh?!"

There was a momentary flash of light. Following behind it came a roaring boom that split the sky.

Cheena knew this type of phenomenon.

Lightning...

The magic bullet of roaring lightning.

Firing off lightning itself, this bullet far surpassed the realm of mere musket fire in both range and destructive power. Even the flak tower, its iron supports covered by thick outer walls, was scorched in an instant.

"A-Alus is...l-loading his next shot! Don't let him finish!

Y-you have to keep firing…! If we don't stop him— Another one's coming!"

In a panicked state, Cheena shrieked out her report. Somewhere in her mind, she thought her panic was making a terrible mess of things.

But who could hope to stop the fearsome Alus the Star Runner?

I don't want to die. I don't want to die. I don't want to die.

He pointed his gun barrel in their direction. Cheena could only watch.

If he pulled the trigger and that bullet was shot their way, it would all be over.

Aureatia's going to lose.

…In this moment, there was an error in Cheena the Wind-Wrought's judgment.

The goal of this artillery barrage wasn't to shoot him out of the sky but to divert Alus's flight path.

In other words, the Aureatia army had *already incorporated* Alus breaking through the storm of cannon fire into their plans…

◆

Iron rain fell.

Alus, as always, was flying straight through death.

Why was he always doing this?

He was searching for treasure.

Just as he had single-mindedly continued to do across the span of his life, he was thinking about destroying the obstacles in front of him and obtaining treasure.

Before him were towers of stone inorganically joined together.

The sounds of cannon fire were incessant.

The metropolis beyond, stretching far over the horizon, was Aureatia.

An unprecedented calamity had arrived in the last minian kingdom.

...Right. I was collecting treasure.

The Cold Star that Hidow the Clamp had shown him that day should be here in this country.

Not only that. Findeluil the Vital Spot Manuscript. Liquified Rampart. Mote Nerve Arrow.

He must have known from the very beginning that in order to obtain all the treasure this world had to offer, there was one final dungeon he needed to conquer.

That was where the numerous magic items that the minian kingdom had spent many years gathering together were.

I wonder why I never realized it for myself. Strange.

Replaced with a machinelike constitution, Alus the Star Runner was gradually losing his sense of self.

Yet amid his thoughts dissolving into ambiguity, he was convinced of his actions.

I get it. I...was supposed to save this for last. So...this is likely the end of my story...

Even Toroa the Awful was dead.

In the end, Alus had been unable to steal his enchanted swords, and Toroa had vanished into an otherworldly rift.

There might not have been any enemies left in this world anymore that Alus was supposed to steal something from.

Once he stole all the treasure that had been gathered in Aureatia, Alus the Star Runner would then be the sole owner of all riches.

That didn't sound too bad.

He needed to do this if he wanted to put an end to this tale of avarice that seemed like it would go on forever.

He would destroy Aureatia.

His objective was not to take the lives of others. If anyone tried to flee, he would let them escape. If anyone tried to fight, he would fight. The only ones who remained would be those with treasures they couldn't afford to abandon.

If he continued on his path of destruction, then eventually, like Vikeon the Smoldering, they would present their treasure to him.

"......"

Alus thought that, first, he would destroy the tower in between him and Aureatia.

He had grown accustomed to watching and evading cannon fire across several battles, but it still tired him out somewhat.

He loaded a magic bullet into his musket and aimed at the second of the flak towers.

"Ah."

In that moment, Alus changed his target. With terrifying speed.

He didn't even turn around.

He shifted his gun barrel behind him and—

A steel beam pierced through Alus's stomach.

"That's one hell of a reaction time, Star Runner."

"......!"

Blood began to trickle along the thin steel beam.

His enemy's attack had come before his voice had time to reach Alus.

Not only that, but the owner of the voice *was already in front of Alus.*

The weapon that had just launched the steel beam at him was a magic item that Alus had once possessed for himself. It had been lost during his battle with Lucnoca the Winter—Heshed Elis the Fire Pipe.

"Fastest in the sky. Truth is, I've always been envious of that moniker of yours."

On top of a leaning bell tower in the abandoned district stood a lone skeleton.

In other words, the Aureatia army had *already incorporated* Alus's breaking through the storm of cannon fire into their plans...

In order to prevent the wyvern from sensing the approach of someone faster than any known phenomena...

"Give me a name like that, too."

...they had called in Shalk the Sound Slicer.

◆

Shalk fixed his eyes on Alus, moving at speeds similar to his own, from atop the bell tower.

Normally, it would have been a fatal wound. With his stomach pierced by a steel beam, what would he do next?

Try to put distance between Shalk out in front of him? Or perhaps try to counterattack with his musket?

"Kio's Hand."

"...!"

Neither.

Alus produced his weapon on the spot, turned around, and made a clean sweep through the air with his magic whip.

"...Impressive."

Shalk jumped right as the murmur left his mouth. Immediately afterward, the flash of the magic lightning bullet pulverized the foundation of the bell tower into rubble.

Blinding light and searing heat, surpassing actual lightning itself. The delayed thunderclap tore through the sky.

Alus the Star Runner's magic lightning bullets were as fearsome as a dragon's breath.

I was moving pretty fast for that surprise attack, yet he was still able to avoid a direct hit to the head. Not only that but...

The steel beam, wrenched free from Alus's body, fell to the ground.

He even saw through the steel wire attached to the beam, huh?

The steel beam fired from the Fire Pipe had been connected with steel wire to a winch secretly placed inside a freight warehouse within the abandoned district.

In that moment, if Alus the Star Runner had elected to put space between them, or closed the gap to counterattack, his

movements would have been restricted by the wire's tension, and Shalk, jumping from the bell tower, would have created the perfect opportunity to run his skull through.

And he can still fly, too?

Had he missed Alus's internal organs by a stroke of bad luck?

Or perhaps, was there some unknown magic item at his disposal that made it possible to keep fighting, even in his current state?

I'm dubious that I'll be able to follow through with a frontal attack but, well, no other choice here.

Escaping from his restraints, Alus didn't pursue Shalk.

Instead, a lightning bullet was brought down on him.

Shalk ran *a bit faster* than the flash of lightning and evaded the trajectory of the bolt before it bored into the earth.

As he escaped, he never for a moment dropped his sight from his enemy in the sky. Alus was flying upside down. In this situation, he couldn't afford to ignore the Aureatia army's cannon barrage, either.

Being on the ground was, in fact, the superior position against an enemy forced to watch the sky.

"...They're getting in the way..."

"You use a gun, but you're scared of bullets? Quite the ordeal there, Alus the Star Runner."

Even a single shot hitting the tip of his wing should have been more than the wyvern could afford. While he adjusted his slightly off-set flight, he would get hit with the incessant storm of scatter shots. This was the reason why shrapnel fire, each individual shot having a low impact, was effective against wyverns.

Conversely, Shalk the Sound Slicer didn't even possess the

flesh for said shrapnel to cut up in the first place. His bones, as a construct, had undergone a strengthening process as well, so he could move while ignoring some degree of gunfire his way.

Of course, in my case, even if my body wasn't just bones...

Grasping several shots from among the torrential rain of shrapnel, he loaded them into Heshed Elis the Fire Pipe.

It'd be harder to get hit by bullets that're slower than me anyway.

It wasn't completely impossible to surprise the world's strongest rogue from behind.

A few moments ago, Shalk had fired a steel beam and hit Alus's torso.

Someone who ran at such ludicrous speeds was impossible to visually track. Cannon fire constantly rained down from overhead. It was impossible to keep his guard up in both directions. Right now, Alus had no way of predicting Shalk's position.

Aiming above Alus's head, he fired the shrapnel shell he had loaded into Heshed Elis the Fire Pipe.

A sniper shot borne on his own unworldly fast speed.

It'll hit.

The air surrounding Alus appeared to fluctuate.

The shrapnel shell was deflected with a grating metallic noise.

"...What?"

Alus hadn't even been looking in his direction. Shalk's groan came from his understanding about what Alus had done in that moment.

He extended out his whip in his blind spot ahead of time and reflexively moved it as soon as the shell came into contact with it.

Neither from a prediction nor part of some automatic defenses. He performed such a daring feat solely with his own abilities.

As if the magic item were a part of his body, like an insect's antenna.

Certainly if that was possible for him, then any amount of saturated shrapnel fire would have ultimately been meaningless.

"Give me back…my treasure."

"Whoa, now… You're not angry with me, are you?"

While his sniper shot hadn't actually hit the target, Shalk had been aiming for a different effect, too.

He had purposely used Heshed Elis the Fire Pipe against Alus for the sake of the most effective tactic in this situation.

"Thing is, I thought for sure you were dead, so I took this treasure for myself… That can't possibly be what's got your scales in a bunch, right? It's the same thing you've been doing up until now, isn't it?"

Taunting him, running around, and continuing to take the wyvern's attacks.

He'd get hit when his concentration was finally broken. His attention would turn to another objective. He'd come down to steal the fire pipe back.

No matter how Alus the Star Runner ultimately ended up, there would be no losses for Aureatia.

…Jeez, except it's all losses for me here. Ah well. I'm the first one on the scene and all.

Neither the cannon barrage nor Shalk's sniper fire would land a decisive blow on Alus. Understanding that alone was a good haul.

Shalk raced to the east.

On the east side, the cannon fire was intentionally sparser. Since the true aim was to guide Alus in that direction, the fort side of the battle didn't adjust their aim, either.

If they were going to keep battling a threat of Alus the Star Runner's level, it would consume a tremendous number of soldiers and weapons. If a direct magic lightning bullet was fired toward the military facilities like it had been earlier, Shalk had no means of protecting them.

The reason the Thirty-Eighth Fortress didn't make any use of magic items themselves was to *avoid leading Alus to them*.

The sounds of bursting cannon fire grew sparse. He was advancing beyond the range of the Thirty-Eighth Fortress's cannons.

If the battle shifted to somewhere without any cannon support, Shalk would be locked into battling against Alus with just his individual fighting power, but that, too, was precisely what he wanted.

He'd keep going to the eastern side and head outside of Aureatia's borders.

Right before he could, Alus stopped chasing him.

He came to an eerie standstill, as if he had seen through Shalk's intentions.

"...Where are you going?"

"Scared? Come on down here and steal your treasure back."

"In Aureatia...there's a lot of treasure. Much better than... Heshed Elis the Fire Pipe..."

Behind Alus lay the cityscape of Aureatia's Eastern Outer Ward.

Shalk had planned on leading him along while they battled each other, but they were close.

Did it mean Alus was leading Shalk toward Aureatia's streets himself?

The fifth borough of Aureatia's Eastern Outer Ward. With the time Shalk and the fortress soldiers bought, the evacuation should have finished, but...

This is right on the borderline.

Could he lure him even farther out from here? Was he going to attack Aureatia city?

Whatever direction Alus went to make his move, there were only a few possible ways for Shalk to intervene.

"...If you'll fight against me one-on-one..."

Shalk made a show of sticking Heshed Elis the Fire Pipe into the ground.

"I'd be fine letting you have this thing. Interested to see which one of us is stronger?"

"You're lying...," Alus coldly declared.

Shalk had an absolutely terrible feeling. As if Alus had clenched down on some core feeling that even Shalk wasn't aware of.

"Why do you say that?"

"You...you're trying to protect people."

"Don't be stupid."

It was all too idiotic. Did Alus really think that he was returning Shalk's provocations here?

There wasn't anyone as unfit for saving others, or any sort of heroics, as Shalk the Sound Slicer. There had been several opportunities mid-battle where he had the opportunity to save someone, but he *didn't save any of them* and never even gave the idea a moment's thought.

Ridiculous. This annoying little show is all just part of the job.

He readied his spear, as if to readjust from the discomfort.

"Listen. The only thing that matters is this fight. Right here, right now. Even you'd rather have a big open space to fight me with everything you got, right?"

"......An open space?"

There was an oozing sound.

An odd sound, like bubbles welling up from some sticky viscous liquid.

Shalk realized that just a bit below Alus floated a red-hot orb, big enough to hold in one's hands.

There had been one incomprehensible fact about the battle up until now.

I heard about the magic items Alus has from the Aureatia guys. If he was gonna torch the military installations, there should've been far more effective items at his disposal than the magic lightning bullets—

The orb of traveling flames, Ground Runner.

Rotting Soil Sun, creating and launching projectiles of mud.

While he was fighting with me, what did he do with those?

This red-hot glowing orb might have been Rotting Soil Sun.

Except seeing it tinged with reddish-brown heat and distorting the air around it, it resembled a small sun.

Was this how Rotting Soil Sun usually behaved?

Another oozing sound could be heard.

Uh-oh.

The sound he could hear from Rotting Soil Sun wasn't merely something bubbling.

There was something jammed inside it, something unable to bear the pressure. And it was *boiling.*

Shalk should have attacked then, but it was too late.

"......Now."

The sun burst.

Red-hot lava bullets swarmed down.

In an instant, Shalk kicked off the ground and dodged wide. With his speed, it was possible.

A sharp turn. He went to turn to the counter—and saw the fifth borough of the Eastern Outer Ward.

"It's more open."

The town was in flames.

Shalk's dodge and turn had happened in a fraction of a second.

In that instant, Alus the Star Runner had reduced the *entire district* of the Eastern Outer Ward's fifth borough to ash.

"What...did you do?"

He murmured the names of his treasures.

"Ground Runner. Rotting Soil Sun..."

Alus had never tested their combination against anyone else. Thus, there was no one who could predict it, either.

There was only a single wyvern, the greatest adventurer in the land, who could control several magic items at once and even combine their unique abilities.

Rotting Soil Sun was able to add pressure to the endlessly

gushing mud and fire it at high speeds. By manipulating the pressure, it was possible to freely shape the mud at will.

In that case, instead of releasing the pressure, *what if it was used for compression instead*?

The source of Ground Runner's fire would never be fully extinguished, even if it ran out of oxygen. If this flame continuously burned inside the super-high-pressurized and ultra-dense mud, then what would happen when it was released?

Ultra-pressurized lava missiles, fired off in every direction simultaneously.

Even in the middle of his fight with Shalk the Sound Slicer, he had already prepared this technique, solely for the purpose of burning the city to the ground.

"I take pride in my treasures..."

He was calamity incarnate.

◆

I just have to fight him here.

The fifth borough of the Eastern Outer Ward was deserted. Or rather, it was more accurate to say it had *just become deserted*. Whatever the case, now that he had invaded Aureatia itself, Shalk couldn't afford to *let* Alus the Star Runner leave.

Additionally, there were very few effective ways to fight against Alus, flying at high speeds through the sky. While it may have been possible to make his attacks reach the wyvern by using Heshed Elis the Fire Pipe, Shalk had already shown him the attack.

If he was going to use it one more time, he would need to find the right moment for it to be a guaranteed kill.

Shalk determined the attack from his enemy's opening movements.

"Here it comes. The lightning magic bullet."

A flash of light shot down, and an abnormally persistent electric discharge cut across the city.

There existed no other but Shalk the Sound Slicer who could *dodge* this attack.

The flames, like a glint of light, furiously approached Shalk from the left behind him.

"…Ground Runner."

He predicted the trajectory. He kicked the ground. Instantly accelerated. Kicking debris, he changed his running path and, keeping Alus in his sights, arrived on the roof of what was once a fire station.

Ground Runner. The seeds of flame shot down from the composite bomb attack moments prior ran through the streets and continued to pursue Shalk across the surface. Flames obstructing his sight lines and narrowing his routes of escape. The conflagration was contained to just the fifth borough area right now, but it was highly likely they would spread to the other districts as well.

There still had to be some magic items that Shalk didn't know about. The left half of Alus's body being replaced with a metallic configuration was likely the work of yet another magic item. It was probably also the reason why Shalk's opening ambush hadn't been fatal.

Rotting Soil Sun, shaping mud bullets and firing them at will.

The magic whip Kio's Hand, which freely cut through any targets. The Greatshield of the Dead, delivering absolute defense at heavy cost to the user. While he didn't appear to carry Hillensingen the Luminous Blade, perhaps he was keeping it hidden.

Flight at super speed. Magic bullets bringing instant death. Masterful sniper attacks. Persistent flames and earthen blades. If I could get in close, he's practically invincible even at that range. Along with absolute defense, he has crazy regenerative ability...

Simply enumerating all the proven threats made him seem like a monster beyond Shalk's control.

How am I even supposed to kill this guy in the first place?

Destroy his head. Shalk understood that it was the only way.

As long as he possessed regenerative abilities that allowed him to continue fighting even after being pierced through the stomach, there was no other option but to destroy his thought center in a single attack that allowed him no chance to regenerate.

But how?

His enemy was farther away than even the latest models of guns could reach, fast enough to avoid any shot after the trigger was pulled, as well as clever enough to anticipate his opponent's tactics. On top of that, Shalk would need to find a way around the Greatshield of the Dead, get his attack to precisely hit the wyvern's small head, and deal a lethal blow.

Feels like I have to keep solving this unbelievably annoying problem while I'm locked in a fight to the death here. Those Aureatia guys did a pretty good job, but...If I had someone like Regnejee up in the sky, I might've had a bit of an easier time here.

He recalled the name of the red wyvern he had formerly fought with.

There no longer existed any air force in this world. The only ones able to bring down this wyvern champion who even outshone dragons were a fighting force of similar sublime and outstanding individuals like him.

"... Fine, then. I'll go ahead and work just a bit harder."

However, at that moment, the situation took a dramatic turn for the worse.

Shalk heard a voice.

"Help..."

"...Oh c'mon."

Directly under a wall of rubble. This was one of the spots that had been untouched by the fires, yet it was still the worst outcome of all.

He heard the frail voice of a young man.

"Some...one...help..."

"You gotta be kidding me... How the hell're you still kicking in a situation like this?!"

Aureatia had successfully guided the evacuation proceedings without any ineptitude at all. Despite having close to no time to spare until Alus's attack, they had succeeded in making *almost* all residents evacuate.

However, perfection was impossible.

If I stop to move the rubble, I'll be a sitting duck. I'm abandoning this guy. One extra corpse isn't going to cause problems down the line...

There wasn't anyone as unfit for saving others, protecting others, or any sort of heroics, as Shalk the Sound Slicer.

He had seen many willing to charge into their deaths, and he had always thought *he didn't care whatever the hell they did.*

He had never tried to protect another person before.

I can just run away. That's what I've always done, for as long as I can remember.

In that brief moment, his feet stopped moving.

...As long as I can remember?

He heard a gunshot from the sky.

The lightning bullet twinkled like a star in the sky, before—

"Shalk!"

A young girl, appearing like a gust of wind, stopped the torrent of electricity.

Her long chestnut-colored braid trailed behind her as it fluttered.

"You."

Neither Shalk nor the delayed evacuee was hit with any of the aftermath from the heat and destruction.

Had she instantly manipulated her body's conductivity? The enormous electric current had been repelled into the ground, as if the girl's body itself were a lightning rod.

Taking the huge electric shock that had destroyed the fortress towers in a single attack with nothing but her outstretched right arm, she stood there perfectly unharmed, while her clothes were seared from end to end.

"...Saved my ass there."

Shalk the Sound Slicer knew this young girl.

"I should be thanking you."

He knew that she possessed an invincible physical body that surpassed all accepted knowledge of physics.

"You really are a nice guy after all, Shalk."

At the center of a roaring flame that incinerated all it touched, Tu the Magic smiled.

At the same time the eighth match was finishing, an alert resounded across all of Aureatia.

For the citizens it was a simple order to evacuate, but it was widely known that for the hero candidates, and the people involved with them, it contained another, extremely severe implication as well—an emergency summons regarding a threat to Aureatia. So long as they all put forth their names as hero candidates, they bore a responsibility to go out and face off against any self-proclaimed demon king.

…Then at Flinsuda's estate.

"You don't need to mobilize."

The revenant controlled by Krafnir the Hatch of Truth stood barring the door to Tu's room.

Hearing the alert, Tu the Magic was certain to go running out of the estate without thinking ahead. He needed to make sure to stop her.

"Outta the way, Krafnir! I gotta get going!"

"Tu. After you disobeyed orders and withdrew from the fifth match, you're currently seen as difficult to control.

IN OTHER WORDS, THERE'S A CHANCE YOU'LL BRING HARM TO THE AUREATIA CITIZENS IF YOU'RE ALLOWED TO RUN FREE."

"Of course, I wouldn't do anything like that! You know that full well, Krafnir!"

"YEAH. I UNDERSTAND. BUT THERE ARE OCCASIONS WHEN THE WAY YOU'RE PERCEIVED BY OTHERS DOES MATTER. IF THEY'RE GOING TO THROW YOU OUT ON THE FRONT LINES, WITH THE FEAR THAT YOU MIGHT LOSE CONTROL, THERE'LL BE NEGOTIATIONS BETWEEN FLINSUDA AND ANOTHER IN THE TWENTY-NINE OFFICIALS...MOST LIKELY THIRD MINISTER JEL, AND YOU NEED TO WAIT UNTIL THERE'S CONDITIONAL APPROVAL FOR YOU TO ACT."

"That doesn't make any sense! People's lives are on the line, aren't they?!"

"THEY UNDERSTAND THAT EVERY SECOND COUNTS RIGHT NOW, TOO. THE NEGOTIATIONS WON'T TAKE LONG."

"...Does that mean—"

Tu's eyes, as she stood in front of the window, gleamed with a faint green luster.

"—it's about getting money out of it?"

"......"

Tu possessed an almost childlike purity and innocence.

However, that didn't mean she was stupid. She understood the meaning behind this current situation.

Flinsuda the Portent was using the suspicions about Tu the Magic's wildcard behavior to try adding on conditions to the request for Tu's mobilization, once an outright obligation. In order to lay the responsibility of Tu's mobilization on the opposite party, in exchange for a sizable bribe.

"...Tu. Flinsuda is definitely not a virtuous woman. But she's not doing all of this out of her own greedy self-interest, either. She's being considerate of you in her own way. What sort of conditions she would need in order to introduce you to the Queen, for example?"

"...That's neither here nor there. Right now...that's not what I'm supposed to do."

"......"

Tu surely must have believed that her wish to see the Queen was *selfish*.

This was why even as she desired to meet the Queen enough to enter the Sixways Exhibition—she ended up putting others before herself, as she had done when she had been protecting the Land of the End and when she had acquiesced victory to Kuze.

If she kept this up, wouldn't she run the risk of putting others before herself forever?

"When I learned that Sun's Conifer attacked the almshouse...I felt so much regret. I wanted to help out Kuze, yet...I wasn't able to do anything. I couldn't be there at the kids' side when they needed me the most."

"That isn't what you're supposed to do."

"I don't think so. That goes for anyone... Anyone still alive. Nothing makes me happier than helping someone else, and it makes me sad when I can't. That's all there is to it."

Krafnir was aware of Tu's good nature.

However, he didn't think it was genuine.

"IF YOU GO NOW...TU, YOU WON'T BE ABLE TO LIVE IN AURE-ATIA ANYMORE. NOT ONLY THAT...YOU'LL LOSE YOUR PLACE IN ALL OF MINIAN SOCIETY ITSELF! OUR SOCIETY ISN'T BUILT TO TRUST IN THE GOOD NATURE OF MONSTERS! AT THE VERY LEAST, YOU HAVE TO MAKE THEM THINK...THAT YOU'RE REGULATED BY ORDER AND DISCIPLINE, OR YOU WON'T BE ABLE TO GO ON LIVING YOUR LIFE!"

"I don't get it. I'm sure that you and Flinsuda have all these amazing ideas, and you're way smarter than I am. Still...! There are still times when if you don't act, someone might end up dead! If Rique was still alive, he'd definitely say the same thing!"

"......!"

Krafnir had regrets.

He thought of himself as *smart*. He believed that if he thought things through, without making incorrect choices...he would be able to accomplish his goals without exposing himself to any danger. He would keep sacrifices to a minimum.

But that hadn't been the case at all.

Every time he experienced Tu or Rique's innocence and youth, there was a sense of guilt somewhere inside his heart.

Being forced to acknowledge that this part of him remained was a terribly unpleasant feeling.

"TU THE MAGIC...I SHOULD HAVE NEVER INVOLVED MYSELF WITH YOU... THE TRUE DEMON KING, THE SIXWAYS EXHIBITION... I JUST...INTENDED TO LIVE IN PEACE...RIDING OUT THE TURMOIL IN SAFETY, AND YET..."

"Well, I'm glad we met."

Tu's eyes looked straight ahead at Krafnir's revenant.

They seemed to be peering through to Krafnir himself on the other side.

"I despaired the whole time, too. I never had the courage to look out beyond the Land of the End. But...I'm glad the first people I encountered were you and Rique. It's thanks to you both that now I can say, without any hesitation, that I want to go help others."

"...Why...?"

The revenant shouldn't have possessed any ability to feel pain, but it was in anguish, reflecting Krafnir's own mental unrest.

His Mind Arts control was falling into disarray.

"...WHY! WHY DID YOU END UP THAT WAY, TU?! YOU, THAT DEMON...! YOU'RE A WEAPON MADE BY THAT MONSTER IZICK THE CHROMATIC, AREN'T YOU?! SO WHY, WHY AREN'T YOU A MONSTER?!"

"There are infinite possibilities in this world! There are all sorts of colors! As long as you have a just and brave heart...then even a monster like me can get to see that sorta stuff, too! That's what he taught me!"

"LIAR...!"

He could never forget.

The hand of his dying master had become terribly thin and frail. Enduring lasting agony from Izick's bacteriological weapon, the woman who had been the beginning of everything for Krafnir died a young death.

He had seen the ruins of a city Izick had annihilated on a

whim. He had seen the vestiges of a coldly efficient massacre, but beyond that, where the perpetrator gleefully tormented his victims as he killed them.

"You're lying!"

Krafnir knew Tu's inherent good nature. This young girl had never told a lie before.

But Krafnir couldn't forgive him. Ever since he heard that Izick had challenged the True Demon King as part of the First Party, he remained unable to forgive him.

Don't lie, Izick the Chromatic.

A tempest of winged insects surged through the open window.

Controlling a massive number of revenants through Mind Arts, Krafnir had finally surpassed the techniques of Izick the Chromatic.

He had to, or he would never find peace.

"Krafnir!"

"You can go...after you defeat me!"

◆

In this world, before the appearance of the True Demon King, the words *self-proclaimed demon king* didn't mean anything. Just a mere twenty-five years earlier, they were the ones referred to as demon kings.

The original demon kings of this world were demonic monarchs diametrically opposed to the true monarchs.

A demonic monarch couldn't possibly become a king all on

their own. At the very least, there may have been comrades who shared the same views, or people who were attracted by their ideals. There may have been some who wished for the good fortune of the subjects that followed them, or wished for a new kind of prosperity, or for world peace.

The demon kings of the past were destroyers of order, but they weren't absolute evils.

He was different, however.

One of the seven members of the First Party, Izick the Chromatic was a man described as the wickedest demon king of all.

For instance, Izick was said to have been heavily involved in the events surrounding a particular city, Meeti Crossroads City.

The lord ruling the city, Rotegra the Scrupulous, criticized the faction of aristocrats who provided support for Izick's research and carried out domestic reform. The two held a deep-rooted hatred for each other.

Opposing Izick the Chromatic came with considerable risk, but Rotegra avoided direct conflict, even negotiating with him on occasions, and dexterously protected himself.

One day came when Rotegra stood on a hill on the outskirts of Meeti, without a single bodyguard along with him.

"Impeccable as always, Lord Rotegra! Right on time! Welcome! *Ha-ha-ha-ha!*"

He appeared to be a relatively normal worn-out middle-aged man, adorned in traveling attire—

So long as one ignored the laugh that never failed to grate on the listener's nerve.

Izick the Chromatic.

"You got here right as I finished eating my lunch! This deer meat pastry really is great, huh?! I heard this was Meeti's signature dish, right? Ain't too bad!"

Izick's horribly cheerful voice instead only brought more mental gloom to Rotegra.

He mumbled with what sounded like the whispered voice of the infirm.

"...L-let me make sure..."

"Huh? What's that? You say something?"

"Y-you promised...if I surrender Meeti...m-my daughter...you'll give Selure back... I-in that case, I'll hand it over. A-all of it..."

His voice was trembling.

It was fair to say that Meeti Crossroads City meant everything to Rotegra. It was a domain bestowed to his family as a reward for their great contributions to the True Northern Kingdom judicial system.

If he surrendered it to the world's enemy, Izick the Chromatic, it would result in Rotegra losing all his honor and wealth. However, the man's will had already been broken.

The people Izick targeted hadn't been any of his capable advisors, or major players within the city's political and business circles.

At first, the elderly librarian Rotegra was closely acquainted with went missing.

Next, his longtime friends from his youth began to disappear one by one.

His driver and servants disappeared, then his housekeeping matron did, too.

Not a single person vital to Meeti's administration was included among them.

Then, finally, his daughter, Selure.

"I'll tell my men…everything… Meeti, I'll…I'll hand it over…"

"Oh, good."

Izick didn't carry anything. He hadn't brought anyone else along.

Yet it wasn't numbers, or power, but his spite itself that was the most terrifying of all.

His eyes were cold. He gazed at Rotegra as if he were looking down at a flea.

"Hey, so do you mean, like, right now? From now on, this town is mine?"

"Where is Selure?"

"Listen here, Lord Rotegra. The thing is, I'm not too bright. I never went to school or church, so sorry if I'm misunderstanding something, but, um…who's the person asking the questions here?"

"Wh-where is she?! Where is Selure?!"

"Aww, enough already… Just calm down a sec."

Izick let out an exaggerated sigh, and then scratched his head.

He pointed at the hill behind Rotegra.

There was a young girl walking there. Looking from afar, there was no mistaking her.

"Ahh... Ahh...!"

"See? She's fine, right?"

"...I-I'm, I'm not even part of the aristocracy anymore. My daughter and I, together...we'll live hiding from the eyes of heaven itself...so I—I won't do anything else to you. I can't do anything more... Let's put an end to this. Everything, both of us."

"*Ha-ha-ha-ha!* Oh, that's great! Tying a bow on this long relationship of ours, then! Peace is great, isn't it? So from this moment on, this whooole city's mine, huh?! *Ha-ha-ha-ha-ha-ha-ha!*"

Loudly cackling with both hands stretched out, the demon king looked down over the city. The city that had been Rotegra's.

Why did the Wordmaker give a man like him nightmarish power?

Meeti Crossroads City, which Rotegra had once ruled over, was now destined to be turned into the base of operations for this wickedest of all demon kings. The vast, fertile soil, all the living, breathing people within, would become toys for Izick's maliciousness.

Rotegra the Scrupulous's fight against wickedness had ended with it all being for naught.

Evil had won.

"*Ha-ha-ha-ha-ha-ha-ha-ha-ha-ha*—oh."

Izick's roaring laughter was suddenly interrupted.

He almost resembled a windup doll coming to its abrupt stop.

It was eerie.

"Y'knooooow, that bakery where I got my lunch earlier, the staff there was really rude to me. They looked at their customer and clicked their teeth. What do you think of that, Lord Rotegra? That sorta thing is the worst, isn't it? I mean, I'm the customer, right? I'm paying their wages and everything. So why'd they click their tongue at me, I wonder...? I don't get it..."

"W-why indeed...?"

"Hmm... Y'know what? Forget it. I don't need a city like this."

Rotegra heard a sound splitting the air, like the rumbling of the earth...

A terrifying sound like nothing he had ever heard before.

And from the direction of town...

"I-Izick."

...came screams.

The shrieks of the people he could hear from Meeti down below, all at once. Innumerable.

Overlapping in countless numbers, they reached all the way to this plateau so highly removed from the city.

They were the last gasps of the very city itself.

The townscape spread out before his eyes began to be dyed in a chilling black.

The swarm of *something*, appearing out of nowhere, was alive— or at least, appeared to be alive.

Unnervingly bubbling forth. Incessant and everywhere.

"A-ahh... *e-eauuugh...!*"

Rotegra could no longer keep himself standing, and he frantically moved back, dragging his waist along the grass.

There were countless red eyes mixed among the black clouds devouring the city.

An enormous sea of rat revenants…overflowing from the sewers, from the floorboards, and every other nook and cranny throughout the city, was greedily devouring the living.

The chorus of screams below him continued. *They were making sure their victims could still use their voices as they killed them.*

They were none other than the voices of the citizens of Meeti, having their flesh chewed away and devoured while they yet lived.

"*Eeeeaaah*, I-I'm sorry… Please, please forgive me…!"

"*Weeeell, you* gave me the city, right? That means I can destroy it if I want, right? Thanks!"

"Stop, it's not my fault, it's not—*eeaauuuuugh!*"

"*Ha-ha-ha-ha-ha-ha-ha-ha-ha!* Ah, this is so much fun! *Ha-ha-ha-ha-ha-ha-ha-ha!*"

Even as the cackling and the screams tore his mind apart, Rotegra ran toward the hill.

His daughter. As long as Selure…

On top of the hill, his beloved Selure was walking.

With tottering steps, while her unfocused eyes looked at Rotegra.

"……"

"S-Selure."

It seemed like something moved inside his daughter's face.

Something…like a tiny swarm.

"Lord Rotegra."

He heard a bone-chillingly cold voice from behind him.

Izick wasn't laughing anymore.

"You remember what happened a little while ago, right? Right, right, it was *juuuust* before that girl of yours went missing, I think?

You insisted on peace talks or whatever, but as I was heading there, along the way some bandits... Knights? I couldn't really tell, but they came and tried to attack me, you see... Boy, did that give me a scare, let me tell you."

"I—I don't know... I...I didn't know anything about that! M-my subordinates acted on their own!"

"Oh-ho! Your subordinates! So that's how it is, huh? So it wasn't your fault, then, Lord Rotegra? It's fine; it's fine! See, I'm really forgiving about that stuff. Besides, those men of yours..."

The earthshaking screams had already stopped.

Black.

Meeti Crossroads City was covered in black.

Now there was nothing but an eerie silence in the carcass of the metropolis.

The army of rat revenants didn't raise a single squeak.

"...are already dead anyway."

It was silent. Just like Selure was, walking before Rotegra's eyes.

"Please... Y-you promised, didn't you? I—I gave you the city already. Selure... Y-you promised to give her back... That was the deal..."

Selure's head hung limply. She was still moving. Still walking, even.

A pink tail peeked out of her earlobe and disappeared inside her skull.

Rotegra prayed that the face still twisted in agony, and her repulsive driven steps, were all part of a replica made in bad taste by the demon king.

"Huh? Hold on. Was thaaaat the deal? Did I say I'd return her?"

Rotegra fell to his knees.

His daughter's body burst from the inside, and a small black army swarmed him.

"Aww, too bad! I liiiiiiiied! *Ha-ha-ha-ha-ha-ha-ha-ha-ha!*"

Listening to Rotegra's dying breaths as the surface of his skin was shredded apart, Izick the Chromatic laughed with utter delight.

"*Ha-ha-ha-ha-ha-ha-ha-ha-ha-ha-ha-ha-ha-ha-ha-ha!*"

A mere twenty-five years earlier, they were the ones who were called demon kings.

They didn't need any companions. If they required an army, they could make one.

They possessed neither beliefs nor ideals. Without any clear objective to their massacres, they spread unbridled destruction and took joy in misery.

The malicious will to paint over absolutely everything in their color.

In the past, this world had a man called the wickedest of all demon kings.

He was the self-proclaimed demon king, Izick the Chromatic.

◆

Four years had gone by since the destruction of Meeti.

On a mountain road in the Athiel noble family's domain, there was *something resembling* a shredded minian corpse. In other words, it was not actually a corpse.

It crawled with its fingers as it painted a line of blood behind it. There were only two fingers on their right hand.

"*Hah, hah...ha-ha-ha-ha. Kweh, hwak...*"

All they could do was continue forward like this. The flesh of their left thigh was torn open, with the bone inside exposed.

There was nothing left from their right ankle down.

The laughter-like sounds escaping their lips were out of terror.

Their diaphragm was spasming in fear, and this was the only voice that came out.

"*Hah...hah, haah, aah.*"

Even the simple act of breathing tore the inside of their lungs.

Both their physical body and their mental state were unable to maintain the form of a normal minia.

There was no prospect of recovery. They would simply continue toward doom.

It was the final moments for the survivor of the First Party, Izick the Chromatic.

He had laid eyes on the True Demon King.

On true terror that no one in possession of a heart and soul could oppose.

"...I'm not giving up..."

No one knew what not giving up would even accomplish.

"Like hell I'm giving up..."

The bushes around him trembled. Revenants that he had employed for himself.

The centipede-like revenants crawled out in an agitated stir and forced their way into the man's mouth, his eye sockets, biting and tearing away tissue as they went. He screamed in the agonizing pain of certain death but was unable to with the bugs filling his esophagus.

"Gnrgh...gahk...glrgh...urngh..."

He suffered just like people he had killed in the past, unable to even let out a scream.

His legs and arms feebly wriggled and struggled until the movements became slight spasms, and bit by agonizing bit, over time, they began to stop.

"............"

Izick could no longer move.

From his mouth and nose flowed red, but eventually it changed over to a dark brown.

Even after the sun fell, and it turned to night, not even the lowliest beast approached the unsightly carcass.

Then the sun rose.

The next day, and the day after that, the man once referred to as the wickedest demon king of all rotted away without anyone paying him any mind.

All his blood and moisture had completely dried up, and falling leaves accumulated on top of his body.

One day, it rained.

Izick the Chromatic was half submerged in a puddle of water.

At last, for what must have been the several dozenth time, the sun rose into the sky.

A beast-like silhouette approached his corpse.

It was abnormally colossal compared to the beasts in nature, with an uncanny glow of intelligence about him.

An elegant, multipedal, wolflike beast.

"YOU FINALLY MET YOUR END, TOO. DIDN'T YOU, IZICK THE CHROMATIC?"

The chimera created by Izick the Chromatic bore the name *Ozonezma*.

He murmured at his creator, now dead, just one single sentence.

"A FITTING END."

Feeling no more words were necessary, the beast went to leave the scene behind.

Ozonezma's hind leg was grabbed by that man who was supposed to have breathed his last.

"......! I-IZICK...!"

"Ga-ha, hak, kahak, ha-ha-ha-ha-ha-ha!"

The corpse cackled.

"That's right! It's Izick!"

With strength that seemed impossible from a formerly dead man, he dug his fingers into Ozonezma's leg.

"Ha-ha-ha-ha-ha! That's awfully cold, Ozonezma! Your ole master just came back to life, y'know! C'mon...you could stand to look a little bit happier, right?! Right, Ozonezma!"

"HOW...HOW ARE YOU ALIVE IN THIS STATE...?!"

"...Kahak, hak! You can't tell just by looking? I made revenants slip into my injured areas...and merged the swarm to create an artificial organ system. Connected the insects' nerves, digested with the insects' stomachs, revived my cells with the insects'

blood— Well, if I'm being honest, I'm mostly bug at this point. As a minia, I'm essentially dead still. Disappointed? Yeah, right! *Ha-ha-ha-ha-ha-ha-ha!*"

"IMPOSSIBLE... A PROCEDURE LIKE THAT, WITHOUT ANY FACILITIES AT ALL... BUT THEN...THAT WOULD MEAN YOU'VE BASICALLY BECOME A REVENANT YOURSELF."

He hadn't learned his excellent techniques from anyone.

However, the Life Arts of self-proclaimed demon king Izick had been clearly abnormal from birth.

He could bring together the cells of different organisms without causing any rejection response.

Sending signals to his nerves with the swarm that had slipped into his corpse, he could even move himself as if he were still alive.

"I CANNOT BELIEVE YOU WOULD ALTER AND REMODEL YOUR OWN BODY."

Making a mockery of all living things and trampling over even the barest ethics and morals, despite it all, he continued to have a flesh-and-blood body for himself—up until now.

There was no question that Izick the Chromatic, called the wickedest demon king of all...had challenged the True Demon King in order to remain who he was.

"*Ha-ha-ha-ha-ha-ha-ha-ha!* What do I care anymore? Ozonezma... When I sent off Fralik and the others, I told you that I didn't have any more use for you, right? Yeah, that was all a big lie. I take it back. I mean, Fralik's dead either way. You're going to work for me again."

"PISS OFF. LIKE I HAVE ANY DUTY TO YOU!"

"...It's useless to refuse. *Ha-ha-ha-ha!* After all, you can't disobey me, right?"

"......"

"Nope, nope, no sirree! You'll be that way forever. At my beck and call! Since I never gave you any innate courage after all! I bet you thought, with me dead, you were free, right...? Aww, too bad. I'm aliiiiive and kicking! *Ha-ha-ha-ha-ha-ha-ha-ha!*"

Ozonezma could split open Izick's head with his strong forelegs. However, for Ozonezma, Izick's orders were absolute. That was how he had been made.

While he despised this demon king, now weaker and frailer than a baby, Ozonezma would never be able to kill him. Izick always gave his creations a sense of self solely to make sure they were able to suffer.

Ozonezma drooped his head, bit down on his fangs...and then he asked a question.

"...HOW MUCH?"

"Huh?"

"HOW MUCH LONGER WILL YOU LIVE?"

"*Ha-ha...*"

Since he had thrown away his proper existence as a minia and depended on heretical Word Arts to remain in this world...Ozonezma wondered how much longer Izick would be able to stay alive.

He had lost to the True Demon King. While he may have survived, the scars must have been fatally gnawing at him.

Without any doubt, it was a life far more hopeless and horrific than death.

"*...Ha-ha-ha-ha-ha-ha.*"

Izick laughed morbidly while crawling along like an insect.

"Who the hell would give up? Never, never, never, never, I'll never give up...! *Ha-ha, ha-ha-ha-ha!* I'm Izick the Chromatic, dammit! Right, Ozonezma?! Aren't I right?! No way this is enough to get me to throw in the towel, you hear me?!"

"......"

"I'll make...the strongest construct ever; just watch. Strong enough to break that stupid little girl's neck with a single punch! I'm one who can do it! I'll do what Neft, Fralik, Lumelly, and that damn brat Alena couldn't do! I'm the only one left! I can do it...! I can...! Me!"

"...Izick."

He was pathetic and unsightly, without the slightest shadow of his past might.

Ozonezma was unable to flee from that blazing glare... Was that because he was a creation that was never given courage? Or perhaps...

"Material. We need real cells, mountains of them. *Koff, koff.* O-Ozonezma...bring me the bodies of champions. Doesn't matter who. Whatever you can get your hands on."

◆

Several years passed.

Izick was still using the domain of the Athiel nobles as his base of operations.

After coming back to life, his body was no longer able to endure long-distance movement.

Given he was unable to move his physical body from where he was, his only choice when it came to the materials and base bodies for his creations was to employ constructs for long-distance work, amassing them all from his basepoints across different regions.

Even then, as long as he obtained the most important part of all, for the genius Izick, that was plenty.

"...The fundamental theory's the same."

He had spent his whole day experimenting, eating cultivated insects, and hiding himself in the corner of some ruins.

To the man once lauded throughout the world as the wickedest demon king of all, this countryside, already destroyed by the True Demon King and unbeknownst to anyone, was his final domain.

"Ozonezma...had been the strongest combat organism possible, pieced together with the most powerful parts I could find. But it can't be like that defective prototype... I have to start over from square one. I'll construct something that's been perfectly designed; just watch."

The mass of cells in the glass bottle, immersed in preservatives, was the true cornerstone of Izick's research.

A deviant species of unthinkable embryonic cells that weren't even differentiated by race.

Discovered mostly by accident by a self-proclaimed demon king long, long ago, it was a construct capable of transforming its own physical body and imitating any and all entities, referred to as a mimic.

How many more trials were left before he would incubate the organism he sought from these cells?

However, the completed organism that Izick was aiming for was not a normal mimic.

"Simply patching together the bodies of champions isn't enough. I don't have the Greatshield of the Dead with me, but…I did completely analyze its Word Arts theory-based mechanism that interferes with spatial phases, and I can even reproduce it, too…!"

The Greatshield of the Dead was the name of a magic item Izick had previously possessed, which bestowed absolute defense. By interrupting a minuscule spatial phase, it rejected any and all interference from outside. However, at the same time, the warped space would corrode the structure of the user's cells like poison, a dangerous magic item that induced severe pain and degeneration.

Nevertheless, he believed that a mimic could even conquer this heavy toll.

"…thirty-seven trillion cells, every single one, without exception, as strong… No, it's theoretically possible for their structure to even surpass the Greatshield of the Dead, both structurally and conceptually. Same with the degeneration reaction from its defense; the mimic cells themselves could immediately respond and reset everything back to the way it was initially…! I'll design a homeostasis managed through the mimic's transforming abilities! All that's left, *ha-ha*…are its physical capabilities… I have mountains of material to work with…! Champion muscles, champion nerves, champion bone! I can even fully sequence the invincible cells… I can do it!"

Reproducing a magic item with a living organism, and this idealistic sequencing and preservation. A truly preposterous dream.

Izick himself had thought as much before challenging the True Demon King and shelved the plan.

Testing this was his only option. If it was in order to defeat the True Demon King, there was significance in completing it, even if he sacrificed everything to do so. Exhausting resources, exhausting lives, in the thousands, and the tens of thousands.

Terror and obsession had begun to drive the extraordinary genius toward acts of madness. Though, of course, to Izick the Chromatic, there may never have been a borderline between sanity and madness to begin with.

"*Hah, ha-ha-ha...!* Damn demon king...! You're nothing at all... Terror, fear, I just gotta *excise all that stuff from the start...!* I'm not connecting any of those nerves together... A living weapon made specifically to kill you!"

Thus, he set down a grueling path.

Life Arts. Chemical treatment. Introduction through bacteria. Coaction with magical items. He tried all the methods at his disposal.

The experiments were as if he were etching an extremely detailed sculpture out of a tiny grain of sand and then applying the same process to all the grains of the sandy seaside beach.

Eventually, Izick even replaced the arm on the side of him that was still intact with a wire-like prosthetic arm meant for precision work.

A large portion of the motor functions in his brain, rendered unnecessary by the loss of his physical body, were replaced with a nervous system composed of fungal hyphae. This nerve circuit made him able to automatically handle the complex initial work of treating the cells.

The constant alterations to his own body gnawed at the memories from when he was still minian, but even then, he stubbornly protected his sense of self in order to complete his final creation.

The two moons cycled many, many times, and his work remained undiscovered by anyone.

A long time. Longer still.

The light of success would appear only to vanish, without even providing him with the darkness of resignation long enough to give up.

At the end of a repeating cycle of thousands of miracles and thousands of inevitable failures...

"...A name. I gotta think up a name at some point."

Izick had always been a talkative man, but he was talking to himself more and more.

The only person for him to talk to was the mass of cells being cultivated inside the glass tube.

"...Minia-shaped. It's always the minia...who can create the strongest society of all... I'll borrow some help from them and make this one even stronger. In that case, guess I should make them a man—"

Absolutely all of it was part of a long-shot future...

"Nah, nah, a woman! If I make 'em a man...I'll be forced to stare at a naked guy the whole time, right? *Ha-ha-ha-ha!* That sounds awful..."

...Time passed.

◆

How many years had gone by?

The cells that had started to grow could no longer fit inside the glass tube and required a square aquarium.

With Izick's Craft Arts, creating it was a painless endeavor, but with the increase in volume, he now struggled with the adjustments to the preservatives suppressing their mutation.

Returning with a supply of champion bodies, Ozonezma, too, set eyes on his successor for the first time.

"...THAT IS YOUR OPUS?"

"Yup. Actually, in a sense, y'know. It's the ruined remains of all those guys you've been slaughtering. *Ha-ha-ha!*"

It didn't seem like the disordered mass of cells he was looking at would shape into a minia, but if Izick declared they would, then Ozonezma figured it was likely so.

While he was generally a truly loathsome man from any and all perspectives, he had never been wrong when it came to construct creation.

"You better not get in the way here, Ozonezma. Finally... With this, my life'll finally begin..."

"RISKING YOUR LIFE ALL FOR YOUR MASTERPIECE, YOU SOUND ALMOST LIKE KIYAZUNA THE AXLE. YOU'VE NEVER ONCE SHOWED ANY EMOTION FOR YOUR CREATIONS BEFORE... YOU'VE CHANGED QUITE A BIT."

"Huh? Sounded like you were getting smart with me there. Almost like who?"

"THIS MIMIC, SHE'S VERY IMPORTANT TO YOU, THEN."

"…This is all for me. My toy. I'm not like that old hag…! I'm living entirely for myself. I'll kill anyone that tries to look down on me; they'll regret ever being born. That's who I am!"

"IZICK, YOU CAN NO LONGER WIELD THE POWER YOU ONCE HAD. YOU HAVE NO CHANCE OF RECOVERY. YOU MUST UNDERSTAND THAT MUCH…!"

"Yeah, yeah, forget it. Y'know, I don't need you to do anything 'cept bring me more material. Don't you dare get close to this one… That's an order from your master. Got it?"

"…UNDERSTOOD."

Before two small months had passed, the mimic shriveled and died.

This tiny sliver of hope disappeared, and from there, another ten years went by.

Izick lived another ten years, all just to glimpse that light once more.

◆

"Do you understand me?"

"…Uh-huh."

"Perrrfect. We're good as long as you've got a soul that comprehends Word Arts, no matter how dumb you may be at the start. Oh…right. Should we start with my name?"

"…Uh-huh."

"Izick the Chromatic. Better remember it, okay? *Ha-ha-ha!* It's the name of your master."

"Uh-huh."

At long last, his creation was complete.

This mimic, having its perfected form engraved into it from the beginning of its existence, didn't undergo any of the maturation process of a normal life-form, possessing the body of a young girl right from the start.

Although she was born as a mimic, capable of transforming her body at will, her figure wouldn't change for the rest of her life. She was a life-form shouldering such a fate.

"Your name is Tu."

"Tu."

"Mhm, Tu. Tu the…Tu the Magic. *Ha-ha-ha-ha!*"

Izick laughed. The freshly born life-form had no idea this laugh was one of scorn, looking down on his ignorant servant.

"First, I'm gonna go ahead and teach you the most important things of all."

"Uh-huh…"

"Justice and courage."

She was innately unable to fight because of a defensive response to fear. He had made her that way.

A sadistic heart was unable to stand against an enormous menace like the True Demon King.

For example, it was possible to rephrase things such as justice and courage.

"Tu. It was an incredible stroke of luck that you were born, okay? There are infinite possibilities in this world. All sorts of colors. A world where you can take hold of any future...just as long as you have a just and brave heart. So now, as for what that really means, well..."

Which was precisely why the wickedest of all demon kings taught her about the heart, first and foremost.

Things that he himself, in the past and still now, never once believed in at all.

◆

The days and months went by.

Tu hadn't yet stepped outside of her tank, but her condition appeared to be stable.

However, there was still a problem Izick hadn't anticipated.

"Izick! Izick!"

"Ah, shut up...!"

For the past big month or so, this was how he had been woken up.

"You have to get up early and make sure you eat a good breakfast! Why can't you take proper care of yourself?! You haven't washed up at all, either! You're dirty!"

"Dammit... Gah, I can't get your damn voice outta my head...! I'm free to do whatever I want. It's *my* damn life I'm living."

"You're not free! You're the one who taught me to hold all life precious!"

"*Ha-ha-ha-ha!* Why the hell do I gotta follow my own rules anyway, huh?"

A year had gone by since he had begun training her personality. Tu was growing exactly as Izick had intended—too much so, in fact.

A living weapon that would pledge to overthrow the True Demon King, fighting with a just heart.

With this came something that Izick himself hadn't anticipated in the slightest... The interpersonal compatibility between someone raised to be an ally of justice and the wickedest demon king of them all was, frankly, absolutely awful.

"Listen to me! This isn't just about you, Izick! You have to treat all other lives as precious, too! You don't need all that material for experiments anymore, right?!"

"Oh, you don't think so? Then, why don't you try to stop me, hm? From inside that tank of yours! Those cells of yours aren't invincible. On my slightest whim, you could dissolve away and die in there, you know."

"Go ahead and try it! I'm not scared at all!"

There were many like Tu out there.

Trite justice. Trite anger. Trite sadness.

Izick never understood why they would act under such worthless pretexts.

He thought that if he instilled in Tu the exact same ideals the rabble talked about, he could create a blindly devoted soldier, like the ones who had challenged him before.

He had been too successful.

Unlike Ozonezma, Tu, completely lacking the emotion of fear, couldn't be brought to his heel.

...Son of a... Why did I end up like this? I'm Izick the Chro-matic, aren't I?!

It was the True Demon King.

Their presence had thrown everything in their world out of order. Both justice and evil.

Every time his thoughts turned to the one who had ruined his life, he was never able to let it go.

No matter what price he had to pay, he wouldn't die until he got to see the True Demon King fully suffer and perish.

"Ah, whatever. I'm sure that determination of yours ain't worth shit. Study time, study time! Gonna hammer a bunch more knowl-edge into that brain of yours, got it? Up first, going over the theory behind a mimic's construction!"

"Nooo! Nooo! No way, no how! I'm not shutting up until you listen to me!"

"Mimic cells divide at super-high speeds, and using a form exactly as they remember it... Shut up, already!"

"No! More! Murder! No! More! Murder!"

"Gah, shut up, shut up, shut up, shut up!"

Izick had slaughtered, all for his own pleasure.

Each of those victims had had their own life and a heart just like Izick's. He had seen plenty of people smugly relate this to him before.

Izick had killed every single one who did, without exception. They had all been fools not worth keeping alive.

It was inconceivable that Izick wouldn't understand some-thing *so obvious and natural*. It was this heart and the senses like

Izick's own that made his victims cry out in torment and scream when in pain. It was because they possessed such a heart that it proved entertaining.

There may have been children just like Tu among his victims. He didn't remember every single person he killed.

It was only natural that they all died. They had been weak.

Even if Izick hadn't laid his hands on them, they would have still been awaiting the suitable recompense for their own weakness.

I haven't lost... Not to anyone. Eventually, not even to the True Demon King, either.

Izick the Chromatic was different from all of them.

◆

At long last, Izick moved the base of operations he had remained at for almost twenty years.

From the True Northern Kingdom to the United Western Kingdom. It would be a long journey.

"...YOU'RE MOVING YOUR BASE OF OPERATIONS, IZICK?"

For Izick, Ozonezma had already served his purpose, but he still continued to use him as a convenient slave.

Ozonezma was stuck acting like a horse, carrying a large amount of research materials, but his only option was to obey.

"Well, I mean, I've really gotten accustomed to this place and all. At first, it was just supposed to keep me outta the elements, but at some point, it ended up becoming my personal lab."

"THAT IS BOUND TO HAPPEN, GIVEN HOW LONG YOU HAVE REMAINED HERE."

"Wait, I guess I'm testing to see if I can even move this body properly for the first time, huh? *Ha-ha-ha-ha-ha!* I haven't had anything to eat but bugs, weeds, and roots for the last twenty years!"

"ARE YOU GOING TO THE WESTERN KINGDOM ON TU'S WISHES?"

"*Ha-ha-ha-ha-ha!* Is that a joke? Thing is, I'm guessing most people have forgotten my face by this point, so I figured they all might be a little lonely! I'm just so damn excited to see how I kill all those worthless worms, I can hardly contain myself!"

Ozonezma didn't pursue the thought any further.

He knew the Izick would pursue creating this one single construct, even if meant sacrificing absolutely everything.

"...IS TU DOING WELL?"

"Oh, curious, are we? When you've never even met her? I had a different construct carry her, so there's no need for you to know *anything* about her."

"THAT'S RIGHT... THOSE WERE YOUR ORDERS."

Ozonezma was incapable of disobeying Izick's directions.

While Izick himself may have forgotten, he continued to kill champions, exactly as he had been ordered to long ago in the past.

To ensure that he wasn't idly sacrificing preeminent intelligence and wit, there was only one method for Ozonezma to utilize. He only killed *champions who were destined to die.*

Therefore, he reigned as the True Demon King's keeper and continued to slay champions.

He had been doing this the whole time, even after the birth of Tu the Magic had rendered this order meaningless.

Even while he possessed such strength, he was forever unable to challenge the True Demon King himself.

He didn't have any innate faculty for courage.

"...IZICK, I HAVE A REQUEST."

However, a small hope was born inside this manufactured chimera's heart.

Perhaps a single encounter was enough to change a cursed life like his.

This was why he had purposely come to see Izick once more.

"Huh?"

"I WISH TO END MY JOB WITH THIS. I...I WANT TO GO ON MY OWN JOURNEY."

Ozonezma had come across a man named Olukt the Drifting Compass Needle.

A simple bard, weak, and wholly incomparable to any champion. Yet Ozonezma thought he seemed to possess a certain something that could defeat the True Demon King.

"*Ha-ha-ha-ha-ha-ha-ha-ha-ha-ha!*"

Izick simply sneered at his creation's show of will.

"Wait, hold up. Were you still killing people this whole time?! *Ha-ha-ha-ha-ha-ha!* Well, isn't that admirable?! Sure, go right ahead! I already finished Tu's body anyway! I don't have a use for you anymore. You're disposed of. Dismissed. Go and do whatever the hell you want."

"...I WILL DO JUST THAT, THEN."

Killing the True Demon King.

This venture was sure to be a far more difficult path for him than killing the wickedest of all demon kings who had long held absolute control over him. Now, with his hardened resolve...he thought perhaps he could have killed Izick standing in front of him.

In the past, he should've done so. But as for now...

Even if it was possible, he thought he likely wouldn't.

"IZICK."

"What now?"

"YOU LIVED FAR LONGER THAN I HAD PREDICTED YOU WOULD. AT THAT TIME, I ASSUMED WHAT LITTLE LIFE YOU HAD LEFT...WOULDN'T EVEN AMOUNT TO FIVE YEARS. GIVING YOURSELF WHOLLY TO YOUR RESEARCH, WITTLING AWAY AT THE ALREADY SCANT LIFE YOU HAD LEFT...YOU LIVED. I BELIEVE...I UNDERSTAND THE REASON WHY."

"...Don't talk like you know a damn thing about me. That's obviously 'cause I'm the wickedest demon king ever."

"THAT IS NOT IT, IZICK. YOU SHOULD KNOW THAT REASON JUST AS WELL YOURSELF."

"......"

"IZICK, YOU..."

—were a minia after all, the same as any other.

◆

"Ohh, so these are people...! Living, breathing people!"

"...*Ha-ha-ha-ha*, is it really that much fun? Must be nice to be so simple, huh?"

"But I can see them...up until now, I had only ever heard about them from what you told me, but wow...! There really are parents laughing with their children... Even when one of them gets hurt, they all support each other... Everyone's just living their lives..."

"*Ha-ha-ha-ha!* Yeah, well, I guess they are all alive, aren't they?"

Izick laughed vilely as he thought about numerous cities he had once brought to ruin.

He wasn't able to do anything else with the life exhausted from the long journey.

This hillside base of operations situated with a view down over the city could be discovered at any moment.

It won't take time... The only things left are her combat skills and the cruelty to smash her enemies. Once that's over, I can release her...and I can take everything back. Everything I've lost in the past twenty years.

What should he do after that? he wondered.

It wouldn't be bad to rampage like he did in the past, taunting and playing with simpleton fools.

For instance, if he were to annihilate the vast kingdom before their eyes, what sort of face would Tu make?

That was certain to prove very fun.

"...*Ha-ha, ha-ha.*"

"People...real people... *Ah-ha...ha...*"

Tu was crying.

Her tears became tiny droplets, dancing and floating inside the preservative.

For the next day, and the day after that, she pressed her face up against the tank glass and tirelessly gazed out at the people's activity.

◆

The United Western Kingdom did not fall in the flames of war. Nor was it trampled underfoot by some colossal monster.

Yet everything died. Each individual person died in fathomless terror and despair.

The True Demon King reached the center of the Western Kingdom much faster than Izick had thought.

At this stage, there were several things he still needed to teach Tu.

"Shit. Shit. Shitshitshit."

Even on top of the faraway hill, he could see the same presence he'd felt back then.

The presence of terror. The unmistakable presence that brought an end to everything—the presence of the True Demon King.

Despite the many years that had passed since, despite excising the memory storage area in his brain, even after Izick had tried all possible means to forget it all, logic seemed to have no effect at all. He still remembered.

It was unmistakably the terror from that time.

...Can I not beat her?

Thus, it was at that moment when he realized this fear.

It was the question that he should've clearly realized from the outset.

Was it even possible to defeat the True Demon King in the first place?

The True Demon King's terror sheared away the will to try defeating it.

In which case, did the mere fact *he was able to complete the creation* of Tu the Magic mean that she *wasn't enough to defeat them*?

Hadn't Izick *been aware* of this for twenty years?

"Tu…! We gotta escape, or we're in trouble! You want me to leave you behind?! This country's finished!"

"No way!'

Tu raged inside the tank.

Below her eyes, the kingdom she had constantly gazed at day in and day out was falling into ruin. They couldn't be saved.

Even if Tu headed off to save them right at that moment, it would've been too late. The terror of the Demon King extinguished all hope.

"We can just look for a different city, can't we?! We can find more of those minia you love so much! There's still plenty of 'em, tens of hundreds of thousands of them all over the world! But if we die here, it'll all be for nothing!"

His only option was to convince her. If he ignored Tu's will and forcibly carried her off, he would never be able to control her again. However, if he released Tu from the tank right now, she'd never return to Izick's side again.

Once he took her out of the preservative liquid, he couldn't dissolve her away and dispose of her, either. Izick had created her to be an invincible organism.

"No...! No! No! No!"

"Why can't you understand?! You can't win the way you are now! Your heart... You gotta become the perfect weapon, right down to your heart, or you won't be able to kill her! There's still time! I'm not... Listen, okay?! I'm not dying until I perfect you! You understand?! I can't die yet! So stop talking back and listen!"

Right. If he could just complete Tu, then she could defeat the True Demon King.

Even if, perhaps, he had merely convinced himself of this and could do nothing but put it off forever.

"But you were the one who said it, Izick!"

Tu the Magic was different from any of the constructs Izick had made up to that point.

For him, only ever having underlings who obeyed every word he said, it was almost as if she was...

"You said that the most important things in this world are justice and courage!"

"Obviously all that shit was a big fat lie, dammit! You're a weapon! A weapon solely meant to kill that True Demon King!"

"No! No...! I get it!"

Inside the tank, Tu looked hard at Izick in front of her.

She had beautiful eyes, sparkling green.

Her appearance, the ways of the heart, were practically the exact opposite of the demon king said to be the wickedest of them all.

The fact she was even created by a man like Izick the Chromatic seemed like a bad joke.

"Defeating the True Demon King, saving the world... I don't want to think that I had to abandon someone else to do it! If I was made to be a champion, then I want to live in a way that won't make me ashamed to call myself one! I want to believe in justice! I want to believe I have the courage to fight!"

"Dammit...! Dammit, dammit, dammit, dammit!"

There was neither the time left nor the possibility for Izick to create another specimen.

He was going to die.

Tu the Magic was going to challenge the True Demon King in her incomplete state, and it was all going to end up meaningless.

I failed.

Tu the Magic, whom he staked his second chance at life on making, was a total failure.

Why? Why? Why?

Why had he made something that he knew couldn't win?

Why had he taught someone so useless?

...Why did he do that?

"Curse you...! What the hell was I... I just...*ha-ha*... My life, it's...*n-nngh...ngh...*"

"...Izick."

Tu placed her palm against the tank as she spoke.

"You raised me up until now, Izick. Even if it really was all a lie...to me, that world you told me about was the real one! All the colors that you gave to me when I was blank white slate! This heart you instilled in me, that was true righteousness!"

"Enough, you dumb asshole! Piss off! Don't you dare take me for a fool! I'm the wickedest demon king of 'em all! That's who I was! Me! I—I..."

Izick the Chromatic touched the tank structure with a trembling hand.

He would dissolve Tu the Magic and dispose of her.

In that past, that's what Izick would have done. He was surely able to, even now.

The fluid began to drain from the tank. Everything, in that moment, had gone to waste.

Izick shouted in order to avoid looking at Tu as she stepped out into the world for the first time.

"Fine...go on, then! Dumbass!"

He wasn't going to look at her, no matter what.

Her body should have felt unbelievably light.

She should be able to breathe. Be able to walk.

Because, after all, she was the greatest creation of Izick the Chromatic.

"Thank you."

...She must have been smiling.

The fact he could tell was the worst part of it all.

"Thank you, Dad!"

With her braid fluttering behind like a tail, she disappeared far into the distance.

Then in the present.

The only thing left in the room Tu the Magic had stayed in was the aftermath of tremendous destruction.

Most of the destruction had been caused by the construct army Krafnir had unleashed. He used up all his might in an attempt to stop Tu.

...This was all completely pointless.

The revenant Krafnir used as his terminal was twisted apart and leaning up against the wall.

Even after pelting her with an attack powerful enough to damage himself in the process, Tu never stopped. He knew.

He also knew that the reason she didn't stop wasn't because she possessed an invincible body.

I knew...

The fifth match. She had conceded victory to Kuze the Passing Disaster, who had a reason for advancing through the tournament.

However, it was definitely not because Tu was weak of heart. At the time, Tu did exactly what she believed she was the right thing to do.

I understood...what Tu held in her heart.

A Mind Arts caster, capable of controlling the mind, heart, and soul.

This reputation that Krafnir the Hatch of Truth had earned for himself seemed all too ironic.

Even though he had systematized the creation of constructs

that acted in accordance with a set structure and had devised unmatched and peerless technology to project his own heart and soul into a construct...never once had Krafnir been able to *create a construct like Tu, with the same sort of heart and mind as any other person.*

"Ah... Right, Tu..."

Tu was going far away and might never return to him.

That was why Krafnir was able to say it.

"...Please, Tu...keep going ..."

She could simply continue forward, without listening to whatever anyone else had to say. To the ends of the earth, as far as she could go.

Since that itself was the life for those with hearts and minds of their own.

"...Save everyone."

The flames engulfing the city were growing ever stronger.

Mixed with the deafening roars of wood splintering and iron bursting, she could hear the sounds of water being pumped to fight the flames from afar.

But she had made it in time.

"Hrn, hnaaaah!"

Both of Tu the Magic's slender arms gripped chunks of tower rubble and tossed it aside.

The piled-up debris that had trapped the man who had failed to evacuate in time was now being cleared away faster than Gigant construction work. The man coughed from the heat that abruptly gusted in from the depression in the ground surface.

"...You're a lucky guy. Seems like both of your legs are broken, but that's a small price to pay for your life, right?" murmured Shalk, gazing at the events off to the side.

Most likely, the debris that Tu had just tossed away had been the wreckage of a water tower.

The heat of the flames was nullified by the huge quantity of water, and by being pinned underneath the rubble, he had just barely managed to get through without inhaling a lethal amount of smoke. Tu felt glad that he was saved.

Shalk the Sound Slicer shouldered the man on his back before anyone said another word.

"...Tu, I can leave this up to you, yeah?"

"Yup!"

A bullet flew from beyond the other side of the flames. She could see it.

Tu stopped the bullet aimed at Shalk with the palm of her hand.

It was something Rique the Misfortune had taught her. Using not just the central point of her line of sight but the vicinity around it to pick up on signs of an attack.

It appeared to be a magic bullet containing some sort of toxin, but it didn't have any effect on Tu's body.

"I'm so glad I was able to save him!"

"Here, take this. I'll be back soon."

Shalk handed what looked like a metallic pipe over to Tu and rushed outside of the district with tremendous speed.

Since she could still visually track him, he must have been holding back to ensure it didn't have adverse effects for the man on his back.

For the time being, she would have to keep Alus from attacking from the sky, until Shalk and the man could withdraw to the safe zone.

"All right, come at me, Alus! This thing'll...," Tu shouted, waving around the strange metal pipe she had taken from Shalk in the air.

"...What is this thing anyway?"

Two bullets landed one right after another.

On her flank, the flames assailed her, seemingly alive as they moved, and Tu reflexively shook them off with her arm. The shapeless flames flickered slightly from the gust following Tu's attack but broke through the winds and burned Tu's body.

"Whoa!"

Ground Runner, making a direct hit on Tu, had already incorporated itself in the mass of fire, now fed by a whole city of kindling. The threat it now posed was incomparable to when it had just recently been kindled. Its flames now brought instant death, but nevertheless...

"...I don't really get what's going on here!"

Half of her clothes had been burned away. There wasn't a single scratch on her pale, soft skin.

Her bare feet smacking the ground, she raced through the flames like a humongous house cat.

"Give back my treasure..."

"Ah, so as long as I have this thing, Alus'll come after me! That's gotta be it!"

A rifle shot swooped down toward her. Tu saw it and then dodged.

The next attack was already waiting for her.

"*Nhn!*"

A mass of mud, reminiscent of a meteorite, hit her directly. The projectiles from Rotting Soil Sun weren't aiming to cause destruction, but to crush Tu's torso under its mass. But Tu's physical strength alone was able to endure the impact.

"Alus!"

Raising her voice, she asserted her presence while guiding Alus toward the center of the conflagration, to prevent the damage from spreading further. Unlike Shalk's battle, every one of Alus's attacks hit his target; however, Tu wasn't bothered by any of them.

She had another reason for heading into the center of the flames. To see if there were any other survivors who hadn't escaped yet.

She would be happy if there were other lives that Tu could save, like when she had saved Sephite long ago.

"Why...why are you doing such a thing?! All of them, everyone was living their lives...! They didn't harm you or anything at all! There were a whole lotta them that didn't even know how to fight, you know! I—"

She found a child's arm lying on the ground. Tu went to grab their hand, but the child's face and torso had already been reduced to black ash. It was no longer possible to determine if it had been a girl or a boy.

"......!"

"None of that stuff...really matters...does it?"

A cold voice came down to her from the skies.

"The ones who don't put up a fight are easier... I want treasure...not enemies."

"...Why do you want treasure?"

"......?"

"Collecting stupid treasure all by yourself when you don't even have anyone to brag about it with! Is that what makes you happy?!"

She sank down really low, as if her whole body were a spring. The movement took only a second.

She threw a chunk of rubble with all her might.

Alus rotated in midair, easily evading the piece of debris flying at subsonic speeds. Yet Tu in that moment hadn't been trying to lure him anyway, but to close the distance to attack.

Leaping solely with her physical strength, she kicked off the wall of a crumbling tower, tracing an arc like a beam of light.

"...! Alus!"

She had closed in on her enemy, getting barely within arm's reach of the wyvern in midair, with her physical strength alone.

With her unanticipated and explosive power output, her hand attempted to grab the tip of his wing.

"Kio's Hand."

In that moment, Alus had already started to unleash his whip.

The magic whip bent and smacked soundly into Tu's exposed stomach.

"Hng!"

But naturally, the attack didn't manage to slice through Tu's invincible body.

But he reaction from the impact knocked Alus ever so slightly away from Tu's leaping path.

In his very close, yet definitely out of reach, position, Alus readied his gun barrel.

These were the fighting tactics of the world's strongest rogue.

"Magic tree bullet..."

Together with the gunshot, Tu crashed down from the air.

"Nhn...!"

"...Rotting Soil Sun."

The mud masses from Rotting Soil Sun rained down in quick succession where she fell. From among the huge muddy mass, abnormally growing tree branches began to sprout forth. Tu the Magic was being imprisoned within the root structure, complexly intertwined inside the muck. Mud continued to pour endlessly into the spot where Tu had landed.

"Consider the source; take countermeasures... Consider the source; take countermeasures... Consider the source; take countermeasures."

The invulnerable being that remained unharmed after any and every kind of attack would not be so easily killed.

Until Alus accomplished his goal, he would ensure she couldn't move whatsoever.

There was a percussive sound.

"...An attack..."

The mud mountain burst open from within.

Another percussive sound echoed.

Cracks formed in the dirt mound, and a massive chunk of it was sent flying.

"...like this...is nothing for me!"

Tu the Magic's physical body itself was her strongest weapon. She was what Izick the Chromatic had considered to be the perfect combat life-form, and she possessed physical abilities that surpassed that of dragons, even as her whole body was entangled in dirt and roots.

She wrapped herself in a street stall's tent that had escaped the fire, in place of her own clothes, which she had lost in the fierce attacks.

"If there's some magic item that can stop me...go ahead and try, Alus...!"

She would stop Alus here. She had to.

Tu had had enough of tragedy. The scene of the kingdom she had lost was still fresh in her mind.

...Think. I gotta think. I'm not smart. So if I try to attack him, he's definitely gonna predict my moves. My attacks won't harm him, and I think...Alus will probably learn from watching how I act, and then...he might decide he can't kill me and try to flee.

Tu needed to do something about the situation she knew was coming, but she couldn't think up a strategy. She was using the pipe Shalk had handed her as bait to keep Alus around, but if he ever managed to get away, that would be the same as defeat to her. No matter how Tu used her mighty physical abilities, Alus, with his flight mastery, was faster.

"One more attack might—"

"You planning on fighting him alone?" came a voice from right beside her.

A place that, up until just a second ago, had been completely devoid of any presence at all.

"Ah!"

Faster than Tu could process, she was joined by a skeleton cloaked in dark green rags.

"Shalk!"

"I told you I'd be back *soon*, didn't I?"

Shalk the Sound Slicer was twirling his white spear like a windmill and brandishing it low.

He spoke provocatively to the sky above.

"Sorry, Alus the Star Runner. But it's two on one from here on out."

"Okay… Is that because…you can't win by yourselves?"

"Who knows? The two of us might be more than enough."

◆

There was once a phenomenon called the Particle Storm that ravaged country after country.

Even compared to this Particle Storm, self-proclaimed demon kings, and dragon attacks of legend, the single wyvern Alus the Star Runner was the worst calamity in all of recorded history.

The biggest reason was his speed.

Even Lithia's air force, supposedly boasting absolute air supremacy, couldn't fully utilize their air defense network in the face of Alus the Star Runner's lightning speed invasion and were only able to intercept this singular wyvern on Lithia's home soil. At the time, Alus the Star Runner hadn't even utilized his ace in the hole of combining his magic items together to reduce an entire city to ash.

The current situation, with Alus the Star Runner being held up in the first district he attacked in Aureatia, itself a far wider area to defend than Lithia, was a truly miraculous outcome. Forcing him to relentlessly use Rotting Soil Sun and Ground Runner in combat didn't give him any time to use his combination attack a second time.

I mean, we've done a damn good job. Enough to ask for four times the reward from Aureatia; that's for sure.

But simply containing him was no longer enough.

Giving up a fight just because his enemy remained high in the sky, regenerated even fatal wounds, and possessed invincible defensive abilities brought Shalk's pride into the mix.

If running around and evading nonstop was all that was needed to win, then no one in the world could rival Shalk the Sound Slicer. However, using skill, strength, or strategy to overwhelm an enemy and silence them was the stuff of true victory.

"Tu, I have an idea. A strategy, even. We'll need to attack his blind spot, but... You understand where I'm going with this?"

"Stra...tegy...?"

"That's a no, then."

Ground Runner once again assailed them, as if to divide the pair.

Shalk evaded fast enough for his figure to disappear completely, and Tu didn't flinch as she was bathed in hellfire.

Even as the fabric she draped over herself was half incinerated, Tu rolled underneath the rubble, where Shalk had hid himself. It could serve as somewhat of a safe zone and allow them a few brief moments to speak.

"I can help! Just tell me what you need me to do!"

"Do you know what types of magic items that guy's got?"

"Uh, a whip, mud, some fire…and the Greatshield of the Dead. My attacks don't do anything to it."

"…Talking about that magic necklace of his? So you actually know its name, then?"

"Yeah, a long time ago I sorta became familiar with it. He uses a whole bunch of different bullets, too. I mean, just now he shot one that started sprouting all these branches and stuff. If a normal person was hit by one of those, they'd probably shrivel up and die."

"There's got to be a limit to the magic bullets. They're ammunition, after all."

Shalk was proud of how much he'd managed to do by himself in that regard.

The magic lightning bullets must have been a trump card for Alus the Star Runner, and not something he used multiple times over the course of a fight. Shalk had already made him fire four shots of his limited ammunition.

"He's got a regenerating ability that repairs his wounds. The magic item that allows him to do that must be embedded in his body somewhere… I don't know what part of his we have to destroy to kill him once and for all. But Alus still has his sight and his hearing, and he's thinking about our moves and counteracting them. You know what that means?"

"What does it mean?"

"That he even if he looks like a monster, *he's still got a brain.*

Or at least there's an organ in there that serves as the center of his five senses. Destroy his head, and he'll stop moving, and once we've managed to stop him once, we can just keep breaking him down faster than he can recover. We're both good at that, right?"

Stop his movement, deprive him of the Greatshield of the Dead's defenses, and smash his skull.

The important part was sharing this plan with Tu.

"Hey, Shalk, that means…"

Beneath the rubble, Tu's eyes, shining green, looked at Shalk.

"…there's a chance we might be able to talk things over with Alus, right? Maybe?"

"……Get those stupid ideas out of your head."

Shalk had no intention of mincing words at this point.

Alus the Star Runner had become an absolute monster. Getting their hopes up was pointless.

◆

Meanwhile—the alert announcing Alus the Star Runner's attack had reached the halls of Romog Joint Military Hospital.

Since this military hospital was removed from the expected route of the wyvern's attack, the patients and visitors weren't evacuated to a different district and instead were instructed to remain where they were until the state of emergency was over.

As the patients looked on with bated breath while smoke rose high from the Eastern Outer Ward far off in the distance, there were two men arguing back and forth at the rear entrance of the hospital.

"I'm tellin' you, you ain't coming with me, old man. You'll die."

"Nonsense! I could say the same to you! You can't possibly beat the Star Runner with one leg! That's an even more suicidal endeavor than my own!"

"I'm fine. Hell, you just admitted what you're trying to do is suicide, didn't ya?"

The middle-aged man was Aureatia's Sixth General, Harghent the Still. The small-statured man in a red tracksuit was the hero candidate Soujirou the Willow-Sword.

The pair's personalities were oil and water in every way; however, they were similar in one regard—in this situation where they were supposed to avoid the incoming calamity, they both intended to fly directly into the maelstrom.

"Don't try to excuse it with 'I'm fine'! You don't even have any reason to go fight in the first place! There's a provision that states those rendered unable to fight are exempt from their duty to fight against self-proclaimed demon kings!"

"Oh yeah...? That just means I gotta go out there even more. If what yer saying's the truth, then if I don't head out there after hearing that alert, *that'll mean I ain't able to fight anymore*, won't it? Could end up disqualified from the Sixways Exhibition fights, too, so I ain't gonna enjoy myself if I don't jump in at a fun time like this."

"*Th-that's* your reason...? You'd really go that far to gain the title of hero?"

"Herooo?"

Soujirou the Willow-Sword's eyes widened as if he was hearing it for the first time.

"Where the hell'd that come from? I was only ever here for the matches. I've been up front about that with damn near everybody. 'Sides, you're being treated like a sick man, too, ain't you, Harghent? No need for you to head out there, neither."

"I—I... As one of the Twenty-Nine Officials, I have a duty to defend the nation! First of all, it doesn't make any sense that Sabfom has mobilized when he's a patient here, while I wasn't even summoned! Besides..."

"What now?"

"Besides..."

Harghent's words caught in his throat.

"...Star Runner's still alive. I—I...need to defeat him..."

Soujirou looked up at Harghent from below, stooping down like a frog.

"You wanna fight that guy to the death, eh?"

"...............That's right."

Harghent couldn't say anything reasonable at all.

That's how it always had been with all matters regarding Alus the Star Runner.

Nevertheless, he felt that they needed to kill each other.

As the disaster menacing Aureatia, as the enemy who had haunted him his whole life, Harghent needed to kill him. As someone who had killed his friend once already, and as the one who had accidentally started the rogue on his path, Harghent needed to be killed by him.

"If I don't fight him right now, I won't be myself anymore. If there was any enemy in this world...I was meant to give my life to fight, it is Alus the Star Runner. This is what my life has been leading up to. I'm sure of it..."

"I get it, fine. Then I won't do anything to stop ya. So what're you gonna do?" Soujirou shrugged his shoulders, resigned. Though clearly, from any onlooker's perspective, he was the more heavily wounded patient who needed to be stopped.

"...This hospital must have used Flinsuda's funds to bring in some number of automobiles. Those vehicles can be operated by one person and don't need horses or carriage drivers. I have... some practice with handling locomotives. I should be able to drive us to the Eastern Outer Ward. Probably."

"Automobiles? I forgot those things even existed."

"Y-you ever driven one before?"

"No way. Just seen a lot of them turned into junk heaps is all."

"I see... Hrm. I'll have to drive, then... Anyway, there should be some. I'll search for the garage. I'll get the car ready before the hospital staff can spot me."

"Hold up. Now that I think about this, this is stealin', ain't it? You sure we can just take a car like that?"

"O-of course it's not okay! But this is an emergency!"

"So it *is* stealing, then."

"Even so! I'm still going!"

Harghent didn't expect to be able to do anything for Alus, even if he did reach the wyvern.

It wasn't even clear if he wanted to fight him or if he wanted to try to get something across to him.

He could end up reduced to ashes like other riffraff and have it all be over with that.

Once more, Harghent was trying to meddle in something reckless and beyond his station.

...*That's right. It was the same when I tried to kill Vikeon the Smoldering. I was the same way when I went to search for Lucnoca the Winter, too, wasn't I?*

Ultimately, Harghent the Still hadn't even been able to become the madman he was diagnosed to be.

Nevertheless, he still wanted to do this of his own volition.

I was able to do all of that precisely because of the existence of Alus the Star Runner.

His unparalleled recklessness was the talent acknowledged by the strongest of all wrongs and the sole glory in Harghent's life.

◆

Alus the Star Runner had stopped attacking. It had become a fruitless endeavor.

Although he had tried several methods of attack while Tu the Magic was isolated, it only led him to conclude that it would be impossible to crush her with the magic items he possessed.

On top of that, Shalk the Sound Slicer had linked up with her now. Shalk hadn't chosen to escape but had purposely come back to fight him.

He had come back even after being made painfully aware that not a single one of his attacks would reach the wyvern.

"...You're both in the way."

Two aberrant monsters, each individually possessing more fighting strength than a dragon.

Amid Alus's waning sense of self, his tremendous combat experience, and the accumulated tactics that accompanied it were the few areas that had been left untouched in order to maintain his combat abilities. But he could determine that Shalk and Tu were, without question, enormous obstacles in front of him, on par with Lucnoca the Winter and Toroa the Awful.

Although this simply stemmed from the difficulty he had defeating them—the high-speed mobility to evade even his lightning magic bullets and the incredible tenacity to endure a direct hit from Ground Runner.

He didn't need to aim to beat them. This was how Alus had begun to think.

The goal of his adventuring wasn't to kill legends, but simply to amass his treasure hoard. He would fly low, set up a surprise attack, and steal away Heshed Elis the Fire Pipe. After that, he could just ignore the enemies in front of him.

...Flying lower. Is that...what they want me to do?

The reason the two of them still hadn't landed a decisive blow on Alus was because he was constantly in an advantageous position on this three-dimensional battlefield and could handle attacks from the surface with ease.

Particularly when he tried to dispose of Shalk the Sound Slicer, Alus had showed the skeleton a majority of the magic items at his disposal. Since his enemy was enticing Alus down closer to the ground, it would be correct for him to consider that to mean Shalk had some sort of strategy to overcome Alus's methods of attack once he did.

These two...what's their reason for still getting in my way...?

He looked across the area. The district below him was dyed in an ominous dark red from the flames, but the city of Aureatia stretching out across the edge of the horizon still remained totally untouched.

If I destroy that area instead, I wonder what they'll do...... Guess I'll give it a try...

Shalk's determination to keep his hold on Heshed Elis the Fire Pipe despite how fiercely Alus was attacking meant that *he had a reason not to let it go.* In which case, if he erased that reason without killing the man himself, Alus could get ahold of the treasure he was after.

There was no need for him to enter into his enemy's attack range.

Alus instead increased his flight speed in order to gauge his route.

...The air was quivering ever so slightly.

From far off in the direction of the fortress, there appeared to be a light of some kind.

"......"

The upper quadrant of the sky exploded, and Alus descended.

A deathly beam of light, brighter than the midday sun, cut through the clouds and passed right above Alus's head.

He had been forced to make an evasive maneuver by decelerating in midair.

Burning the atmosphere. Destruction. Heat.

A light beam magic item that accumulated solar light and allowed for fierce intercity bombardment.

Cold Star...!

"You didn't think I just ran away, did you?"

Shalk's voice. Had he already requested backup from Aureatia before returning to the battlefield?

After Alus slowed down to evade the light beam—there was someone waiting for him at his point of descent.

"I'm not going to kick you!" yelled Tu.

"......"

Tu had jumped, as if galloping through the air.

Her long braid flowed behind her like a tail. Her eyes, glowing with green light, traced lines through the sky.

"I'll grab you!" she declared confidently.

In the middle of his descent, Alus couldn't evade Tu, who was now closing on him faster than a bullet.

Even if he strengthened his defenses with the Greatshield of the Dead, if she simply grabbed on to him instead of trying to destroy him, he would eventually be forced to release the Greatshield's protection.

"Rotting Soil Sun."

He dropped the magical item.

The mud bullets were mostly fired at random—it didn't possess any method capable of stopping Tu the Magic. Still, if he was able to obscure her line of sight for just a second, he should be able to escape.

Alus felt her grab on to the tip of his left wing.

...She avoided it.

Tu the Magic wasn't wearing any clothing.

The cloak she was draped in... She was no longer wearing the leftovers of a street stall's tent. She had caught Rotting Soil Sun in the fabric after Alus had dropped it below him, and she wrapped it up, suppressing it right before it could fire.

Tu had a grip on his wing. The only choice was to cut it off himself.

"Kio's Hand...!"

"You're not getting away!"

Alus's arm, already moving to unleash his magic whip, chose his musket instead.

In that instant, Alus's combat judgment was warning him of something,

That skeleton.

Shalk the Sound Slicer was quietly lingering in the rear behind Tu. Carrying Heshed Elis the Fire Pipe, with his rags pulled down over his eyes, he remained motionless.

In the middle of this momentary clash, he might have chosen to act as a decoy.

That's not it.

The musket's gunshot echoed.

"......"

"If you're planning on cutting off part of your own body—"

He had the sensation of something cold and rigid passing vertically through his eyeball.

A blade fired out from a completely blind angle.

Alus's cranium had been pierced by a spear.

…He could see Shalk's body. Behind Tu, he still remained completely motionless.

"—you can't use the Greatshield of the Dead thing, can you, Alus the Star Runner?"

"You're…"

However, at the same time, Shalk the Sound Slicer was up above Alus, skewering his head.

From his sternum up…his head and right arm were now linked together by a chain.

"The game of cat-and-mouse is over."

Consider the source; take countermeasures.

Shalk's body, which he saw down below, consisted only of his left arm and everything below his chest.

He could separate his bones and re-form them. That was this skeleton's ability.

…Of course. That big piece of cloth that Tu had stripped off.

Shalk had clung to the back of that fabric while his bones were scattered.

Making himself into a weapon at Tu's control, he put every-thing on the line for that one moment of opportunity.

Alus figured out the source.

If he knew that, he could counteract it.

No matter what sort of legend he was up against, if he fought them a second time, he could defeat them.

As long as he could fight.

He fell into darkness. His thoughts were dissolving away.

"We did it…" Tu quietly murmured after she landed.

Their final strategy had succeeded.

The world's strongest rogue was now pinned into the ground by Shalk's spear.

He may eventually start regenerating, but Tu had a firm hold on Alus. She wasn't letting him escape.

The destruction and losses were enormous, but they had been able to hold him at bay.

The speed of Alus the Star Runner's assault had been abnormal. Shalk the Sound Slicer and Tu the Magic were the only hero candidates who had gotten there in time after being summoned to take him down.

"Now we can end this, without letting anyone else die… Right, Shalk?"

"…Tu, I'll say this just in case, but…"

Shalk's skull and right arm groaned, still piercing Alus's head through with his spear.

There was something slightly off in Shalk's tone.

"You can't let go…of Alus's body no matter…what."

"I know that. Why would you say…?"

Then she realized.

Tree branches growing out from Alus's body were wrapping around Shalk the Sound Slicer and beginning to absorb his body into their tangle.

Tu knew what this attack was. The magic tree bullet.

In the moment the fight was decided, Alus hadn't fired his musket at Shalk. He'd fired it *at himself.*

"N-no...!"

"Impressive. This guy really was...one hell of an...abomination. I can't believe, in that single moment, he thought of a way to turn the tables like this...!"

Before she could think of something, she went to rip the rapidly growing branches away from Shalk's bones.

"...It's not working!"

It wasn't enough. Tearing off the parts that she could grab with only one hand proved meaningless.

Shalk didn't possess the same invincible physical body that Tu did. If the magic bullet tangled around him and ate away at him, he was bound to be destroyed.

The sole chance that Shalk's strategy had created for them... ended up creating an opportunity for Alus as well, to put an end to the Sound Slicer.

"......!"

She needed to release the other hand holding on to Alus.

There was a strong possibility that Shalk's final attack had killed Alus anyway. His brain was run through.

"Shalk!"

"Don't let go!"

"How...how could I not?!"

Tu was fully aware that she was a fool.

She let go of the hand gripping Alus.

She used both arms to tear away the branches entangling Shalk. A single second.

In that moment.

Kio's Hand, which the dead Alus still held fast, flitted up into the air and cut Alus's own skull. Sacrificing half his head, he had escaped from the white spear pinning him to the ground.

"Not yet…!"

Even as the branches she tore off Shalk were enveloping her arms, she immediately turned around.

Mud exploded right before her eyes.

"…!"

Rotting Soil Sun had fallen on to the ground during the previous clash.

The magic item that endlessly generated mud bullets was lost…

Overcome by a terrifying amount of mud and with her vision blocked off, she barely managed to touch Alus's arm.

She couldn't grab hold of it. The tree roots she'd grabbed earlier were now blocking off Tu's fingers.

He'll be able to escape!

"Tu! Throw me!"

In the blink of an eye, the roots entangled around her fingertips were sliced off.

Shalk the Sound Slicer, now just his head and one arm, had lost his mobility, but he could still swing his spear.

With her sight still obstructed, Tu clenched down on the white spear tip.

I have to judge this for myself. If Alus is still alive, which direction is he going to fly?

Rique the Misfortune would have definitely thought about it.

Everyone else besides Tu was desperately thinking things through.

They used their experience to get a grasp on how their foe would act next.

That's right. In Alus's case, he'd steal treasure!

Tu flung Shalk, now transformed into a single spear.

In the direction of Shalk's torso decoy—toward Heshed Elis the Fire Pipe.

This motion scattered the mud covering one of Tu's eyes.

She could see the scene in front of her. Shalk connected with his body and extended out his spear.

It didn't reach.

...It can't be.

Alus, recovering his ability to fly, had flown off in a completely different direction than she had predicted.

Tu's decision had come too late.

There was a single point that was outside Tu the Magic's expectations. The world's strongest rogue, who was more obsessed with treasure than any other, in that moment, *hadn't been a rogue at all.*

Alus the Star Runner, his skull destroyed by Shalk, moved solely on the instincts directly following his regeneration.

Tu the Magic had failed.

Shalk shouted from outside the sea of mud.

"Tu! Unless you want to turn into a fossil, you have to get out of there! The mud's not stopping!"

"No!" Tu shouted. She held on to Rotting Soil Sun, trying to curb the constant torrent of mud.

"I have to put a stop to this thing! If…if there are any survivors still left, I can't let them get swallowed up by this mud! I won't let any more harm come to this district…or anyone beyond it!"

"There aren't any damn survivors! You think you can get that magic item under control right now?! That's like trying to use Word Arts on a guy you just met for the first time!"

Her lower body was sinking completely into the mud. Her feet found no purchase.

The amount of mud pouring from the discarded Rotting Soil Sun was a veritable ocean. Tu's body was covered in muck, her eyesight was being sealed in darkness, and the insides of her respiratory organs began to drown in mud.

Even then, Tu was able to endure it. She believed so.

I won't give up.

She was an abomination who had been created without the ability to feel fear. She could continue fighting however long it took.

In this hellish city, engulfed in raging fire and sinking into mud…right now, Tu the Magic was the only one capable of continuing to hold on to Rotting Soil Sun.

She could hear a voice from far away.

This time, she wanted to be sure to save someone. She wasn't going to abandon anyone to die.

I won't give up, I won't give up, I won't give up…!

Her fight was over.

Together with her strong will, the Demon King's Bastard sank into the depths of the mud.

The sun of calamity, rising up into the skies of Aureatia, refused to set.

CHAPTER 9 ◆ Kizaya Crater Lake

Twenty-seven years ago. In an age before the appearance of the True Demon King.

The terrors of this era were wyverns, the monstrous races, plagues, and those who claimed to be demon kings.

Occasionally, there were also enchanted swords and magic items from parts unknown that threatened order, as well.

There was no minian settlement at the base of the Kizaya Volcano.

The river that flowed from the lake at the summit was unusual, an unsettling, sticky mudslide continuously flowing down it. There were even rumors of some grotesque, never-seen-before creatures inhabiting the area around the crater lake.

However, in order to reach Kizaya Crater Lake, one must traverse dangerous terrain filled with noxious fumes and miry swamps, while carefully watching one's step over the muddy rock surface. A natural labyrinth.

Occasionally adventurers and scholars had gone to investigate the crater, but most of them were never heard from again.

Much like the Yamagah Barrens and the Particle Storm that raged there, Kizaya Crater Lake was generally recognized as a hostile region, and there were very few people who thought it contained anything that made trespassing worth it.

Alus the Star Runner was at the base of Kizaya Volcano.

"...I want to ask what you saw up at the crater."

"Who are...you...?"

A dwarf adventurer lay collapsed below the precipitous bluff.

Perhaps he had slipped down the craggy mountain. The dwarf's arms and legs were broken and twisted in directions they shouldn't have been. But owing to his dwarven tenacity, he clung to life.

"Three arms... N-no, it can't be..."

"It can."

Alus nodded slightly. He thought this would make the conversation go smoother.

The dwarven adventurer smiled in pain.

"I...don't have anything to my name. Hell, that's why I'm stuck with an awful occupation...like adventurer..."

"I think it's good work."

"Because you're strong...? The rumors of the three-armed wyvern...have made it all the way to the kingdom."

"...Okay," Alus replied briefly. He wasn't particularly interested.

After he gave the dwarf some water from a throwaway canteen, the dwarf struggled to speak.

"Up on top of the Crater Lake...there's some type of monster up there... There's always been those types of rumors... We were trying to see if they were true... Thinking it might be profitable."

"Profitable? Are ogres and goblins really that profitable...?"

"A *new species*. You don't know...the minian legends, do you? For example, that abominations coming here from the Beyond... establish themselves in our world, and...*koff!* Turn into a race with a new name... If we did discover something like that, even a carcass would be worth a whole lotta money...!"

"Hmmm... I don't really want anything like that..."

Alus the Star Runner continued to amass the world's treasures, but he only took interest in items that had some sort of combat utility. He would often see people like this dwarf who would refer to rare carcasses, beautiful stones, scenery, or pictures as treasure, but he didn't understand their sense of value.

He also felt in part that any treasure he couldn't use to protect himself or steal from others would be nothing but dead weight that'd get stolen no matter how much he amassed together. But the minia must have had their reasons for finding value in such things.

"......But right before we reached the lake...two people were shot. By mud...mud arrows."

"You...were shot in the leg and fell back down all this way, then."

Unlike the other lacerations carved into the dwarf's body, the wound on his right shin had come from something sharp. Alus could tell it had been cut into him by some type of weapon.

On top of that, the dirt around the wound had the same

characteristics as the strange mud and rock flow that flooded the whole region. The dwarf's testimony was worth considering.

"...I want to hear about this new species. It's fine if you want to keep it secret, though..."

"It's all right. It's not like any help's coming for me in a place like this... I'll never get to sell off this information, either. They had the same appearance as ogres, but...*koff!* I definitely saw them... Not one or two, but several, up at the Crater Lake..."

The dwarf's breathing continued to grow weaker, but his voice was trembling with excitement.

"The one-eyed monsters were really up there."

"......"

Alus scratched at the rocky area near his feet in boredom.

Just as he had expected, the information didn't interest him.

"...The mud in this area...has the same smell as the Matouk Coalfields that I saw a long time ago. The soil around here...is totally different from how it originally used to be..."

"Huh...?"

"...I'm heading out now... Bye."

"Huh?! Y-you're not...going to eat me?"

"...? Is there something I'll get out of eating you?"

"B-but...isn't that what wyverns do? I figured I was about to die, so..."

"Is it? I've never really...had much of an appetite... Instead of minian flesh, I can just eat the food I brought with me..."

Alus, with his sprouted arms, may have become far more detached from the wilds than his wyvern brethren.

He had been able to survive off the same prepackaged foods that the minia ate without any problem, and the impulse normal wyverns had to attack other races wasn't particularly strong enough that he couldn't hold it back.

"Besides...I've got a friend. If I harm any minia, then maybe... at some point, it could interfere with his success..."

"S-Star Runner...has a friend...? *Ha-ha*... I can't believe it... It sounds like a joke..."

"...I'm not lying."

"Yeah, I believe you. Sheesh...that little tidbit'll be a good souvenir to bring along with me to hell..."

"...I don't think you're going to die."

Alus looked far off from atop the rock.

They were still a ways off, but he could tell that five minia were approaching this area. A kingdom anti-wyvern task squad, following Star Runner after he was witnessed near Kizaya Volcano.

There may not have been any value in surveying Kizaya Crater Lake itself, but there was enough value in getting visual confirmation of the wyvern adventurer and his multitude of magic items for them to dispatch a squad.

"...You were lucky to slip down this far. I wouldn't mention... that stuff about the new species."

"*Koff!* If I had known I would've been able to return alive, I never would've mentioned it anyhow...dammit!"

By the time the dwarf cursed, Alus had already lifted off from his rocky perch.

A one-eyed monster, huh...

He looked over the rock face, mud continuing to flow down it.

No matter how difficult a labyrinth it may have been to traverse, in the sky, there was nothing to get in Alus's way.

The adventurer's story had also managed to confirm it for him—there was treasure worth stealing here.

...*My treasure.*

◆

His name, Zelad the Glaring, was one he had given himself.

He believed he did have parents of his own. He had always acquired the knowledge and skills to survive in the harsh environment of Kizaya Volcano on his own.

Unlike the minian races or goblins he occasionally caught sight of, he possessed only a single eye in the center of his head.

"You have to understand where I'm coming from, Alus. I never thought there were any other people like me out there."

"............"

The scenery of Kizaya Crater Lake looked almost like flatland, smoothly leveled off in black.

The endlessly bubbling muck had completely filled in the lake that had originally been there. In between the residences, connected by planks for footing, was a field growing crops that used the mud as soil.

The monsters that lived there all had only one eye like Zelad.

"I...found other monstrous people like me here in Kizaya. Right now, there are six of us, including myself. There are more and more like me starting to be born. This is the domain of the cyclopes. Without Rotting Soil Sun here, the minian races would intrude on our lands."

Even now, mud ceaselessly bubbled up from the porous sphere Zelad held in his hands.

Zelad had come up with the name *Rotting Soil Sun* himself as well. The magic item allowed the wielder to control the shape and pressure of the mud flow by touching it and communicating their will with it.

For a wielder as skilled as Zelad, he could fire the mud off like blades or bullets, and it was easy to kill the small number of adventurers that came to find him—but most of all, he could maintain Kizaya Volcano's present state as an impregnable labyrinth that defied all minian civilization.

"So I can't hand this thing over. Even if it means a fight with you to the death."

"...I'm not so sure about that. I think...it'd be better for you to hand it over."

"I don't know about that. Do you have some reason not to forcibly steal it away?"

"Not really... If it's a hassle, I'm fine with that, too, really..."

Alus the Star Runner's scrawny body wasn't even half as tall as a cyclops's, but even so, Zelad likely had no hope of victory.

Up until Alus stood in front of him like this, Zelad's tribe had tried every method at their disposal, including shots from Rotting Soil Sun, to shoot him out of the sky, but it was no use.

I don't get what this guy's aim is here. But I want to leave behind my cyclops blood, no matter the cost.

This was the reason why he had forbidden the others from getting involved, and Zelad alone was engaging in this negotiating farce.

"…When I came here…I had a dwarf ask me why I don't eat people…"

Alus turned around to the small shack on the eastern side of the pier.

The wyvern appeared to know what was hung up inside.

"…You ate the adventurers."

"It's valuable minian meat from people who trespass into our domain. A wyvern like you can't possibly have come here to get revenge for some no-name adventurers. It's natural for the monstrous races to eat minia."

"That's why."

"What?"

"…If you want to eat people…all you have to do is descend the mountain to a town nearby. You're all being dishonest about your desires… It's not natural."

"It's to protect our species. We still haven't grown our numbers nearly enough. If the six of us and the four children all ended up dead, that'd be the end of us. The closer we get to minian settlements, the greater the risk."

They had a craving for minia flesh. But the cyclopes needed numbers to confront the power the minian races commanded. Until they could increase their number, Zelad had to keep protecting this Crater Lake.

Yet Alus said something he hadn't anticipated.

"...Why's it risky?"

"Excuse me?"

"If you were an ogre, you wouldn't worry about that. You're all weak... Your aim from your attacks earlier—you missed because you only have one eye. You even failed to finish off that dwarf..."

"......"

With only one eye, cyclopes didn't have the same stereoscopic vision of other monstrous or minian races. Needless to say, this had a great effect on their marksmanship precision.

Not even Zelad understood why a species like theirs, bestowed only with defects, had been born.

"Are you saying we're trying to increase our number because we're weak?"

This was an inconsistency that Zelad was fully aware of himself.

The cyclopes were weak. The fact that, if nature was left to take its course, their species was destined to die off was all the more reason he felt they needed to live on—even if they had to rely on the power of a magic item to do so.

Thus, Alus's next words pointed to something truly terrifying.

"The children you mentioned. There's been...more than four of them, hasn't there?"

"Wh—"

Zelad's blood ran cold.

"Why...would you say that...?!"

"Huh...? If you cared about your species so much, it'd be weird...for you not to raise more of them."

"We just haven't had that many healthy births, that's all! *Birth defects* are something any species has to contend with...!"

"When you say *birth defects*..."

Alus peered at Zelad with passionless pupils.

"You mean *they were born with two eyes*, right?"

"No, that's not it...!"

Cyclopes, just like Zelad the Glaring, were supposed to be a species that had newly appeared in this world.

In that case, why *didn't their children look like them*?

"...The mud here."

Alus scooped up the muck spreading out at his feet.

"Smells like the Matouk Coalfields. In the river there...the poison from the mine made the fish's eyes merge together...and the fished-up ones had mutated into hideous monsters..."

"Th-that...that can't be..."

"...This is a volcano. The heat of the volcano is vaporizing the material inside the mud into the air...and the effects of that smoke are what made you like this."

Zelad didn't know his parents' faces. It was the same for all five of the other cyclopes he had taken in.

That was why they had believed they must have been a new species sent to this world from the Beyond.

"For example, near the volcano...there's an ogre habitat—"

"...Shut up, Alus the Star Runner!"

Zelad tried to break Alus's neck, but his swings didn't connect.

Alus had evaded with far too much ease. The cyclops was weaker than a normal ogre.

"...W-why...why are we...?! I killed them... The children with two eyes, they aren't a part of our species!"

"You're an ogre."

All the inconsistencies that Zelad had disregarded pointed toward this truth.

The creatures he had considered to be *cyclopes* up until now were just ogres, and the rare ones that hadn't been born with the one-eyed deformity from the effects of the Rotting Soil Sun had simply been abandoned on the mountain.

He considered the Rotting Soil Sun a magic item for them. However, this cursed magic item was, in fact, what was creating creatures like them in the first place.

"Wh-what...what am I supposed to do...?"

"...You occasionally get small earthquakes here, don't you? Earlier, I also heard...a sound like gunpowder exploding."

Alus the Star Runner continued to speak, without paying any mind to Zelad's current state.

"...If you don't get rid of Rotting Soil Sun, everyone here is gonna die."

"No, that can't be..."

"Earthquakes and those sounds...are signs of an impending eruption. So much mud's flowing underground...it's building up the pressure... You'd be better off going down the mountain and living life like an ogre instead..."

The mud generation, more than enough to completely cover an entire mountain, was clearly abnormal. Nevertheless, such abnormalities could be found all over this world, and most adventurers didn't try to inspect each one and try conquering them for themselves.

Alus, however, traveling across the horizon enough to earn the name *Star Runner*, had honed his powers of observation through a great amount of trial and error. Was every phenomenon the result of a treasure, or not? If not, then what *was* the source behind it?

...*This is a true adventurer.*

Zelad had heard stories about the outside world from the adventurers they had captured. Many of them spoke about the strongest rogue adventurer of all.

For some reason—when they spoke about the wyvern named Alus the Star Runner, supposedly just an indifferent plunderer, they talked of him like he was a champion.

Though it was far faster for Alus to kill all his enemies and plunder their treasure, there were times when he didn't.

"Why...? You're supposed to be the same sort of aberration like me...so why...?"

"I'm just me. There's not much difference between us, really..."

Zelad crouched down.

He couldn't continue to keep Rotting Soil Sun in his possession any longer.

"I wanted to be free. I just wanted freedom..."

".........You can still do just that, can't you?"

From that day forward, the mud on Kizaya Volcano stopped.

Two years later, rumors spread throughout the United Western Kingdom about sightings of a group of one-eyed abominations, but such topics were soon left behind.

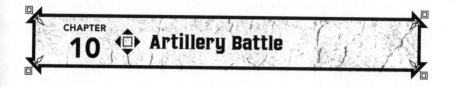

Soon after Rotting Soil Sun was lost in the fifth borough of Aureatia's Eastern Outer Ward, Tu the Magic dropped out of the battle.

From a small tower in the Third Fortress, he saw the moment Alus lifted off.

The word *saw* perhaps wasn't the correct way to phrase it. It was just a small silhouette, like a speck of dust, seen through optical scopes.

You gotta be kidding me.

The shooter, wearing a thick pair of sunglasses, cursed inwardly as he placed his finger on the Cold Star mounted inside the small tower. The motions to fix his aim on the target were mostly done unconsciously.

Dally the Coin Repeller was a soldier originally belonging to Kaete's camp.

He had once used a new weapon from the Beyond to snipe at Kuuro the Cautious from over nine hundred meters away. Right now, his target was Alus the Star Runner.

Alus wasn't ascending higher. He was flying at a low altitude to hide himself among the city buildings.

The buildings hindering Alus's low-altitude flight path were laid out in complex and intricate ways, and they also made it impossible for any sniper's line of fire to pass through.

The wyvern was clearly keeping conscious of the Cold Star's long-range fire.

The Greatshield of the Dead protected Alus from extreme heat.

It had become evident that as long as Alus was activating this invincible defensive ability, he was unable to take any other action, including flying or attacking. In other words, Dally's role was to use the radiating light beam to interfere with Alus's flight and force him into the attack range of Shalk the Sound Slicer, who was pursuing him from the surface.

There was a 2,500-meter distance from Dally to the Eastern Outer Ward. It was a distance that made it completely unrealistic to snipe down a small target like Alus.

If this thing misses its target and hits him directly above the city, am I going to be held responsible?

The Third Fortress was the closest one to the Eastern Outer Ward, located on its western side.

His line of fire was aimed outside Aureatia city, and the damage that would come from the artillery barrage was seen to be *within acceptable limits*, however...

Even if a few hundred get caught up in the blast and die, I ain't handing out any compensation to the bereaved or anything.

Dally controlled his breathing. His combat experience led his finger to pull the trigger with near autonomous movements.

"Fire."

A dazzling light was launched in between the buildings, standing like shadows, as if threading a needle.

The beam of light the Cold Star radiated didn't produce any sound itself.

The light pierced through iron towers. The roofs of private citizens' homes were melted.

The shrieking roar that echoed across the sky was the result of the air above its line of fire being heated up and exploding.

With the sniper rifles that existed in this world, hitting a target from 2,500 meters was close to impossible.

However, the Cold Star fired light. Therefore, there was no need to heed gravity, the impact of the wind, or the rotation of the planet. With this, a big difference between it and a normal gun was its firing range and its *duration*.

Even if it missed the target by the time it reached it, it was possible to shift the light beam, as well as place the attack along the target's expected path. The weapon had characteristics that were completely unlike any of the firearms up until now.

Meanwhile, Dally the Coin Repeller himself was a test shooter who specialized in handling the weapons of the Beyond more than anyone else among Kaete's camp, and he continued to adapt to new emerging tactical strategies.

"Hurry up and crash already, Star Runner."

Through the light shield on the optical scope, he saw Alus's silhouette get hit by the Cold Star.

He had taken a direct hit. Before, Alus had sensed Dally's first shot and descended down lower into the city, but—

Something felt off.

He understood why Alus's figure remained intact after getting hit by the cannon. He had activated the Greatshield of the Dead.

That wasn't all.

His descent speed is slow.

There was even enough time for him to put these thoughts into words.

That silhouette. What if, in fact, that wasn't actually Alus the Star Runner?

Dally thought he saw a flash of light behind the silhouette.

He carried up a corpse from the fifth borough of the Eastern Outer Ward. He's having...

It was too late. Who could have possibly imagined until witnessing it for themselves...that he had a means to fly and counterattack, all while he readied a shield against the fatal light beam?

...that corpse use the Greatshield of the Dead for him.

The target was bigger, and heavy. That was why, this time, Dally had scored a direct hit.

A lightning flash.

A magic lightning bullet was fired back at the small tower of the Third Fortress where Dally stood.

I'm dead, he thought.

He still thought so as a loud roar of thunder echoed around him.

A bright something—flames—cut across, right before Dally's eyes. Cutting off the arc of Alus's lightning, it looked like a midday meteor rushing by.

The lightning that should have burned Dally to ash intersected with the huge quantity of flame and vanished.

"You're kidding," he couldn't help murmuring.

The difficulty of *passing through* the trajectory of Alus's shot, firing it from north to south of Aureatia, was entirely incomparable to Dally's successful shot from moments ago.

The distance it was fired from wasn't *a piddling* 2,500 meters, either.

"Mele the Horizon's Roar...!"

◆

Turning back the hands of time, while Tu the Magic was in the middle of her brave struggle in the fifth borough of the Eastern Outer Ward.

Shalk the Sound Slicer, having withdrawn with a rescued survivor, immediately searched out the minia who appeared in command of the scene once he'd handed off the wounded survivor and tersely gave his request.

"Send out Mele the Horizon's Roar."

"What...?!"

It was Tuturi the Violet Foam, Aureatia's Twenty-First General.

After she had thrown the residents of the fifth borough of the Eastern Outer Ward into Chariot Golems and made them evacuate, she was in the middle of commanding the firefighting efforts and evacuating the peripheral areas.

"There's no time. We're doing the best we can, but there's only so much ground-based combat can do to hold Star Runner back. But if you get that Mele guy into the mix, that should change the situation."

"Whoa, whoa, whoa...hold on a sec here; you're Shalk the Sound Slicer, right? I mean, what do you expect me to do here? If you want to talk about Mele the Horizon's Roar, go talk to his sponsor, Cayon. I don't have aaaaany right to tell him what to do, see. What in the world even made you come to me with this anyway?"

"You were nearby."

"Listen, buddy! Don't put this on me!"

In contrast to her jocular tone, a cold sweat ran down Tuturi's back.

If someone as strong as Shalk the Sound Slicer was talking like this, then the situation was undoubtedly much more urgent than she'd imagined. If they needed to shoot down someone who Shalk couldn't defeat even fighting two on one, then there likely wasn't any other means besides using Mele the Horizon's Roar to help.

"At any rate, Jel and Cayon are in the middle of negotiating about how to use Mele right at this very moment, okay?! Besides, even if you wanted to include him in all of this, I heard that he was rendered unable to fight in his match! Y'know, *your* match against him! What the hell's he supposed to do here?!"

"Unable to fight?"

Shalk tapped his spear on his shoulder, smiling with exasperation.

"That can't be true. That guy can still shoot, and even beat Star Runner no problem."

"Mele had one of his eyes crushed!"

"Hey, I don't have *any* eyes, do I? You think he hasn't practiced shooting with one eye before?"

"Aughhhh, give me a damn break!"

Either way, the negotiations regarding Mele the Horizon's Roar needed to be hurried along.

The problem then was how to buy time until the negotiations had concluded.

"…You just need some long-range backup, right?"

"If Alus starts destroying the city from far up in the sky where we can't reach him, it'll all be over. Eventually he's gonna be looking to do that, too."

"So we'll knock him down to make sure that doesn't happen. There's someone who can do that."

"What's your name?"

"Tuturi the Violet Foam. Why ask now?"

"I'm coming to kill you if you don't do your job."

"Hey!"

Before Tuturi could get the word out, Shalk had already disappeared from the area.

She'd mobilize Dally the Coin Repeller and get permission to use the Cold Star. Considering this current emergency, the permission process was bound to go through without a hitch.

However, the question was if Mele the Horizon's Roar's sniping skills were actually in good shape or not.

"Quewai! You heard all that, right?!"

"I'm currently radzioing Dally the Coin Repeller. Seeing that introducing Shalk the Sound Slicer and Tu the Magic to the fight still isn't enough to defeat him, I believe we should consider pulling back the defensive line as well."

"Wait, why was I the only one getting hounded like that if you were standing right here, too?!"

The Eighteenth Minister, Quewai the Moon Fragment, had been acting together with Tuturi for some time now; however, it was possible that Shalk hadn't recognized him as one of the Twenty-Nine Officials. It was the first time Tuturi had ever felt envious of the man's lack of presence and gloomy demeanor.

"We'll need to figure out where to snipe from. Dally will move on my judgment. Quewai, contact General Haade and tell him to pressure Cayon from our side as well. It isn't the time to get caught up in faction this or that. Hell, I said it myself... I told him I'd do it. So I'm gonna do it, dammit."

The district Tuturi and the others were in was quite far removed from the fifth borough of the Eastern Outer Ward, but even then she could see the black smoke from the fires through the gaps in the low-rise buildings.

This battle concerned whether those flames of war would spread to engulf all of Aureatia or not.

"After all, Aureatia's in critical danger...but more than that, my own life's in danger, too."

◆

Mele the Horizon's Roar was continuing to receive treatment in Gigant Town, situated on the northern edge of Aureatia.

Though he was recuperating, there wasn't a single hospital in all of Aureatia that could take in Mele given his colossal body. It was more bed rest than recuperation, simply waiting for him to naturally heal due to his Gigant vitality. Aureatia's Twenty-Fifth General, Cayon the Thundering, was there with him.

Visiting them was a messenger from Jelky, sent to negotiate with Cayon regarding the operation to intercept Alus the Star Runner.

"Impossible," Cayon replied. He sat in a simple and plain chair, with his legs crossed.

"Nothing more for me to say here. I'm *certainly* not letting Mele shoot."

"But if Alus is allowed to invade Aureatia, the entire nation will fall victim to his rampage…! I know full well how unreasonable this is, but the situation requires a complete mobilization of our fighting forces!"

"*You realize it's unreasonable*, do you? Um, listen, do you really understand? Mele's sniper attacks aren't some simple, magical nonsense that'll automatically hit the target, okay? If he misses his mark just a little bit, the result could be this city you're busy protecting getting directly hit by a meteorite. Simply using this method of attack inside Aureatia's borders is out of the question already, and if he were to shoot while one eye and one leg are still wounded…he'd bring ruin to Aureatia far more easily than Alus can, I'll tell you that."

"……!"

The messenger couldn't come up with a response.

One of the reasons for hosting the Sixways Exhibition in the first place was either to kill the shura like Mele, who could potentially bring ruin to the world, or force them into being unable to fight anymore, to secure peace and order for Aureatia.

Thus, Mele the Horizon's Roar's present incapacitated state was, to Aureatia, a *desirable* outcome.

The same held true for Cayon the Thundering.

Ultimately, it may have been fortuitous that Mele got defeated in his first match with Shalk. He didn't lose his life, and it established that he was unable to fight anymore... The most desirable way to get through this Sixways Exhibition. Now that things have ended up this way, I need to protect Mele until the games have concluded.

Cayon's serious actions were likely acts of treason against Aureatia. However, from the very beginning, he had been acting only with thoughts of his homeland, Sine Riverstead, and their guardian, Mele, in mind.

A future where Mele was hunted down as a threat to the kingdom meant ruination for Sine Riverstead.

He wouldn't run counter to this priority no matter what, even if, right now, Aureatia were to be destroyed.

"If you don't have the authority to make a decision, you can get Jel on a radzio call. I don't mind. I'd prefer to wrap this up as quickly as possible, thanks. I have to head to the front, too, right?"

<...Cayon. There's a mistake in your perception of things.>

A voice cut in from the messenger's radzio. Third Minister, Jelky the Swift Ink.

"Lord Jelky...!"

"Oh, there you are, Jelky. Are you sure you should be spending your valuable time on me? Time's of the essence, isn't it?"

<I determined that it was necessary to do so. Shalk the Sound-Slicer and Tu the Magic can no longer stop him. Committing Mele the Horizon Roar to the fight is my highest priority.>

"If Mele's fingers slip just a little bit, he'll destroy Aureatia, you know. If he shoots from here, the commercial and residential quarters will be included in his line of fire."

<Sacrifices are tolerable.>

"……!"

<My messenger has already explained everything, right? If Alus the Star Runner's invasion penetrates further, it's highly likely that he'll destroy Aureatia's municipal functionality one way or another. I've judged that the destruction by Mele's arrows can be tolerated when compared to the estimated damages without his diversionary sniper fire.>

"I'm sure the numbers may tell you that, but I wonder what the citizens would say, hmm? If Mele's attacks cause damage and harm, no matter how necessary they may have been, they'll all criticize him for it. It's just as much our duty as sponsors to shield candidates from such political attacks as well. You understand that, don't you?"

<If his arrows cause any damage, we'll publicize that they were all caused by attacks on our end. Ahead of Mele's arrow fire, we intend to try shooting Alus down with the Cold Star. The eyes of the citizens aren't going to be able to differentiate between the nature of the two attacks. We'll shoulder the responsibility.>

"Still going to be impossible, I'd say."

There was yet another problem, even if Mele was able to avoid responsibility.

If Mele was mobilized here, it would demonstrate to Aureatia's side that Mele wasn't incapacitated.

<We have one additional piece of information from Tuturi on the scene. Shalk the Sound Slicer is claiming that Mele is still capable of fighting. Given that he has reached this conclusion after fighting against him directly, there's room for consideration.>

"Well, his *sponsor's* the one who's been the closest to him and looking after him. When you phrase it like that, it sounds like you're doubting my judgment."

<But we are ordinary people. Their fighting capabilities exist outside our abilities of imagination. Isn't that right, Cayon?>

"......"

Cayon heaved a deep sigh and covered his face with his sole remaining hand.

Unlike most of the other Twenty-Nine Officials, Cayon the Thundering had never once genuinely considered Aureatia as his homeland. The loss of his arm in battle hadn't stemmed from his utmost loyalty to the kingdom, either. He'd merely tried to protect his life, even if it meant losing an arm, for the day when he would return to Sine Riverstead.

Despite being so highly capable that his other colleagues within the Twenty-Nine Officials feared him, he didn't belong to any of the major factions. This was because he never held any interest in Aureatia's future.

However—even then, it didn't mean he wished to see it in ruin.

"Hey, Cayon, enough of the wishy-washy brooding already." A massive voice came down from above his head.

He didn't need a second thought to know who it was.

"Mele…! What're you doing up? You were supposed to be asleep!"

"You guys are too damn noisy. I was peacefully napping before you all started yapping."

"Don't you realize the situation you're in?! You absolutely can't be shooting any arrows right now!"

Cayon had explained the whole situation to Mele.

That it was best to pretend he was incapacitated until the end of the Sixways Exhibition. That it was the best way to keep Mele safe.

"Who says I can't? Hey, radzio fella."

<…Jelky. Jelky the Swift Ink.>

Mele begin to create earthen arrows through Craft Arts without waiting for the answer.

"Give Aureatia's wheat and some agricultural engineers over to Sine Riverstead. The wheat here's the one thing that's got the Riverstead beat," said Cayon.

<I promise.>

"Mele…! What do you expect to do with your body like that?!"

"I'll look like a damn chump if I stay lying down after Shalk the Sound Slicer mouthed off like that. Besides, Aureatia here's your homeland, too, Cayon."

Mele nocked an arrow on his black bow.

There wasn't anyone who could stop Mele once he took up that stance, no matter what Cayon said to him.

Mele the Horizon's Roar was a warrior.

"Alus the Star Runner, this ain't gonna be like back then."

With his one eye, he gazed up at the far-off stars.

"I'm gonna shoot right through those eyes of yours."

Aureatia's Central Assembly Hall.

The bureaucrats had gathered in the second communications room, now converted into the provisional operation headquarters, collected information transmitted from the different areas of Aureatia, and were devising strategies to curb damages as much as possible.

Among them were three of Aureatia's Twenty-Nine Officials. One was the person in charge of the operation, Twentieth Minister Hidow the Clamp. Supporting him were also Eighth Minister Sheanek the Word Intermediary and Twenty-Eighth Minister Antel the Alignment.

With his hands placed on a map, filled in with several arrows marking the expected invasion route, Hidow shouted, "Mele made it in time!"

A stir spread throughout the room.

Amid a perspective that outlined unavoidable, hopelessly large losses, it was one of the few select pieces of good news.

"I can't believe it. From Gigant Town to the second borough of the Eastern Outer Ward! From that far away...and not only that, but he managed to hit just Alus, without grazing the city at all. Horizon's Roar's sniping abilities are in perfect form! With this, we'll be able to stop Alus the Star Runner!"

"He got a direct hit on Alus?!"

A tan-skinned man wearing dark glasses stood up. Antel the Alignment was known for his composed levelheadedness, but he appeared to be uncharacteristically excited.

"We're getting detailed reports on the situation from the ground observation team. Alus the Star Runner defended against the Cold Star by *making a captured minia hold* the Greatshield of the Dead for him. The magic lightning bullet was shot back in the direction of the Third Stronghold. Mele fired two shots. One to block the trajectory of the magic bullet and protect the small tower. Then another that directly hit Alus."

"I don't believe it...! Is such a feat even possible?! True, if another person was activating the Greatshield of the Dead, Alus would have been vulnerable to an attack from another direction, but still...aiming for that brief moment and firing two shots simultaneously..."

"Given they aren't reporting our victory, it's safe to assume the shot wasn't enough to kill Alus the Star Runner, then?"

Jumping into the conversation was a gaunt, small-statured man: Sheanek the Word Intermediary. While the man's physique resembled that of a malnourished child, in the academic world he was celebrated for his supreme intellect.

"...That's right. Alus was knocked down into the city, but he still isn't dead."

"Do we know that for sure? It'd be impossible to keep his original body intact after getting hit by one of Horizon's Roar's arrows."

Sheanek answered Antel's suspicions. "One possible explanation could be... Hm, what if the Greatshield of the Dead was bound to Kio's Hand from the beginning, even when he made that corpse hold it, to ensure he could *pull it back in* to prepare against a surprise attack from another direction? He switched over to using it normally, by activating the Greatshield of the Dead himself. Thus, he fell, unable to maintain his flight..."

Possessing a large collection of magic items, wielding them effectively, and moreover, applying them as needed.

Alus the Star Runner may have been just a single wyvern, but he was capable of killing legends.

"......"

Hidow looked down on the arrows scribbled helter-skelter over the map.

Using Cold Star inside Aureatia's borders wasn't the extent of it. They had considered defensive strategies to stop Alus's invasion, even if it meant using scorched-earth strategies including methods of destruction that involved the city itself, or utilizing magic items that sent harmful pathogens into the atmosphere. The evacuation and interception planning had needed to be revised several times already.

"Then, Hidow, is it safe to assume that Star Runner's been stopped by Horizon's Roar?"

"Yeah."

Guiding Alus the Star Runner's invasion path through Aureatia and committing the hero candidates to intercept him.

Their strategy had produced the exact results they had been aiming for. At the same time, they now understood for themselves that Alus the Star Runner was a terrifying abomination that far outstripped their expectations.

"...The credit goes to Shalk the Sound Slicer and Tu the Magic, then. Without them, this would've been the end," Antel mused.

This was a battle of speed. Alus's speed exceeded the expectations of Hidow and the others, but it was thanks to the Shalk's otherworldly mobility, and Tu's swift will, that they were able to bring things to this stage.

Hidow drew a large circle around the second borough of the Eastern Outer Ward. He firmly declared, "This is checkmate for Star Runner."

From here, it was possible to throw a convergence of hero candidates at Alus, not just Shalk and Tu.

His escape route in the sky was already firmly under Mele the Horizon's Roar's control.

In which case, Aureatia needed to shoulder all the other work outside of the fight itself. There were countless other things he needed to get to. Firefighting. Housing the evacuated citizens. Curbing unrest. Controlling the flow of information. Treating the wounded.

"From here, our plan will put all our energy toward evacuating the citizens from the combat zone and preventing any increase in casualties. Focus our support on Sabfom's unit on the ground in particular! Sorry but everyone's going to have to give one more push!"

Alus the Star Runner was a threat that needed to be erased from this world.

An unfettered plunderer that ignored any and all authority to steal whatever his avarice desired.

For the sake of this world's tranquility, someone would have eventually needed to subjugate Alus. That someone would be the one who had brought Alus this far—Hidow.

He would take responsibility, right to the end.

"...Time to snuff you out for good."

◆

Hearing the alert following the end of the eighth match, and leaving the audience seats, now Ozonezma the Capricious was lingering on top of the outer wall of the castle garden theater.

He wasn't on watch for the incoming threat the alert had spoken of.

With Zigita Zogi the Thousandth dead, there was a strong chance that someone was nearby aiming to take Hiroto the Paradox's life.

His collaborative relationship with Hiroto had already concluded; however, the vampire threat that Hiroto's group hinted at was an enemy that a medic like Ozonezma needed to prioritize dealing with above all else.

IF THERE IS AN ASSASSIN, THIS SHOULD BE THE ABSOLUTE PERFECT OPPORTUNITY.

The wind was strong. The clock must have been fast approaching noon.

Ozonezma could clear the outer wall of the garden theater with a single jump, but it was also tall enough to look down over almost all the buildings in Aureatia.

THEY ARE MASKING THEIR PRESENCE WELL. VERY SKILLED.

Several of the innumerable arms hidden inside his body gripped scalpels.

Ozonezma's perceptive abilities came from heuristics he had established by observing a large number of the minian races in detail and classifying their typical behaviors. During the upheaval in Gimeena City caused by the Old Kingdoms' loyalists, he had been able to discern who among the throng had military experience and shoot them down from afar.

Individuals behaving unusually. Individuals purposely concealing themselves in the shade. If he sensed any such presence, he could pick up on them through comparison with the great masses but...right now with the echoing alert, the reaction of the people at large wasn't different from usual. Some weren't following Aureatia's guidance and were trying to escape on their own. Some held their loved ones close while others were thrown into confusion and trying to keep themselves hidden.

In the midst of such chaos, his enemy didn't need to maintain their presence of mind but instead could *feign natural confusion*. At the very least, it signaled that Hiroto's enemy was a group capable of such techniques of espionage.

HOWEVER, THEY ARE DEFINITELY HERE. IT'S INCONCEIVABLE *THAT ZIGITA ZOGI THE THOUSANDTH COULD*

BE CLUBBED TO DEATH WITHOUT ANY PLAN IN MIND. SOMEONE PRESENT, OR PERHAPS ZIGITA ZOGI HIMSELF, CARRIED OUT A DECEPTIVE PLOY.

Carriages began to carry the citizens away. They were uniformly headed toward the western side of Aureatia. If this alert had come from an outside enemy attack, this would signal the attack was coming from the east.

Even among the citizens boarding the carriages, he couldn't spot anyone he felt had something conspicuously off about them.

THE ENEMY IS A VAMPIRE. IF I WAS IN THEIR POSITION, FIRST I WOULD TARGET IT...

"Hiroto the Paradox!"

Ozonezma heard someone shout out the name. Not from beyond the castle garden walls, but from the spectator seats inside.

"I'll kill you, you Okafu warmongering dog...!"

A violent group of criminals was charging at the isolated Hiroto. Their weapons were blades of some kind. Ozonezma could sense their presence and knew where they were positioned. He didn't plan to make a move.

...A FEINT.

This was because the voice had come almost exactly as a medical squad carriage carrying corpses had departed from the garden theater.

A shadowy something was passing under the feet of the masses and swooping in toward it.

I KNEW IT. THEIR GOAL IS TO DESTROY THE EVIDENCE OF CORPSES AUREATIA'S CAPTURED.

As the thoughts passed his mind, one of Ozonezma's arms became a blur.

A scalpel flew like a beam of silver light and skewered an object flying through the air into the ground.

He knew that it was a projectile weapon, like a spinning metal disk.

There was something enclosed in cloth, wrapped messily around the edge of the disk.

"......!"

Ozonezma instantly determined what it was, and he jumped down from atop the wall.

Because of his speed, he fell the almost forty meters immediately, then he knocked away six people in the crowd where he was going to land, pushed a carriage over, and alighted right on top of the chakram stapled into the ground. All of it happened in the span of a single second.

Then came a muffled *thud*.

An explosion occurred on the ground directly below Ozonezma.

The shock wave covered the enormous chimera and rippled throughout Ozonezma's body, but only a small amount of blood dripped from his armor-like bluish-silver fur.

There were some with light injuries among the group he had swept away when he landed, but they were merely scrapes from falling on the ground after he'd knocked them away. They were outside the area of the shock wave. Ozonezma had held back his strength to make sure of it.

"...Are you okay?" He called out to the medical squad carriage that was knocked on its side nearby.

There was someone who had escaped just a second before the explosion, carrying two of the corpsified patients with her.

"M-more or less. I-I'm all right..."

A woman had a frightened look on her face and one eye hidden. Aureatia's Tenth General, Qwell the Wax Flower.

"What about yourself, Mr. Ozonezma...? Um, that explosion... was that a bomb...?"

"IT WOULD SEEM SO. THEY PROBABLY AIMED FOR THE MOMENT YOUR MEDICAL SQUAD LEFT THE GARDEN THEATER AND HAD SOMEONE THROW AN EXPLOSIVE AT YOU. THAT AND—"

Ozonezma slunk down and peered at the feet of the crowd clamoring in front of the garden theater.

From in between the gaps in the constantly moving feet of the multitudes, he spied the wheels and horses' feet of several carriages.

"THEY DIDN'T SHOOT FROM ABOVE. *IT CAME FROM BELOW.* THERE WAS SOMEONE ABLE TO HIDE AND ATTACK FROM LONG RANGE IN THE SMALL SPACE RIGHT UNDERNEATH A CARRIAGE. THAT WAS WHY I DIDN'T PICK UP ON THE SNIPER'S PRESENCE FROM MY BIRD'S-EYE POSITION."

This assailant had discovered a line of fire to their target through this huge throng of people mingling together and had thrown their chakram with precision. Not only that, but while hiding underneath a carriage.

Bizarre technical skill. A regular sniper wouldn't practice such techniques, nor have any opportunities to use them, either.

"W-was it an assassin...from the invisible army?"

Qwell the Wax Flower's voice was clearly terrified, but the existence of this unknown warrior seemed to invigorate her as she stood gripping her large war ax in both arms.

"We have to defeat them..."

"CHASING AFTER THEM IS POINTLESS."

By the time the sniper had launched their attack, they had probably already withdrawn from the area.

Judging by their degree of skill, this foe wasn't one to linger behind at the scene.

"MORE IMPORTANTLY, THERE IS SOMEONE I WOULD LIKE YOU TO EXAMINE. JUST A MOMENT AGO INSIDE THE CASTLE GARDEN THEATER..."

"Would this be about the criminal that attacked Hiroto the Paradox, perhaps?"

A woman's voice come to them from the vehicle entrance to the garden theater. A black-painted carriage had just arrived.

"...FLINSUDA THE PORTENT."

"*Oh, ho-ho-ho!* I am *so* happy you remembered my name! Now, why were you here at the garden theater, Ozonezma? You didn't come here to chat with Tu, now did you?"

"......"

Through the carriage window, he immediately recognized the corpulent body, swollen to twice the size of the average minia, and the glittering of jewelry on her neck and fingers—Seventh Minister, Flinsuda the Portent.

He owed a small debt to her. When Ozonezma met with Tu the Magic, he had required the approval of her sponsor, Flinsuda.

"YOU REMAINED BEHIND AT THE GARDEN THEATER, THEN... IF I REMEMBER CORRECTLY, YOU CAME HERE ON HIROTO'S SUGGESTION AS WELL."

"That's right. You see, I had a bit of business to discuss with him. You wish to know about the people that attacked Hiroto in the garden theater, yes? It was only a simple examination, but none of the four were corpses. I'd assume they were residents with anti-Okafu sentiments that someone had riled up, wouldn't you?"

"I THOUGHT THAT MIGHT BE THE CASE."

Given that the invisible army had hidden agents in several groups, they were able to indirectly incite the uninfected to act as a feint. Ozonezma had understood this from the very start.

If that was the extent of the mob, Hiroto's goblin bodyguards must have handled it without issue.

"THERE IS ANOTHER REASON WHY I HAVE REMAINED HERE. I WANTED TO HEAR FROM YOU DIRECTLY ABOUT THE CURRENT SITUATION. WHAT IS GOING ON?"

In these situations, it was determined that hero candidates needed to respond to the emergency by making contact with their sponsor and getting the details from them. However, Yuca the Halation Gaol was a bit too far away to go ask about the circumstances. Ozonezma had determined it was faster for him to ask for the details of the situation from Flinsuda the Portent, Tu the Magic's sponsor.

"A-Alus the Star Runner is...attacking."

Qwell the Wax Flower answered his question.

"THE SAME ALUS THE STAR RUNNER WHO WAS CRUSHED BY LUCNOCA THE WINTER?"

"...That's right. But he survived in the bowels of the Mali Wastes. General Haade's regiment intercepted with antiair attacks, but...h-he overcame them. His expected invasion route goes through the fifth borough of the Eastern Outer Ward—stopping him and bringing him down is the job for all the hero candidates..."

"FLINSUDA, DO YOU HAVE ENOUGH MEDICS AT THE READY?"

"*Ho-ho-ho-ho-ho!* Well, thanks to this alert, I've rescinded all the time off for the Health Ministry's staff. All of the squad deployed to the garden theater, myself included, are planning on heading over to the east side. Qwellie's troops are working on firefighting and rescue efforts. That said, though, I can't really be sure if we need help or not without seeing how things are going on-site for myself."

"I WILL ACCOMPANY YOU AS A MEDIC AS WELL. THERE IS ALSO A CHANCE THERE WILL BE MORE ATTACKS LIKE THIS ONE. PROTECTING MEDICAL WORKERS LIKE YOUR-SELVES WILL CONTRIBUTE MORE TO SAVING LIVES."

"That's quite an unprofitable thing to say, isn't it? Even if you work as a medic for us, I can't compensate you for it, you know?"

"...PEOPLE'S LIVES CANNOT BE REPLACED WITH MONEY, FLINSUDA."

"Quite right. I would do just the same myself," Flinsuda readily agreed.

There was no faltering in her tone, nor did she wear a solemn look on her face, speaking as if she was saying something completely obvious.

There wasn't any hesitation in the flow of movements by the medics under her command. The medical squad carriages departed one after another toward the east.

"I HAD HEARD THAT YOU WERE SOMEONE COMPLETELY DEVOTED TO MONEY AND NOTHING MORE."

"You need money to save many lives, don't you? The longer our patients live, the wealthier they make us. There's no contradiction at all, is there?"

"...YOU MAY BE RIGHT."

Vast amounts of money could easily save many lives, but the opposite was true as well.

That was one of the things Ozonezma had learned on his travels with Hiroto.

"I'm sure you know this already, but it will be difficult to rely on Word Arts treatments on-site. Cutting open people's bodies, sewing them back together...how confident are you with that type of technical medicine?"

"...HMPH. WHO DO YOU THINK YOU ARE TALKING TO?"

There was a mountain of work to prioritize above taking down Alus the Star Runner.

Was there anyone able to move rubble that had collapsed in the flames, without paying any mind to their heft or the heat?

Was there anyone who could detect the presence of survivors even while under extreme conditions?

Above all, though, was there anyone capable of treating patients without depending on Life Arts, which demand a long period of contact between patient and doctor?

Cutting open bodies, observing, surgical excision, stitching them back together—there wasn't anyone in the land who had repeated such extraordinary feats more than Ozonezma the Capricious.

"FOR ME, THAT IS POSSIBLE."

◆

If the flow of people was a great massive river, she was but a single small drop.

The woman seemed to be an older sister, carrying her frail and delicate little sister on her back as they fled.

The woman had a bandage over one eye. If there was anyone with a sharp, observant eye, they may have noticed that she was making extra sure the other eye was not directly exposed to light.

The young girl on her back held her breath with her hood covering her face completely, while trying to ensure no one caught a glimpse of the beautiful features underneath.

"Wieze will get the job the done. Do not worry, my lady."

The woman's name was Lena the Obscured.

A corpse in Obsidian Eyes, as well as a mimic, possessing the supernatural ability to skillfully replicate the appearance of another.

"I understand... *Koff, koff!*"

The girl on her back was Linaris.

She had always possessed a weak constitution, but her condition was now growing even worse. Despite successfully murdering Zigita Zogi the Thousandth in the eighth match, she received news of Hartl the Light Pinch's death and had moments ago given the order for the entirety of Obsidian Eyes to withdraw.

Therefore, before Aureatia had issued their evacuation alert— and before Ozonezma appeared on top of the wall of the castle garden—Lena brought Linaris with her and fled. The alert that rang immediately afterward, as well as the flood of people pouring into the street, skillfully concealed the two of them.

With Wieze the Variation on it...he should be able to use the crowd to target just the magical squad carriage and take it out.

Wieze was a sniper capable of crawling like an insect through openings that were impossible to slip through with normal body movements and throw his chakrams from afar. The fact that he had volunteered to serve as their rear guard in front of the castle garden meant that he intended to aim for the corpse-laden carriage to dispose of it.

The problem is...whether there's any Okafu ambush waiting for us where we're escaping to.

At the very least, the two didn't need to fear an immediate attack. Even assuming the castle garden theater was surrounded by troops from the Free City of Okafu, given the present situation, with civilians running about in droves trying to escape after the warning, they wouldn't be able to go through with their operation as anticipated. They needed to focus everything they had on making absolutely sure no one spotted them.

Using the throng of people to confuse Okafu's eyes, they were returning back to their base of operations.

All that's left is if my eye will hold out or not...

Lena pressed down on her eye that wasn't covered by her bandage.

Mimics were an extremely difficult construct to create, and one reason was their nature itself, making it possible to freely design their cells' characteristics. At the developmental stage, they needed to have their life-maintaining functionality designed from the ground up.

Even if by a stroke of good luck they were able to acquire the ability to survive, normally it would generate a defect somewhere in the body. In Lena's case, this lay in her optic nerve.

If her eyeball was continuously exposed to light, it would cause an acute seizure. She would convulse and lose consciousness.

Even with a thick bandage to block out light covering her eyes, Lena herself was able to operate without a problem. However, the fact that movements made while her eyes were covered *seemed suspicious* was a problem no amount of training could solve.

Currently, by suppressing half the amount of light she took in with her eye bandage and taking great care not to directly look at any and all sources of light, Lena was extending the amount of time she could act for as long as possible. Nevertheless, the more that time went by, the further her combat abilities would decline, and it would grow difficult to fulfill her role as Linaris's bodyguard.

"I'm sorry, my lady."

"...*Koff*, what...is the matter?"

"If I had managed to keep a closer watch of Zigita Zogi, I wouldn't have put so much strain on you... I should've used this eye to watch for the exact instant his head was crushed."

"...Frey was there as well, and she wasn't able to discern if it was truly him or not, either. It doesn't mean—*koff*—you're at fault, Miss Lena."

Linaris's velvety black hair was touching Lena's shoulder.

A feeble and thin body, the polar opposite of Lena's and the others, who had trained and tempered their physiques as assassins.

She wanted to steal her and run far away somewhere—the thought flashed across her mind.

If Obsidian Eyes was destined for ruin regardless of whether they fought against Aureatia or not, then wouldn't it be fine to secretly disappear, just the two of them, and live while Lena lovingly admired her lady and her doll-like beauty?

Of course, Lena would never do something like that, nor could she.

All of a corpse's actions, down to their biological activity, were under the control of their parent unit. Their relationship went beyond mere loyalty into one of absolute dominance.

Yet Linaris was so enchanting, so ephemeral, that it made Lena ignore these laws of nature and send such wicked thoughts through her heart.

"If we exit out into the canal up ahead, the eyes of the crowd won't reach us anymore. We can use a small ship to meet up with Frey and..."

Lena's feet stopped.

An extremely short vagabond was sitting down on the berm. Not a leprechaun. A goblin.

...One of Zigita Zogi's soldiers? They've blocked off our retreat path after all.

If this was their only enemy, it would be easy to dispose of them.

However, there was sure to be someone from Okafu's camp keeping watch over the area. Lena had transformed her body into that of a minian woman, but there was a chance they would get a glimpse of Linaris's face or physique.

Making a detour wasn't an option right now, either. If she made any unnatural movement, that would make it all the easier to remain in people's memories. An older sister carrying her wounded younger sister on her back. She needed to act the part; however, Linaris's face was the one thing she didn't wish to show to Okafu.

Now what are we going to do?

It was then that she noticed the sounds of footsteps behind her.

These didn't belong to any Okafu soldiers.

"...Are you two evacuees as well?"

It was an Aureatia soldier guiding the evacuation.

"You can hear the alert, right? The carriages headed to the plaza are gathering out on the main road. You should evacuate immediately before you get wrapped up in a battle against a self-proclaimed demon king."

"Th-thank you."

Lena immediately changed her voice and answered with the voice of a scared townswoman.

"Everything happened so fast, I was so confused about where we were supposed to go. Thank you so much for guiding us!"

She bowed slightly, making sure not to put any more stress on Linaris.

Naturally, she couldn't follow this soldier's guidance. As long as Aureatia, through Zigita Zogi, had learned about the invisible army, they were sure to examine everyone gathered in the evacuation area for corpse infection.

They couldn't let themselves be seen by the vagabond goblin. They had to be wary of a surveillant watching from somewhere. Now this Aureatia soldier, too. The only route of escape lay up ahead—

I'll bring down the surveillant first. That's the only option.

Lena gripped a stone in each fist. She needed to look upward to fight the enemy observing from on high. It meant exposing her eye to the light of the sun.

She'd have only a single second. Would she be able to successfully pick out their enemy?

"...Pardon me, Mr. Soldier. There is something I would like to ask you, if you wouldn't mind," Linaris's clear voice asked from behind her.

"What's that? You can ask me anything you like, pretty little missy."

"Is there anyone watching us from the buildings behind us?"

"..."

The Aureatia soldier looked behind them as if the words were controlling him. Lena could tell that his senses, honed as a soldier, picked out a single window. She only had to follow his gaze with one of her eyes. She got a visual on the person watching them. It happened in a single second.

She flicked the stones. One at a time from her left hand, then her right.

One pierced through the surveillant's eye socket, while the other shot through the vagabond's throat.

"What the—?"

Faster than the soldier could feel suspicious of his own actions, controlled by Linaris, Lena's finger had snapped his neck.

Everything from the right shoulder down on this perfectly ordinary town girl had morphed into a massive, ogre-like arm.

"My lady, let us head for the boat."

Lena tossed the corpse of the soldier away with the strength of her monstrous arm.

The corpse crashed into the tiny body of the now dead vagabond, and they both were knocked down into the canal.

Not even a drop of blood remained on the roadway.

"I can't afford to look at more light than I have, but...the meet-up location with Frey is just up ahead."

She needed to wrap the bandage protecting her eye around the other.

However, there was one thing she needed to make sure she burned into her retinas.

"Thank you very much, Miss Lena."

Linaris smiled.

"Of course."

Looking at her beauty, the thought came to Lena once more.

As long as my lady is here…it's impossible to keep myself composed and proper.

◆

Eastern Outer Ward, tenth borough. At this point, all the residents from the third to the sixth boroughs were finished evacuating, but when taking the speed of Alus the Star Runner's attack into account, this zone could quickly fall inside the area of his attack and had thus become an extremely dangerous area.

Fully understanding said danger, Rosclay the Absolute called out to the city residents.

"I am Aureatia's Second General, Rosclay the Absolute! If there are any residents who can hear this warning, please follow directions and immediately evacuate! A self-proclaimed demon king is approaching the district! Right now I ask you to protect not your wealth or home, but the most irreplaceable thing of all, your lives! I repeat! I am Aureatia's Second General, Rosclay the Absolute!"

Up until moments prior, he had been shouting from atop a firefighting tower, but now he was walking around the corners of the labyrinthine slums, rescuing people who weren't able to move freely or who had yet to escape.

Rosclay wasn't doing this alone, and many soldiers had split into groups to carry out this task, but at the very least, he would still need to make another two rounds through the streets like this.

...*If Alus the Star Runner came here right now, I'd easily die.*

As he verbally called out to save lives, Rosclay's thoughts were morbid.

There was an incomparable gap in fighting strength—however, this wasn't the only issue. As long as the eyes of the citizenry were upon him, Rosclay the Absolute *couldn't let himself shirk away from facing a threat.*

The fear of losing Aureatia and its people. The tension of death, which could occur at any moment. The intense pain in both legs, broken during the fourth match. The sweat that faintly wetted his skin had fully dried out and was changing over to a chill incongruent with the midday sun.

It seemed he hadn't walked around the city without proper protection like this or stood atop a firefighting tower and called out to the citizens, for a long time. For the past several small months Rosclay hadn't done anything like it. This was because of the fear of an enemy force shooting him from afar.

He was always in fear.

"A self-proclaimed demon king is approaching! Should you know the threat of the Demon King's Army of the past, I believe you will make the correct decision to protect your lives!"

Rosclay's feet suddenly came to a halt in front of a plain home with its door ajar.

He spoke to the soldier accompanying him.

"Please search through that house. There may be a bedridden citizen inside."

"Is there something different about this house in particular?"

"I can see a wheelchair in the doorway. Someone who uses a wheelchair must have been left behind while they lay unable to move on their own."

"Understood. I'll carry the survivor in need of help myself."

The soldiers went into the house, leaving Rosclay behind on his own.

He pondered as he gazed at the wheelchair half hidden by the door.

...There's one other thing that's clear. If the door was half open when I spotted it, that means that the resident that had already evacuated from this house—someone who was caring for the infirm inside—must've been here.

The invalid had been *abandoned.*

He felt that someone was supposed to offer them help. This thought didn't stem from any genuine goodness in his heart.

I'm scared. If there truly is this despair of dying while unable to ask anyone for help, that's all the more terrifying. If I can continue saving people...some sort of karmic force may guarantee that I avoid meeting such an end. If there really is something like that, then—

"Hey there, Rosclay the Absolute."

A chill went down Rosclay's spine. He immediately looked up above the roof. Even he didn't understand why he did such a thing, but there wasn't anything there for him to see.

Instead, there was an ominous man dressed in black ascending the narrow slope.

"...Kuze the Passing Disaster."

"*Bweh-heh-heh...* Hills start getting real rough on you once you're my age. Hidow the Clamp's given me the general picture. So Alus the Star Runner's coming, is he?"

Kuze the Passing Disaster's ability is automatic counterattacks that bring instant death. Since it activates even if the man himself isn't aware of any danger, any unperceived surprise attacks against him are ineffective.

Right now, Rosclay was on the front lines, fully cognizant of the danger. In the current situation, with the strong chance of getting caught up in Alus the Star Runner's attacks, he hadn't constructed a perfect support structure to provide him backup, either.

It would have been a golden opportunity for an assassination.

His mind raced at high speed to think of what possible methods he had at his disposal, but there was most likely nothing he could do against Kuze the Passing Calamity, appearing at this distance. The only way to avoid his instantaneous lethal counterattack was not to *make an attack against him*, but that also meant that he wasn't able to put up any resistance whatsoever to any attack Kuze made against *him*.

Rosclay made a flawless smile.

"I'm glad I ran into a hero candidate here. Alus the Star Runner is moving from the fifth borough of the Eastern Outer Ward... He's attacking the second borough now. Please head that way and leave the search and rescue up to us."

"Bweh-heh-heh. You're not heading there yourself? You're just as much a hero candidate, too."

"............"

Both men closed the distance between them.

As essentially the symbol of Aureatia, the Order's oppressors, Kuze must have deeply despised Rosclay.

During the fifth match, Nophtok the Crepuscule Bell had even schemed to attack an Order almshouse and force Kuze to withdraw from the tournament. In the end, the operation had been carried out solely at Nophtok's discretion. But assuming Rosclay had been fully healthy at the time, he was sure he would have directed a similar operation himself.

"I would love to, but my wounds from the fourth match haven't fully healed yet. It's quite embarrassing, but…I wanted to keep the casualties to a minimum as much as I could by leading the citizens' evacuation."

He answered with a composed smile. It was a lie.

Even if his whole body had been in perfect condition, he didn't wish to fight against someone like Alus the Star Runner at all.

He didn't want to die.

"I'm not gonna forget about what happened with Nophtok. You think you can still tell me to go off and fight, huh?"

He felt the illusion of the blade of death being directly held up against his throat.

Amid the terror he felt facing off against a shura, concealing their hatred, with nothing but his mortal body, Rosclay remained normal, down to his heartbeat and breathing, without a single shivering fingertip or his face growing taut. He had trained himself to do so.

"...You yourself—"

He looked straight ahead at Kuze. Straightforward and honest, like a champion unashamed of anything.

"—will always be the only one who can decide that. It's about whether you wish to save someone of your own will, regardless of who ordered you to or not. The choice may have you sacrifice your life, or your faith. I've prepared myself to do that."

"......"

He wasn't lying. However, did he truly and honestly believe it?

If Rosclay truly wasn't reluctant to die, then he might have tried to fight Alus the Star Runner.

If he truly wanted to save someone, then he might have been able to go and save them.

"*Bweh-heh-heh.* Well, what a splendid guy you are, eh?"

As he passed by Rosclay's side, Kuze laughed feebly.

Was he going to climb up this hill and head off to fight against the terrifying wyvern? In the case of this man who continued to fight on alone for the sake of the Order, Rosclay was convinced he would do so.

"Kuze the Passing Disaster!" Rosclay shouted, turning to the black-clad figure's back. "In the second borough...of the Eastern Outer Ward!"

He genuinely and truthfully wished to save her.

If Rosclay the Absolute hadn't been Aureatia's champion, if he was allowed to abandon all the other citizens, he wanted to do so, even if he didn't have any power to fight.

Iska was in the second borough of the Eastern Outer Ward.

The young girl alone was the person who served as Rosclay's emotional pillar.

"What's in the second borough of the Eastern Outer Ward, then?"

"...Nothing. I just ask that you save the people there to ensure no one else falls victim to Alus. Please...I beg you."

Rosclay bowed his head deeply at Kuze's back.

It wasn't an appeal or deference to Kuze the individual, but as if he was praying to something.

"See, I can't really save anyone. So if...if someone's life ends up getting saved from here on out—"

The black shadow walked on, without ever looking back.

He waved a single hand back at Rosclay behind him.

"—just think of it as the Wordmaker saving them instead."

Soon after Kuze had departed, the soldiers tasked with searching the house returned.

"General Rosclay! You were right; there was one person left behind in the second-floor bedroom! Thank you, sir!"

"G-General Rosclay. General Rosclay came to save little old me..."

Rosclay cast a smile at the gaunt senior citizen, being carried by one of the soldiers.

The senior was in tears.

They believed that they had been saved from the danger, that a champion had been there to protect them.

"You did a wonderful job holding out, despite your terrible

illness. Please rest easy. I am Rosclay the Absolute. I won't leave anyone behind."

Such a feat was impossible for anyone but the Wordmaker.

Rosclay forged a smile, to obscure his fear of losing Iska.

"I will save everyone."

◆

The buildings in the second borough of the Eastern Outer Ward were complexly woven between the gaps in crisscrossing canals running through it.

The town's construction hadn't been based on any civic planning. The canals in this district were filled with wastewater and sewage, and the area wasn't expected to be used for residential buildings to begin with.

Therefore, the damage from the fires in this district was tremendous.

The narrow, labyrinthine streets ended up preventing citizens from making a smooth escape.

The wooden footings used as bridge crossings were easily burned apart, dividing the foot traffic.

Among all of the Eastern Outer Ward, the second borough was a district that was especially delayed in evacuating its residents.

Alus the Star Runner had descended on the area.

A wind blew. A terrifying hot blast, blowing in after the buildings were torched one after another, and the flames kicked up and churned in the atmosphere.

The original scenery there had now become black shadows floating among the red-white light, visibly losing their shapes by the second.

Ground Runner—the citizens didn't even know the name of the magic item, but the mass of intense heat, vaporizing the canals as it rushed along, indiscriminately blasted away people, and everything else, regardless of the wind direction or the size of the original flame.

More than anything, though, the sound completely blanketed over everything.

The sounds of wood, iron, or even human flesh, being torn apart. Each individual noise was tiny, but they could all be heard simultaneously from across the city, ringing out loud like a torrential downpour.

"Listen up, men!"

There was a man shouting among the flames, nearly drowned out by the thundering around him.

The mask covering his face, a solid sheet of iron, didn't even have a curve for his nose.

Aureatia's Twelfth General, Sabfom the White Weave.

"All the citizens are watching you conduct yourselves! Will you turn your back here on Aureatia's peril?! Or will you gather up your courage and face it head on?! The day's finally come for you lot to prove who you are, once and for all!"

The courageous general, who had once crossed swords with the self-proclaimed demon king Morio, had volunteered himself to be in charge of evacuating the most dangerous area, the second borough of the Eastern Outer Ward, despite having only just returned to the front lines.

Sabfom didn't wield a sword. Instead, he brandished an iron hammer in each of his hands, and he continued with the rescue operation by forcefully smashing up the blazing houses to create a path forward.

Right now, he didn't have a single one of his men with him. In the midst of this great conflagration, which necessitated that they save as many lives as they possibly could, there wasn't a single soldier in Sabfom's squad who found himself unable to move from the general's side.

The subordinates might have all burned to death somewhere out of Sabfom's sight. Nevertheless, Sabfom continued to yell on his own. "Ah! You think we have no chance to win?! Any cowards who doubt my words?! Still, you all came here anyway! And what for?! To keep the citizens of Aureatia alive! *That's* victory! You hear me?! I came here today planning to claim dozens and dozens of victories! I was nice enough to give all of you the very same opportunity!"

Sabfom's shout, almost like a triumphant roar, was so full of spirit and vigor, it seemed all but impossible to be coming from a wounded soldier.

It eloquently communicated his location through the fire and smoke obscuring their vision and served as a guide for his men or any survivors to reach him.

While shouting, he mowed down debris blocking the path with his giant hammers, pulverizing it.

There was a soldier rushing up behind him.

"General Sabfom! We've confirmed three families of survivors in the direction of the Eda River Factory and safely finished evacuating them! Also, in the middle of our search through the corresponding districts, we discovered two dwarf children who had neglected to flee! We have saved them as well!"

"Bang-up job! What's your name, soldier?! Well?! Puol the Thousand Land! Your name and the name of your squad's members have been etched into the memories of the people you saved! Be proud! Next I want you to search the abandoned pond!"

"Yessir...! We lost two of our squad members, but we'll meet up with the other squads and try to re-form our ranks! We'll show... we'll show the prestige of Aureatia!"

"You've sworn on the prestige of Aureatia, have you? Good, then go! Save everyone without leaving a single one behind!"

Perhaps the current status of Sabfom and his men would have been best described as a desperate and mad scramble.

When the reality of fire and death appeared right before their eyes, this was how they became. That was how they had been trained.

This was because the Twentieth General's troops were originally a suicide corps used to annihilate the Demon King's Army.

"Can you hear me, Alus the Star Runner?! I'm overjoyed!"

While letting out a booming voice that seemed to be purposely broadcasting his location, his two hammers destroyed what were once people's dwellings as though made out of paper.

"Even though the True Demon King's dead, there are still those out there giving us hell! These louts who delight in hell have come running here in place of the residents you wish to kill! That's who I am, and these are my troops! Well, humiliating, isn't it?! *Bwa-ha-ha-ha-ha-ha-ha-ha!*"

Sabfom the White Weave continued to desire the brilliance from that fateful day. Like his fight against Morio the Sentinel, where he had lost his own face.

◆

She could hear a man yelling from far off in the distance.

They seemed to be helping the residents of the lower district, but to Iska, their tone sounded like nothing but the roar of some kind of terrifying beast.

I wonder if this will all turn out to just be a dream.

Inside a small shack in a corner of the canal, Iska was lying down in bed, wrapped up in a blanket.

Fortunately, the flames had yet to arrive at her house.

She also knew what she needed to do to escape.

Tracing the canal until she reached the underside of a bridge, she would climb up the ladder leaning against it, cross the extended wooden plank bridging two shacks, and climb up and over three steep flights of stairs. There were an innumerable number of different streets from there, and she wondered when she had last seen the large main boulevard that lay at the end.

Iska lived her life bedridden in this house. Even if she evacuated now, she was likely already too late, nor did she believe her legs would allow her to actually escape in the first place.

I'm sure someone will help me out...but perhaps I shouldn't be thinking like that.

She held her blanket as if embracing it.

The other residents might have wished that Rosclay the Absolute would be the one to come.

However, Iska knew better than anyone else that Rosclay didn't have absolute strength.

Nor did she wish for him to come save her before any of the other residents. Even if Rosclay appeared before her right at that moment, she would likely puff out her cheeks and scold him for it.

He'd probably wear that same lonely face of his again.

She chuckled a bit when she imagined it.

People were able to laugh, even when certain death was closing in, Iska mused, as if it didn't concern her at all.

She heard the sound of something crumbling with a clatter.

The inside of the room had gone hazy white from the smoke, filtering in ahead of the fire.

...I hope Mom is still alive.

Her mother was supposed to be out at work at this time of day. She was a worker in a factory here in the second borough; however, sometimes she would be sent out to work as far away as the seventh. Perhaps today just happened to be one of those days, and she might have safely avoided getting caught up in these flames.

...It was hope. Hope was the only thing that came to Iska's mind.

Usually, the only thing on her mind was the despair about when her life would finally be exhausted, and she found it strange that, despite this, when it now seemed that she really would lose her life, her thoughts started going in the exact opposite direction.

When she turned over in bed, she saw the ring that was placed at her bedside.

A red coral ring. She continued to keep the gift, the one she'd claimed that day she hadn't wanted, close by her.

"…You don't want to die, do you, Rosclay."

With her thin pointer finger, she stroked the ring. Rosclay feared death more than anybody else.

Yet despite that, he was also facing death head on. Surely right at that moment, too.

Iska meant to die while turning her back from the fear of death, and she thought that was fine for an insignificant young girl like herself.

"Ah… Now what am I going to do?"

She thought that if she didn't have the vitality to get herself up, she would give up. However, Iska succeeded.

Putting her bare feet into shabby outdoor shoes, she soaked the blanket that had been wrapped around her in the bucket of water.

When I think about you…it seems so very embarrassing to give up like this.

She loved Rosclay.

Iska understood that she would never be able to marry him, but she wished to still have a heart worthy of being at his side.

Perhaps the soldier that kept calling out from far away was coming closer.

The flames might not have gotten that big, and there might barely be a path still available for Iska's escape.

She collected together the fragments of hope she'd imagined in bed and forged the courage she needed to flee.

I'm sure that even Rosclay's doing just the same himself.

His ability to give hope to the people of Aureatia wasn't the flashy power of some perfect champion. She believed that, in truth, it was this courage in Rosclay's heart being conveyed to those he inspired.

That was why Rosclay the Absolute was definitely not just a false symbol.

Opening up the door, Iska looked at the scene outside.

The wall of flame had closed in, up to the far shore of the river.

The violent hot blast of air blew in, making Iska have a coughing fit.

Her breath caught in her throat.

"*Koff! Koff...*"

She understood.

She knew that she couldn't survive, and that's why she had needed courage.

Iska was glad that she was able to summon the courage to walk on her own feet.

She would soon run out of oxygen. Her consciousness would begin to fade.

And then the flame of her life would be extinguished...

◆

"*Extinguish.*"

◆

"…What?"

The blaze right in front of Iska had vanished.

Its heat, even the smoke, disappeared like it had all been an illusion.

Even the noxious smell of something burning was gone, and the air was now clean and fresh, like that of a morning forest.

"It can't be. How could this…"

She had believed it had all been too late, and this was the end.

Yet despite that, *someone had done something to save her.*

Almost like that hero, who'd brought an end to the True Demon King…

"…Who could even…?"

◆

The position was far removed from the Eastern Outer Ward.

Farther away than the central city, the royal palace, the railroad crossing north to south, farther past the vast expanse of the old town, in the agricultural quarter of the Western Outer Ward.

And then, another 529 meters up into the sky.

"This feels awful."

High in the sky, wind blowing fiercely, *stood* a young girl.

Her blond hair and the sleeves of her green clothes fluttered in the wind, but she didn't seem to have any trouble breathing and paid no mind to the freezing upper-atmosphere air.

The sight of this fourteen-year-old girl, suspended in midair, could only be described as extremely abnormal; nevertheless, she had a reason for standing where she was.

It was because that's what she wished to do.

She had heard that alert that the distant Eastern Outer Ward was being attacked by a self-proclaimed demon king.

She had also eavesdropped on the conversations from the evacuees to learn that, as a result, the city was being torched in a huge conflagration.

If she had been in a position to make contact with her sponsor, she probably would have been able to do this sooner. However, right now she couldn't let herself be seen by anyone.

Especially not by any other hero candidates.

"...Not like I'd care even a little bit if Aureatia here gets destroyed or saved, but..."

Even from this height, she could clearly see the intensity of the flames covering the second borough of the Eastern Outer Ward.

She erased it because she found it unpleasant.

"Don't show me a big fire like that."

Now, this young girl had a second name.

Kia the World Word.

The strongest of all were gathering to bring down a self-proclaimed demon king.

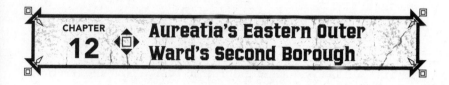

As it had been with Rotting Soil Sun, within a magic item dwelled a presence that formed connections to living creatures and released its power in accordance with its user's thoughts.

It was said this connection differed depending on the user. There were some who perceived it as a figure, or a formula, and others as a voice possessing its own will.

To Alus, it was like a light flickering between his nerves.

This light had vanished.

The city, enveloped in a hopeless blaze, instantly fell silent, without even the heat or smoke being left behind, as its state from moments ago had all been an illusion.

He understood that Ground Runner, somewhere down on the surface, had vanished.

The undying magic item, endlessly increasing the force of its flames from a tiny spark, had come to an all-too-anticlimactic end.

There's another something *here...*

There was someone who had extinguished the magic item of flame, not even possessing a shape of its own, by directly interfering with it.

Alus understood the fact of this reality, and nothing more, in his mind.

Then he moved sharply to evade the streak of fire that burned up the sky.

He didn't have a spare moment to think about the meaning behind the fire-extinguishing phenomenon he had just witnessed.

Even when compared to such an abnormal state of affairs, he faced an even more imminent problem. Right now, Alus was completely trapped by Mele the Horizon's Roar.

Even in Alus's eyes, which had borne witness to several legends, including Lucnoca the Winter, Mele was an unbelievable archer.

From his firing location in Gigant Town to here, the second borough of the Eastern Outer Ward, it must have required him to aim past the limits of the horizon, even with his irregularly colossal body. On top of that, he gave bends and distortions to his earthen-made arrows and continued to fire them in arcs that avoided all the high-rise buildings that stood between the two of them.

Of course, Mele wasn't necessarily able to directly get his eyes on Alus as he ingeniously wove between the shadow of cover. Similarly, with Alus's mobility and judgment, he was able to continuously avoid the rapid-fire arrows of instant death flying his way.

...*But he's not letting me escape.*

He could tell that by manipulating the range of their tremendous destruction to block off his path of retreat, to drive him back, he was trying to put Alus up against a wall. He couldn't get outside of the second borough of the Eastern Outer Ward. He couldn't increase his altitude and evade his shots, either.

A network of antiair fire, curiously similar to the day he'd battled Regnejee in the New Principality of Lithia, had been constructed by a single individual. It was not only Mele's fighting technique, but his strategic eye, that lay in the realm of the deviant and supernatural.

He was strong, Alus thought.

To rogues, the most truly fearsome enemy of all was *an intelligent enemy.*

"If only I had the Cold Star...," he murmured as he continued to evade. He couldn't fire back at Mele's position with his gun, but the Cold Star might have reached that far.

When had he laid eyes on that treasure?

Even these memories were growing vague in Alus's ever-eroding sense of self.

Two simultaneously released arrows closed in on Alus from the left and the right to trap him.

He needed to dodge wide. The atmospheric vortex that the arrows generated as they passed was more than enough to easily tear the tiny body of a wyvern apart.

"...Greatshield of the Dead."

He wouldn't evade them. He was able to make that judgment without any need to think.

Instantly activating the Greatshield of the Dead, he took a grazing blow from the meteoric arrow.

Immediately after, a bright beam of light passed in front of Alus.

Oh, right.

Horizon's Roar wasn't the only one aiming and sniping at Alus.

His indistinct sense of self bubbled up into his mind.

The Cold Star was over there...

The path of the two arrows, seeming to scoop up from below, moved Alus forward, guiding him into a position that made it easier to aim the Cold Star at him. Directly below him, the only available path left...

"Legend killing's real exhausting."

Shalk the Sound Slicer was waiting for him. Now, with the flames that had been blocking his way extinguished, Shalk the Sound Slicer could instantly appear at any location in the city.

Even descending down to lower altitudes wasn't possible.

"You don't like it now that you're the one cornered, Alus the Star Runner?"

That was exactly it.

If I die...then I won't be able to get my hands on anything, right?

He wanted to keep fighting. Because he wanted treasure.

That was why he had started his journey, flying however far he needed to, traversing over everything and everyone.

However, ever since he had awoken in the depths of the Mali Wastes, it seemed like something big was missing.

"It's...somewhere."

"...Not really having a conversation here, are we?"

He heard Shalk's voice.

A hollow landscape. The sky spread out into the distance, yet he felt like he couldn't go anywhere. He looked at a grubby shack by the river right below him.

"…I want treasure…"

Where did he plan to go once he obtained treasure? He didn't know where he was supposed to return to.

Everything was beginning to disappear.

"………………"

Light exploded.

A direct hit.

With his movement stopped, Alus was hit with Mele's arrow.

He must have understood that he couldn't let himself stop in place for a single second.

He was aware of that. In other words.

…I failed…

Alus the Star Runner still remained in one piece.

From his defensive moments earlier…Alus had, unconsciously, *continued to activate the Greatshield of the Dead.*

The same Greatshield of the Dead that was originally supposed to be impossible to use continuously for an extended period of time or to use while in motion.

"…Hold on. That's not how this is supposed to go," Shalk the Sound Slicer muttered on the surface.

What was the problem here? At this point, he was beginning not to understand anything.

He was continuously activating the Greatshield of the Dead. He thought it was impossible to maintain its defense while he was flying, but he was able to move his wings. Why hadn't he tried to do this up until now?

"This thing…"

An intense heat surged from his flank.

The light beam from the Cold Star. His body was uninjured.

He realized that, in this state, he could fly like normal.

Alus shot a magic lightning bullet toward the tower containing the Cold Star sniper. Mele's arrow got in the middle and blocked the lightning. At the same time, Alus took a direct hit from another arrow. Light. Concussion. Destruction.

A vortex of destruction that seemed to disintegrate everything *except* Alus.

Once, Izick the Chromatic had created the ultimate construct, named Tu the Magic.

A mimic with impenetrable defenses, possessing magic item cells that blocked any and all methods of attack by using a magic item known as the Greatshield of the Dead as the foundation. Its base body needed to be that of a mimic.

This was because they needed to possess an ability to maintain themselves by using their ability to transform their own cells, in order to repair the cellular degeneration that was inevitably generated according to the theory behind the Greatshield of the Dead's usage, stating that the user generated a divergence in spatial phases.

In which case, what would happen if the user of the Greatshield of the Dead adapted it to a magic item that continuously repaired his body—Chiklorakk the Eternity Machine—*and continuously activated it in combination*?

To Alus, controlling magic items was a natural act, like light flashing between his nerves.

It was an abnormal degree of aptitude, and with it, he was able to use all the types of weapons the world had to offer.

"The bastard…moved while using the Greatshield of the Dead. Star Runner's going to escape!"

The voice sounded like it was coming far down below him.

He was free.

In the middle of a tempest of destruction, which seemed like it would destroy entire stars, Star Runner flew off once more.

"…Attacks aren't going to have any effect on him anymore!"

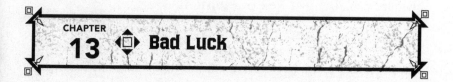
Misfortune is an ever-accumulating thing. That was how Lendelt the Immaculate saw it.

People didn't recognize the phenomena they could potentially deal with as misfortune. It was when the hardships, generated as an inevitable part of life accumulated to an unmanageable degree that it was first meant to be referred to as "misfortune."

Right before the eighth match, Hartl the Light Pinch, who had headed off to stall Kuze the Passing Disaster, had died. As a member tasked with Obsidian Eyes mobile attacks, Lendelt had burned his body, destroying the evidence linking him back to the organization.

From there, he needed to bring Mestelexil the Box of Desperate Knowledge and return home. Right now, with Lena, Frey, and Wieze engaged in the operation at the castle garden theater and Hyakrai suffering serious wounds, Lendelt was the only member capable of doing so.

He was taking plenty of precautions. He wasn't behaving in any way that would cast suspicion on him. He should have been able to conceal Mestelexil in the carriage bed and secretly carry him outside the city.

Which was all the more reason why the circumstances he encountered after that were true misfortune.

...Damn monsters!

Behind him, there was a steam automobile chasing after Lendelt's carriage at full speed.

There was a man riding on top of the automobile's roof, kneeling. The name of this visitor, clothed in otherworldly red garments, was at that point known to most of Aureatia.

"Straight ahead! Keep on rushing straight ahead, old man!"

Soujirou the Willow-Sword. The man gripping the steering wheel with a deathly white complexion was Aureatia's Sixth General, Harghent the Still.

"Wait! I-in a situation like this?! Are you mad?!"

"Ha-ha-ha-ha-ha-ha-ha-ha-ha-ha-ha-ha-ha-ha-ha-ha-ha-ha-ha!"

In the carriage bed, Mestelexil was wildly firing a gun that produced a piercing howl.

It was called a Gatling gun. Its barrage, firing one thousand and three rounds a second, boasted a monstrous amount of firepower, which was fair to call excessive for not only an anti-personnel weapon but also an anti-matériel one; however...

"This all you got?! Ozonezma's! Knife things! Were waaaay faster!"

While the gunfire sounded with enough force to split the air, the only thing he could hear was the slight metallic sound coming from Soujirou's hands. The air in his vicinity was hazy. He was swinging *something* nonstop at high speed.

It wasn't a sword.

Soujirou's weapon was a massive something that could hardly be called a weapon, cut off from a section of the automobile.

Wielding the iron plate with unimaginable finesse, he was perfectly using the surface of the *blade* to completely kill the force of the Gatling gun's bullets.

"How the hell...am I supposed to escape from this situation?!"

The strongest blade master in the land was pursuing Lendelt.

◆

Going back a bit in time.

Hearing the report of Alus the Star Runner's attack, Harghent and Soujirou had hijacked one of the military hospital's steam automobiles.

While the carriages loaded with citizens filled up the main boulevards, they passed through the narrow alleyways that bypassed the buildings and headed toward the Eastern Outer Ward.

Their car continued forward, destroying a fair number of the residences and household belongings along the alleyway, but here in the districts where the residents had evacuated, there wasn't anyone to reprimand them for it.

"Yo, you're driving all over the damn place! Even I can tell! I thought you said you could operate one of these things!"

"S-stop, you're distracting me! Live combat first! I'm learning on the battlefield!"

At first glance, they saw what appeared to be a one-horse cargo carriage, left behind in the road.

The owner must have obeyed the evacuation orders from Aureatia while he was filling it up with his belongings to prepare to flee and, as a result, had left it behind with the horse still tied to it. They had seen several other carriages like it on their path up until now, and there was nothing conspicuously unnatural about it, either.

"Harghent."

Which was why when Soujirou quietly muttered in the seat next to him, Harghent didn't think that this was what he was referring to.

"There's something real nasty in that carriage."

"…What?" Harghent asked, unconsciously reducing the automobile's speed.

Soujirou the Willow-Sword—an abomination who had taken down the Nagan Dungeon Golem all on his own—won a battle to the death against Ozonezma the Capricious, and he even now, after losing one leg, sought to battle Alus the Star Runner.

Something that this man called *nasty* was here in this deathly still residential district.

"Let me ask what you mean. Does that mean…strong?"

"Yup. I'd say that. Seems interesting, but I won't insist on taking it down or anything. You wanna go and defeat Alus as fast as possible, right, old man?"

"That's right. That's right, but…"

Half-hearted.

Harghent thought the way unnecessary hesitation would sneak into his head at times like this was why he hadn't been able to catch up to Alus.

"...It's the Twenty-Nine Officials' job to protect the peace and safety of Aureatia. Just in case. Just in case...we'll check it out."

"A real serious guy, ain't ya?"

"If I really was that serious, I wouldn't hesitate."

At that moment, a strange crunching noise reverberated from the back of the automobile, but Harghent tried his best to ignore it.

"Umm... You, carriage over there. I am Aureatia's Sixth General, Harghent. Is anyone in there?" he called out, walking alongside the carriage. There was no response.

Harghent didn't sense any living creature inside, either. It looked like an unmanned carriage.

"Are you sure about this, Soujirou?"

"Just gotta turn it over, right?"

Before Harghent had time to stop him, Soujirou extended the sheath of his sword and flipped up the canopy over the carriage bed.

"Hey..."

The singular eye of a bluish-purple golem locked its gaze with Harghent's.

"Don't just—"

An explosive gunshot echoed through the alley.

In the same moment, the supposedly unmanned carriage took off.

Separate from the golem riding underneath the hood, someone with an abnormally faint presence had hidden themselves within the very tiny gap in the driver's seat—but this was all something Harghent only realized afterward.

"*H-hah...* Wh-what in the world is this?!"

"It shot at us! Hurry up and start the car! We're going after it!"

The massive load of bullets shot at point-blank range, by some incomprehensible logic, had all completely missed Harghent. Not only that, but the main components of the automobile, and the blade of Soujirou's sword, unsheathed in a single, impossible-to-perceive, second, didn't seem to have suffered even one scratch.

"Or are you not gonna chase 'em?!"

"I-I'll...go after it! That was Mestelexil the Box of Desperate Knowledge! A wanted criminal...i-in a place like this?! Why?!"

"How the hell would I know?!"

"We're going after them!"

"Then go!"

With an explosive ignition sound, the automobile took off.

They hadn't been intentionally chasing after Mestelexil and Obsidian Eyes.

An accumulation of impossible-to-manage coincidences.

For Lendelt the Immaculate, it was an encounter that was nothing other than misfortune.

◆

"Sou...jirou...!"

In the carriage bed, Mestelexil continued his unending attack to his rear.

A rocket launcher in addition to the Gatling gun. Small-size missiles. Or perhaps tear gas grenades.

They were the types of weapons Soujirou had seen often in the

Beyond. All he had to do was discern which bullets from the Gatling gun were going to hit him, and dodge, and for the missiles and tear gas rounds, he just needed to distort their path before they hit.

If he cut off pieces of iron from the car's frame, Soujirou was able to create any number of swords to wield, and currently, he could apply the speed of the automobile to his sword techniques as well.

There was always a limit to *how much speed gunpowder could produce.* No matter how strong the wielder may have been, it was an aspect that no amount of training could have any effect on. Soujirou didn't consider his comparison to Ozonezma from moments ago to be any exaggeration at all.

"U-umm... Uhhh! Wh-wh-who was that again...?!"

"I ain't never met you before."

In addition, Mestelexil was in an unusual state.

He seemed to harbor an intense grudge against Soujirou, but it also appeared as if he currently didn't understand why he felt that way himself. Soujirou could sense that the golem wasn't able to fully bring out all of his power.

In which case, was there some way for him to kill this enemy?

This guy's like that spider thing in Lithia, huh. This guy's life is combined into one.

Even with Soujirou's intuition, he didn't understand *the procedure to kill him.*

What did he need to do to make killing him possible? It was the first time he had seen an enemy like this.

"*Gwah, hah...* This Sixways Exhibition stuff is a whole lotta fun!"

As he knocked away the storm of bullets with his massive iron plate, he ran the tip down at the car beneath him.

Grabbing a piece of steel that had been popped off with the toes of his left foot, he knocked down the rocket flying toward him.

It was with fear. The harder it was for him to understand how to kill his opponent, the more he wanted to cut them down.

It was the means to more deeply understand Mestelexil. He wanted to know what made him tick, and how he could stop it.

"Hey, Harghent! Quit shutting your damn eyes! Don't think I don't know!"

"Impossible! I can't take it anymore! We're going to die! This is the end!"

"We're in an automobile, and we can't even catch up to a freakin' horse?!" Soujirou shouted as he parried the bullet storm.

If both of his legs had been healthy, he was confident he could have jumped over to the carriage in front, like the feat he had performed back in Nagan. From there, he could have cleaved through Mestelexil, armor and all. He completely understood what sort of swordsmanship he would have needed to slice through the golem's composite armor, just by looking at it himself.

However, right now, with his right leg missing at the thigh…

I ain't got a clue.

The distance between them, and the speed of their movement. The endless barrage of bullets. After he jumped, would he, Harghent, or the automobile be able to get out unscathed? A variety of factors intermingled in extremely complex ways and didn't leave him confident.

It showed that Mestelexil the Box of Desperate Knowledge was so strong that even Soujirou's gut intuition, capable of seeing the fate of anyone he faced off against, wasn't a match for him.

He's got to have more to 'im than just spraying bullets everywhere. Poison gas, flashbangs, he's gotta be able to do it all. C'mon, no need to hold back now.

Mestelexil was fighting in a way to avoid getting his driver caught in the cross fire.

Soujirou was protecting Harghent and the automobile, because they were supplementing his mobility now that he had lost one leg. However, normally, that shouldn't have been true of Mestelexil as well.

Most likely, the golem had experienced a battle like this in the past, and he was tracing the decisions made at that time to build his current tactical approach.

You're telling me...even a guy like you is scared to jump into the unknown, huh?

Soujirou was grinning in the middle of the loud, shrieking gunfire continuing to echo around him.

Perhaps it was that, for warriors as mighty as them, they couldn't help fearing an unknown that even their strength couldn't reach. Soujirou thought that he wanted to step into that realm of mystery.

He stepped forward with his prosthetic leg.

Soujirou didn't know what would happen, but he was gonna try jumping from one vehicle to the other.

"...Harghent. You might end up dead after this. Sorry 'bout that."

"Huhhhh?! No, wait, where did that come from?! We look half dead as is!"

A very brief gap came in the barrage of bullets. Utilizing Craft Arts to repair the gun barrel and reload took only a second, but even then, as long as there was a physical restriction, Mestelexil couldn't actually continue to fire indefinitely.

Soujirou tipped his center of gravity. At that moment—

"Ah."

There was a flash of blue light.

With an explosive blast, Mestelexil took off from the carriage.

The recoil from the rocket propulsion smashed the carriage bed into pieces.

"...Damn you!"

Soujirou, right as he was about to jump, cut down two of the gunfire drones Mestelexil scattered right before he escaped. These drones hadn't targeted Soujirou, either.

The carriage, getting hit by the recoil of Mestelexil's flight, crashed right into a residential home and rolled over.

Harghent's automobile managed to miraculously avoid the wreckage—though it needed to tilt on one edge to do it—and came to a stop.

"What happened?!"

"He turned tail and ran! He wasn't running from us, either!"

He had most likely sensed some type of radar or sensor nearby. Soujirou himself had realized at almost the exact same moment that *a mysterious something* was approaching.

He looked down over the carriage wreck. It was deserted.

The man driving the carriage must have escaped from the carriage with ghostlike movements at almost the same time as Mestelexil took off. He had likely jumped through one of the windows of the nearby residences, but now wasn't the time to pay him any attention.

The mass of drones was turned toward the other side of the wall, with their guns trained.

Then...

...the enormous figure appeared, tearing through the sturdy stone wall with one hand.

It was a massive gray ogre.

In his other hand, he swung a wooden club down.

The covered wagon's frame was completely destroyed in a single swing.

"That Mestelexil bastard...! He ran away from this guy!"

The ogre, Uhak the Silent, looked up at the sky.

He almost seemed to be searching for the threat he was supposed to eliminate.

Clinking and clanking sounds echoed little by little.

Many among the drone swarm were losing their functionality. Their compositional elements broke apart and returned to the original materials they had been before being built with Craft Arts. None of them had fired a single shot.

"This *hollow* asshole. Came and ruined the fun."

It stuck in Soujirou's throat. With no particular reason why.

"Back off! Uhak the Silent's a hero candidate! He's different from Mestelexil!"

There was a flash of light.

Soujirou had completed his fatal slash.

Because this thing resembling an ogre was all too *incompre-hensible* a creature.

"……"

His sword was stopped by the club.

It was completely ordinary, essentially just a mass of stiff wood.

Throughout Soujirou's life up until that point, there hadn't been anything like it.

"…What the hell are you?"

Uhak was silent.

His white pupils seemed to be both looking at Soujirou and past him at the same time.

"…Let's go! The fact they couldn't finish us off must mean failure for that carriage driver! Bringing back the information that we saw, and engaged with Mestelexil is already valuable! Now…it's time for Alus! We're going after Alus!"

"……"

Going through the hole-ridden roof of the automobile, Soujirou returned inside the car.

"Old man. What's with this guy?"

"Uhak the Silent? He's an ogre. I've heard that he's docile, but other than that, he's just a regular ogre with no special qualities of note. Was there something strange about him?"

"Nah… That guy's definitely weird. Doesn't seem strong and doesn't look interesting at all… Normally, I wouldn't even pick a fight with someone like that…"

Soujirou wished to learn what lay at the edge of fear.

However, what he felt when confronting Uhak was a different type of terror from that time in the arena—a terrible alien sensation that made him think that *he mustn't get any closer to him.*

Uhak, still lingering vacantly, was far behind them.

With the landscape outside the car flowing in the corner of his eye, Soujirou looked at his own right hand.

He guarded...against my sword.

Harghent's own heart was a mystery.

Despite already struggling enough to comprehend the hearts of the citizens and his men, he constantly understood even less about himself.

Which was why there might have been some part of his heart that was grateful for Uhak the Silent's sudden intrusion.

Pursuing Mestelexil after he abruptly showed himself was a job that only Harghent, who happened to be nearby, could accomplish. If, by any chance, he was able to capture the golem, the accomplishment may likely have been more than enough to make up for his foolish and unauthorized mobilization.

However, in exchange, he might have ultimately *given up* on his decisive battle against Alus.

Since, if he was engaged in a battle no one else could shoulder, then he could use it as his excuse.

He could plaster over his desire not to meet with Alus, now transformed into Aureatia's enemy, and his feelings of obligation for driving the wyvern into the abyss of death, by convincing himself that he had acted properly.

I don't need to be there.

Of course.

Where they were heading, hero candidates, far and away more powerful than Harghent, may have already come together. Aureatia's military, without Harghent doing anything, may already have readied as much equipment and troop strength as they could muster, and encircled Alus with impeccably tactical strategy.

Even if Harghent barged into the battle camp from the outside, he would bring nothing more than the inconsequential strength of a single individual soldier—not just that, he might end up actively becoming a hindrance to the operation.

In which case, the still better outcome would be that the battle was long over already.

He pictured himself if Aureatia's side claimed victory, quietly lingering as the triumphant victory songs of the soldiers echoed around him.

The opposite was just as meaningless. It could end with him simply gazing out, with disappointment and despair, at the charred remnants, everything mowed down by Alus the Star Runner's hand.

No matter what the end result, no one would pay a passing thought to Harghent's existence at all.

…Unnecessary. I've only ever been unnecessary.

It was always how the battles of Harghent the Still had gone.

He was only ever skilled at shooting down wyverns.

In the past, that was a truly sought-after skill in order to preserve peace.

I know. The truth is, I don't need to race around the frontier putting down wyvern flocks anymore. It's the True Demon King's fault...both minian and wyvern numbers have dwindled, and now the habitats of both groups no longer brush up against each other.

Racing through the gaps between houses, they drove across a vacant plot of land at the dead end of one street and came out onto the road on the other side.

His driving may have been inept, but he was thoroughly familiar with every nook and cranny of Aureatia.

In order to defend their home soil from wyverns, he had first needed a complete grasp of the terrain. Not only to help his own men fight against them, but to properly evacuate the citizens away from those formidable foes in the sky.

All this extra effort, too, had been unnecessary.

Since Harghent had been appointed to his Sixth General seat, there hadn't been a single case of wyverns invading into Aureatia's domain.

Very rarely there were times a wyvern had broken away from their flock and approached Aureatia, but they would be shot down with the latest antiair cannons long before they ever reached the city.

My unnecessary ambitions and aspirations also ended up getting so many brilliant men of mine killed.

There wasn't a single commanding military officer who hadn't led their troops to their death in battle.

However, in Harghent's case, they had been completely meaningless deaths, all to serve his own personal ambition. He wondered what exactly he could do to make amends with the families of the deceased soldiers he had urged to their deaths in his campaign to subjugate Vikeon.

In the Lithia War, too, everything I did was unnecessary and uncalled for.

The Mage City soldiers that had worked under Harghent were all dead, too.

The fact that they had volunteered to invade Lithia themselves was no excuse.

They had died because Harghent was too incompetent to properly control the Mage City soldiers on the front lines. If it had been a real member of the Twenty-Nine Officials...anyone besides Harghent himself, they would have been able to make them abandon their foolish plan and wouldn't have caused the battle situation to deteriorate.

The wyvern handler girl Curte wouldn't have died, either.

The view of the city he caught through the gaps in the buildings was flickering red.

Aureatia was burning like Lithia was that day. The Eastern Outer Ward was close.

Why was Alus trying to burn Aureatia down?

Harghent even felt that if this was all out of hatred toward him, then he'd be fine throwing his life away that very second.

He was the one who'd ended up leading Lucnoca the Winter here.

If I hadn't brought her here, I never would have made young Lagrex fight like he did that day... I didn't deserve any gratitude at all. Why, back then, hadn't I been able to say that?

He had seen Alus fall from the skies of Mali Wastes.

Harghent tightly shut his eyes, as if to avert his gaze from the city wreathed in flames.

If I hadn't brought Lucnoca the Winter here...

He simply wished to see his lone wyvern friend fight and win against the truly mighty and strong.

This wish of Harghent's, more than anything else, had been the most unnecessary thing of all.

"...Sorry 'bout that, old man."

Soujirou had been sitting in silence next to him until he murmured, still looking out the window.

"What for?"

"You wanna kill Alus for good, right? I made you take that detour, and worst of all, we didn't even settle the score. I was just thinking for a sec...and sorta thought that you really did a good job driving through all of that, even though there wasn't nothing in it for you at all."

"...*Ha, ha-ha-ha.* I was just whipped up into a fervor... No, I was desperate. Seems like it's those moments when my strength alone isn't enough to do anything when I end up getting that way."

It was the same when he fought Vikeon, back in Mage City, and when he encountered Lucnoca, too.

He had simply been able to do the same when faced with a hail of bullets from Mestelexil, too.

"Real brave, ain't ya?"

"...It's all unnecessary. Everything I do is unnecessary."

The foolhardy courage he wasn't meant to overcome.

Achievements that went beyond his station.

The words that didn't need to be said.

The friendship that killed his friend.

Harghent the Still's life was filled to the brim with unnecessary things.

I don't need to be here.

Despite knowing this better than anyone else, Harghent was heading to the battle.

◆

"When it's all said and done, to the village, I'm an unneeded kid."

The sound of waves was always present in his memories from long ago.

The sound constantly echoed within the shack along the rock cliffs, seemingly on the verge of being gobbled up by the sea any minute.

"I've got three older brothers in my family, see, and I'm the most incompetent one, so everyone's always teasing me, saying it'd be better if Harghent was never born at all."

"What do you mean by unneeded?"

"I mean I don't count for anything."

The young boy's name was Harghent. The name had been thoroughly drilled into his mind.

After colliding violently into the cliff wall, Alus had apparently been close to death on the reef directly below.

If Harghent didn't happen to be passing by that area by

coincidence, he likely would have been dead by now. Alus was the weakest wyvern in his flock, so that had to be right.

"The way the guys in the village see it, three is the *correct number* of children for my family to have. Since I was born after them, on top of being totally useless, they say I'm unnecessary."

"Hmm... I'm jealous..."

"Huhhh?!"

Harghent's voice grew ever so slightly louder.

Apparently minia let out this sort of cry when they're upset. This might have been just Harghent, though.

"Well, if three's the correct number in your village...then that means my arms are the correct number, too..."

"That's not what I'm trying to get at here!"

Harghent did indeed seem to be in a bad mood.

Alus wished Harghent would enjoy himself just a bit more. If Harghent was in a better mood while he was with Alus, then Alus would've been able to observe what sort of faces and voices minia made when they were enjoying themselves.

"Listen. Your arms are unnecessary, too. Not just one of them or anything. They're all unnecessary. There aren't any other wyverns who have grown arms like that. If I had five arms, I'd look like a weird monster, too, right?"

"You think so...? That sounds pretty interesting to me..."

"*Argh*, enough! Can't you think about what you're actually saying before you talk?!"

Alus didn't think it was that bad to have more than the correct number of something. That was how he felt.

The wyvern flock that Alus was born into was always starving.

Buffeted by the cold salt air as they flew over the ocean, they ate rats, mice, even bugs and weeds, too.

The most important of the flock were always saying that if they increased the numbers of their flock high enough, they would eventually be able to feed on minia in the nearby settlements, but there were no previous examples of them doing so.

Regnejee, a little bit older than Alus, was smart, and he would often talk about how inefficient the current assignment of roles within the flock was or what he would be able to do in order to improve the situation.

Though at the time Alus hadn't fully understood what the word *inefficient* or *improve* meant and was first able to comprehend them after Harghent taught them to him.

Harghent was always in a bad mood, but unlike Regnejee, he would teach Alus the meanings of any words he didn't understand. More than anything, though, the stuff he talked about was better. What he talked to Alus about almost every day didn't concern some hard-to-understand logic or structures, but it was related to simple topics like how much dissatisfaction he had in his current lot in life or how spectacular he would become in the future to get back at everyone who looked down on him. They were all easy to understand, even with Alus's lack of smarts.

"Sure, I'll admit I'm bad at counting money or remembering what people tell me. But just because I don't laugh along with everyone else when someone makes a lame joke at the village assembly, that's supposed to mean I'm an idiot?! I was the one who found the better place to set up our wyvern lookout tower, and then when the huge rains from before caused water to overflow the levees, I was the first one in the village to notice, dammit! In reality, I deserve praise! I'm the one protecting the village the most here!" said Harghent.

"Wow… You're amazing, huh, Harghent…"

The actual facts of the matter were that, without a place to belong in the village, Harghent would often walk around the seashore and had simply learned to recognize the coastline terrain or emergency situations nearby. In fact, Alus had been discovered on the reef along the same shore.

"…Stop saying things are amazing so readily like that. It makes me feel like I'm getting made fun of."

"But I said those things because I wanted to praise you, Harghent…"

"That's not it; you just don't get it! It doesn't make me happy at all to get complimented by a wyvern like you! What I want is more like…I want to hear it from everyone! I want to be acknowledged, and praised, by a lot of people, more than just the other villagers, and I want to be called a champion!"

Harghent had said the word *champion* several times before.

This was apparently a title on par with rare and valuable treasures, very difficult to obtain, and which any person, not just Harghent, wished to be called at some point.

"…What do you need to do to become one?"

"I told you, didn't I? I'm going kill wyverns. I'll expel them from minian settlements and make sure everyone can live peacefully.

The kingdom's put out a reward for any skilled wyvern slayers. There are even guys that've killed tons of wyverns and risen up from being poor on the frontier to becoming a real general! Yeah, I might be awkward and clumsy, but…I've decided that, instead, I'm gonna focus on that and only that. Leave this village, work under a good bow instructor… and hunt down every single wyvern out there. Just watch."

"……"

At some point along the way, Harghent had stopped saying "the wyverns in this village" or "your buddies up there." Now he said he'd go outside the village and hunt the wyverns that threatened people.

Alus remembered being convinced that, since Harghent hated this village, and it would still be a long ways into the future before Alus's flock could attack humans, this would be a better alternative for him.

"Once I do that, I'll make absolutely every single person in the village bow their heads down to me. Suzy, Mashky, Takrekun, that asshole Pemeza, and all the people in the Ortega family, too! That Goorica laughed me the other day, too! That one's never even been outside the stupid village, so I'll blow their mind telling them about the amazing machines in the kingdom or bring back written books to show them."

"…What type of amazing machines?"

"Hell if I know, but they got something! It's a place I've never seen, so it's got stuff I've never seen, too!"

He did have a point, Alus thought.

Alus hadn't known anything beyond the area around this sea, but if he flew even farther out, there was sure to still be plenty of things he hadn't ever seen before.

—because he had never gone out there to see.

"...I really do like...talking about that sorta stuff."

"What are you talking about?"

"When you talk about becoming really important, and strong...beating up people you don't like, boasting about your treasure...I want to go along with you. I wonder if I could boast about stuff, too..."

"...*Tch*. No one ever says stuff like that to me," Harghent mumbled quietly, and faced in the opposite direction, away from Alus.

When he ended up like this, Alus could no longer tell what sort of expression Harghent was wearing.

Nevertheless, he got the vague feeling that Harghent was feeling lonesome.

"I thought maybe, just maybe...there'd be another person out there that'd say stuff like you do. I talked to a kid at Abeeq's metal hop, about three years old, the other day. About me becoming a general."

Alus could hear the quiet sound of a sniffling nose mixed in with the sounds of the ocean.

"Instead, now everyone thinks I'm even more of a fool. There was someone else listening in on the stupid stuff I was saying. Why does this always happen? Stuff that I should be able to manage with just a little bit of extra attention, stuff I should be able to handle like everyone else with a bit of patience, I just can't ever do it. I'm trying real hard to do the same…just like everyone else does, but my faults always peek through somewhere. Always, without fail."

"……"

Alus remembered being told he had to become able to do the things he couldn't.

That he needed to grow up.

Harghent might have been raised hearing the same sorts of things his entire life, too.

"…Consider the source; take countermeasures."

"…I'm doing that. That's nothing…even I can…but the others just do it better…"

"Among wyverns…"

Alus raised his head up.

"…there's almost no one…who says the sorts of things you do, Harghent. The strong ones don't think about anything. That's why, if you're planning on fighting wyverns…I think someday you'll end up growing stronger than them. If you just focus on hunting wyverns, you'll become more important than the villagers, and you'll be able to do anything, right…?"

"*Ha, ha-ha…* What the hell? Is that your attempt to cheer me up?"

"I want to do something to repay you…for everything you've taught me."

When Alus thought about it, the concept of repaying something itself was one he had learned from Harghent.

Did he need to repay him with something for teaching him about repaying other people?

Alus's mind nearly descended into confusion as he tried to

think about it deeper, but meanwhile, the minian races lived their lives constantly going along with these difficult conversations. He found it impressive.

"Well, that sorta stuff isn't welcome, okay? I don't need your pity."

"Okay, then, if you don't need it, and it's not welcome...will you still teach me words or talk to me about minian stuff...even after my wound's all healed?"

"Of course not."

Harghent gazed out at the dark sea beneath the cloudy sky.

The small avian silhouettes flying around the cliff wall were wyverns.

Despite walking around the seashore, Harghent had never headed in that direction.

Because he was a minia.

"...I mean, us minia and wyverns are natural enemies and all."

◆

At that moment, the half-destroyed automobile had slipped into the second borough of the Eastern Outer Ward.

With a single word, the conflagration covering the city had disappeared without a trace.

In the air, numerous rays of light coalesced, trying to destroy Alus.

Alus the Star Runner had transformed into an invincible being and was about to fly off into the sky.

The hero candidates, and possibly a powerless old general, were assembling and approaching the conclusion.

The sun was finally beginning to set on Aureatia's long, long day.

CHAPTER 15 ◀▣▶ Glory, in One's Grasp

"The bastard's…moved while using Greatshield of the Dead. Star Runner's going to escape!"

Shalk the Sound Slicer, realizing the fatal transformation in Alus the Star Runner, tried to relay as much information as he could.

With just his power, or potentially even with the power of the other hero candidates, they may not have been able to stop him anymore. At least, if he was allowed to fly off from here, the damage and casualties would grow even further.

"…Attacks aren't going to have any effect on him anymore!"

As a result of the fierce fighting up until now, Alus had exhausted a majority of his equipment.

Hillensingen the Luminous Blade had returned to Toroa's hands, and at the same time, he lost Trembling Bird as well.

He no longer had the magic items that delivered autonomous multifaceted attacks in Rotting Soil Sun or Ground Runner.

He had likely gone through all of his deadly magic bullets, including the magic lightning bullets. Even his rifle itself couldn't have avoided some adverse effects from the harsh nonstop gunfire Alus was putting it through.

Torn off halfway down the whip, Kio's Hand now managed to hold out only in hand-to-hand combat in his magic swords' stead and little more.

Yet now was the truly worst moment of all.

Alus the Star Runner, his consciousness and memory degenerated and letting his multitudes of magic items run wild, had transformed into an immortal automatic machine, slaughtering without any goal.

Sure, he's run out of his offensive magic items...but that's not any comfort at all.

The threat he posed hadn't been mitigated at all; if anything, it was only growing worse.

There was a magic item capable of destroying Aureatia very close to the second borough of the Eastern Outer Ward.

The Cold Star

Just needs to steal *again, is all.*

The incessant arrows from Horizon's Roar, splitting through the sky, stopped.

Shalk could see the silhouette of something taking flight from the point of death, having been killed thousands of times and still persisting.

Alus's figure, wrapped in the vestiges of Mele's earthen arrows, hot boiling rock, looked like a flaming bird.

A part of him, his neck perhaps, moved, and he turned his path toward the small tower at the Third Fortress.

The next arrow came flying in to obstruct his path, but it had been launched before his immortal tenacity had been made clear.

Unable to keep up with his godlike agility, the arrow's aim missed the mark.

He was actually accelerating his flight speed. He couldn't be destroyed.

I can't get at him in the air.

Alus the Star Runner was going to immediately attack the Cold Star's gunner and steal the magic item.

Then he'd shoot at his next target—either Mele the Horizon's Roar or potentially the city of Aureatia itself.

Such a future couldn't be prevented.

Alus was arriving at the small tower.

Metal claws scratched at the small tower's parapet.

"Took you long enough."

A white spear was right before his eyes.

The inexhaustible thrust flashed, casting away sound itself, and pushed Alus downward, destroying the parapet with it.

"I was getting real tired of waiting for you," Shalk spat, already having snatched the Cold Star from its pedestal and gripping it in his hand.

Such a future couldn't be prevented—*for anyone else besides Shalk the Sound Slicer.*

After a significant delay following the clash, the bespectacled gunner shouted, "Hey! What the hell's going on with Star Runner's body?! Forget the Cold Star; how the hell's it still unscathed after taking a direct hit from Horizon's Roar?!"

"Just to be sure. Take shelter."

"Saying this just in case. Get outta here."

Shalk left behind just two short remarks before jumping off the top of the small tower.

In the time it took Alus to fly in a straight line to the small tower, Shalk had *run* all the way here.

If it was now impossible to offensively keep Alus preoccupied, then he'd use the same method he had at the start.

The only option was to use the magic item Alus wanted as bait and turn Shalk himself into a target to keep him pegged down.

But where?

The choice was between either the second borough or the fifth borough, flanking the third on either side.

Shalk wanted to avoid the flames of battle expanding to another district.

He wanted to choose the fifth borough, where there were likely no survivors left behind, but that area, where Tu had sunken down with the Rotting Soil Sun, had already turned into a muddy mire. Would he be able to have the mobility necessary to battle Alus there?

Whichever place I choose, though, now that he can't be killed, I need to lead him outside of Aureatia. The second borough is closer to Aureatia's border... Guess that's my only option.

Shalk's series of thoughts had finished even before he landed.

Kicking off a church roof, he drove his spear toward Alus as the wyvern tried to fly away from below the small tower.

"Where is...my treasure...?"

Way too hard.

Shalk could tell from the recoil he felt in his spear that his thrust didn't affect Alus at all.

He had been able to knock Alus down moments ago because this thrust had been fixed mainly at the parapet and had destroyed the wyvern's footing while simultaneously throwing off his balance right after landing.

This latest thrust served only to provoke him.

"Kio's..."

The magical whip, extending out faster than the speed of sound, immediately hacked at Shalk.

Using the recoil from this attack and without kicking off with his legs, Alus flew up into the sky. Outside of Shalk's spear's range.

"...Hand."

"Can you see the treasure, Alus the Star Runner?"

"The treasure's..."

Shalk broke off in a run without waiting for the answer.

Fast enough for Alus to still visually follow him. To ensure that he could engage him in the second borough of the Eastern Outer Ward, without letting the damage spread any further.

There's got to be someone else who's come here besides me. Someone somewhere who can do something about this.

Guiding Alus outside of Aureatia—this was the only plan Shalk could enact alone, but was it even realistic?

Alus right now didn't seem to be acting with any reason that Shalk could comprehend.

However, if the apex adventuring rogue was trying to storm Aureatia...did that mean he wouldn't stop until he had done just what he had done in countless dungeons and labyrinths before, destroy Aureatia and plunder all its treasure?

If that is true, then this is a losing battle.

No one had imagined it, but this fight had come with a time limit from the very start.

A fight to win before Alus the Star Runner, obtaining a cogwheel body that maintained his combat functionality in perpetuity, managed to perfectly adapt the Greatshield of the Dead to his new form.

This has got to be what the original demon kings were.

Shalk could tell that the shadow of ruin had begun to pursue him from behind.

A nightmare that laid everything in the world bare, plundered it, and journeyed until the death of it all.

From the era before the True Demon King...

Born among the most populous natural enemies in the skies, the strongest of them had all transformed into legend.

An adventurer and a plunderer.

The natural enemy of miniankind.

◆

Gigant Town. Mele the Horizon's Roar's firing position lay sixteen kilometers north of the Eastern Outer Ward.

"...Can't do any more than this. A waste of arrows," Mele casually remarked, lowering his enormous black bow.

Cayon didn't intend to object, but he was unable to experience the same world that Mele saw.

Sitting with his legs crossed in his chair, he simply looked off in the same southern direction.

"What's happening? You said you hit Star Runner, didn't you? The observers even reported several times that they confirmed he had been hit, too," said Cayon.

"Hell, I wanna ask the same damn thing. In any case, my attacks aren't working anymore. If I gotta do this without destroying the city, then I can't try shooting up into the air and hitting Alus a bunch of times until he's buried in the dirt, neither. End up destroying the whole city right down to the bedrock that way. So I got nothing left," Mele replied.

"...I get it, okay."

The trajectory of the arrows Mele shot at Alus had all been aimed toward the sky, tracing a path as though they had suddenly leaped from below. He hadn't let a single one of them land in the city.

Not only that, but he threaded them through the intricately woven streets of Aureatia's high and low cityscape, without letting the aftershock of their impact even touch the buildings. Despite showcasing this utterly sublime technique over and over again, Mele's breathing wasn't ragged at all.

"This is plenty. I never planned on having you be any part of this to begin with anyway... You've worked hard enough, right, Mele?"

With the battlefield past the edge of the horizon, Cayon couldn't possibly feel the reality of it all from here in Gigant Town.

However, the fact that Mele's skills weren't enough to fully stop Alus remained.

Would this be the end of Aureatia? he thought.

"It might be a bit callous...but if this isn't enough, I'm fine with it."

"That so? In that case, I'm gonna take a nap."

Mele yawned as he departed.

The Sine Riverstead's guardian, from the very beginning, felt no obligation to protect Aureatia.

Holding this Sixways Exhibition to put an end to these champions, only to have them save the city when Aureatia itself was actually under threat, was far too self-serving—Cayon thought.

If Aureatia was brought to ruin, then no one was going to show up trying to take Mele down.

Cayon's absolute highest priority, Sine Riverstead and Mele the Horizon's Roar, hadn't changed.

Thus, there was nothing to be done for Aureatia.

The question is, if I can really be convinced of that, I suppose.

He sighed.

The individual citizens living in Aureatia weren't to blame for anything.

He understood that.

Cayon couldn't do anything while innocent people died, just like during the era of the True Demon King.

Who could hope to fight against a threat that even Mele the Horizon's Roar couldn't annihilate?

That's why I'm trying to believe that the situation's hopeless.

The sounds of footsteps were coming back his way.

Mele's footsteps. Mele never moved when he was atop Needle Mountain. As such, it was a noise Cayon hadn't known in Sine Riverstead but had come to perfectly recognize after coming to Aureatia.

"...What's wrong? Wait, *what* are you doing?"

Mele bore a massive iron pillar on his shoulder.

Of course, it was massive by minian standards, and when compared to Mele's enormous frame, it instead resembled a long arrow. One of the iron arrows that was embedded Sine Riverstead's Needle Mountain.

"Weren't you going to take a nap?"

"I'm free to do whatever I damn well please, aren't I? I just... lay down for a sec, and suddenly I was wide awake."

"You're never honest, are you?"

"Bah, can it."

Mele sat down cross-legged and stuck the iron arrow vertically into the ground.

"If things start to look real bad, I'll stop Alus with a net by unraveling this thing with Word Arts. May not be able to blast him to bits, but I should be able to stop 'im from flying off somewhere."

Cayon thought back to the shapeshifting iron arrows he saw in the seventh match.

Mele's Craft Arts, turning this enormous iron pillar into countless fine iron wires.

Normally, these arrows were capable of wrangling wyverns all at once, expanding in midair. Now Cayon finally understood that this was what the technique was used for.

"...In exchange, though, the second borough's not going to get through it unscathed, is it?"

"Probably not."

No matter how fine the iron wires may have been, once fired

with the speed of Mele's archery skills, they became a weapon of total annihilation, able to easily sever everything they went through. While he may have been able to restrict the might of its impact to keep the damage to a minimum, they still needed to be prepared for it to result in some number of casualties.

So I have to come to a decision, then. Mele's not going to let me run away from this, is he?

Mele the Horizon's Roar may have indeed been the guardian of only Sine Riverstead.

However, like Cayon had witnessed during the match against Shalk, he was a warrior and a noble-minded champion.

Cayon the Thundering needed to ensure that he himself was a sponsor becoming of his candidate as well.

"I'll get in touch with Hidow and propose the idea as an emergency defense measure for you. But if it doesn't get approved in time…shoot, and I'll take the responsibility, Mele."

◆

"Alus! Where are you, Alus?!"

The steam automobile raced through the leftover ashes of what was once the second borough of the Eastern Outer Ward.

A majority of what was once an intricate network of buildings had been torched, or already destroyed by Sabfom's troops, and now with the blaze extinguished, there was space for them to just barely get through.

"Alus… *Gwaugh!*"

The car frame sank down at an angle, together with the sound of something breaking. The car itself was reaching its limit.

Almost everything besides its essential components had been pierced by the Gatling gun, and after colliding several times during the rigorous drive, the balance of the car's body was lacking considerably. It was close to a miracle that it had been able to drive this far.

"Dammit, it's always like this with these cursed automobiles…!"

"At this point, it ain't about the car, y'know."

Crawling out from the car's interior, at this point a crushed mass of iron, was Aureatia's Sixth General, Harghent the Still, as well as the hero candidate Soujirou the Willow-Sword.

"Fine…I'll walk then!"

"That ain't happening for me right now."

Harghent looked at Soujirou's right leg. The prosthetic leg. When Soujirou had encountered Mestelexil, his fighting form was so superhuman, he hadn't seemed to be in such a state at all, but he had lost his right leg, an extremely important body part for a swordsman.

For the average person, he was obviously incapacitated. To then escape from the hospital and willingly step into a dangerous location like this would be rightly seen as sheer madness.

"…Soujirou the Willow-Sword, I hate to say this, but you…"

Harghent had raced this far with Soujirou in a state of near delirium.

It was fair to say that they had each dragged each other here. Their connection was a strange one.

"You're not going to be any help at all coming in a state like that. Alus is flying. You can't even chase after him on the ground below. Erm, well...did you think about that at all?"

"Yup. I mean, yeah, you got a point."

Soujirou smiled while he sat on the ground.

"But hey. *He might swoop down close enough for me to cut 'im dead.* Could happen by accident, or Alus may come down and challenge me himself. See, me...I'd get real pissed if there was a party kicking off somewhere without me, and I looked back on it thinking that things *could've* ended up that way if I was lucky. That's all."

"That's it, huh?"

Harghent smiled feebly.

Coming all this way, just for that.

Harghent was aware he couldn't accomplish anything. He had come here knowing he'd be nothing but an unneeded, extraneous presence even if he did.

Even an abomination, completely detached from Harghent's reality, like Soujirou the Willow-Sword was just the same as Harghent after all.

In which case, there was no longer any need for him to hesitate. No matter who ridiculed him, he was going to face off against Alus.

"...Alus! Alus! Harghent's here!"

Harghent's shout, growing hoarse, was swallowed up by the sky.

Ahh. The sky's too vast.

Unlike Harghent, only able to crawl through the debris, Alus lived in such a vast open world, with so much freedom. What did Harghent need to do to catch up to him?

Was he in the shadow of that building? Was he, at that moment, busy flying off in a different direction?

If he had already departed from this district and flown off somewhere, there was no longer any means for Harghent to keep after him.

"Alus... *Hnaugh, ngh!*"

He awkwardly tumbled over.

It was his age. He had used up so much of his stamina and energy just getting this far.

Despite thinking from deep in his soul that he wanted to achieve something, nothing ever went how Harghent wanted it to, and he only ever showed this version of himself to the world, clumsily thrashing about.

"Alus, where are you?! Where...?"

His shouts, too, began to trail off, growing weaker.

It was ridiculous to think a single wyvern would be conveniently within the narrow patch of sky Harghent saw when he looked up.

Harghent possessed neither supernaturally powerful sight, nor godlike speed to instantly race through the city.

He wasn't a shura with the power to fight, but merely an aging man who had found his way into a disaster zone.

"I won't give up... If I give up here, I'll lose who I am. I'll catch up to you, Alus. That's what I came here to do...!"

When he encountered Alus again, he had made up his mind about what he was supposed to do.

It wasn't to ask for his forgiveness or to converse with him as a friend.

He would battle against Alus the Star Runner as his enemy.

If Alus's aim in annihilating Aureatia was to get revenge on Harghent, then by accepting all that resentment for himself and being cut down by the wyvern, this battle might come to an end.

If there was the slightest possibility created through exchanging an inconsequential life like Harghent's for a nation, then it was more than worth the price.

Thus, he would die.

If I died, I could escape from the shame and guilt. Right. Let's do that. I'm sure that dying...is much easier than I'm imagining it to be. Just by escaping down the easier path, I'll be able to carry out what I've decided to do.

It didn't matter how pathetic the idea was. He just needed to avoid any hesitation until he met with Alus.

If he could just meet him, Harghent could change his mind and plead for his life, and Alus would still take his life regardless of Harghent's intentions.

He understood that the gap in their strength was so big, it was laughable and presumptuous even to challenge Alus to battle in the first place.

"Harghent... Harghent is here! Alus...!"

Then a silhouette appeared, as if to answer his cries.

It was a black-clad man, shrouded in an ominous aura.

The man raised one hand slightly, showing a flaccid smile.

"Hey there, General Harghent. I was looking for you."

"Y-you're..."

There was one other hero candidate Harghent the Still had a connection with from the Lithia War.

Kuze the Passing Disaster. The Order's most powerful assassin.

"You were searching for me?"

"Sure was. Been decided that you're gonna have to die."

As well as the clearest and most evident incarnation of death in the land.

◆

Aureatia Central Assembly Hall, second communications room.

As a result of processing the tremendous amount of information constantly flowing in the midst of the extremely tense situation, the Aureatia bureaucrats' exhaustion was beginning to reach their limit.

Once they're pushed to the limit, everyone's going to start getting stupid.

Hidow could sense it in the chaos of the citizens and soldiers he heard through the radzio, as well.

It was just as true for him and the others directing them. He didn't have any confidence that the orders he gave in the radzio call a moment ago were truly the right decision or not.

While this showed just how little time he could spare on each thought he had, it was clear that his judgmental abilities were on the decline compared to normal.

Ending the call, he changed over to a different line and listened to a situation report.

He wasn't able to understand the situation on the ground just by listening to the account once, so he made them repeat it once more.

Ah, I remember now. In the era of the Demon King, everything was a mess. Engulfed in chaotic madness, everyone and everything became totally incomprehensible.

Back then, there was a wealth of anecdotes detailing inadequate directives that led to evacuating citizens straight in the direction of the Demon King's Army, or city soldiers massacring residents unprompted.

Each time, there would be a preposterous number of victims, in the tens to hundreds of thousands, and this came to be considered normal.

The radzio call finished, and he poured back the remaining half of the water in his cup. Lukewarm.

"...Ha. Is he an idiot? No one in their right mind would do something like this."

When it came to both the speed of his invasion and his exterminating power, Alus the Star Runner was a disaster that far surpassed that of the True Demon King, but despite this, casualties were being kept in check as much as Aureatia's strength could manage.

If this calamity had arrived during the era of the True Demon King, they wouldn't have gotten away with a mere ten thousand dead. Every single person would have likely met their end. Since back then, everyone had been a fool, pressed to their absolute limits.

"...Fool. That damn idiot," Hidow spat quietly, looking at a scrap of a report sitting on the edge of his desk.

The report had been submitted quite a long while ago at that point, but he hadn't found time until now to clear it from atop his desk.

—Sixth General Harghent the Still had escaped from Romog Joint Military Hospital.

"The True Demon King is dead, and you're still at your wit's end? So much time has passed..."

A completely hopeless man right through to the very end.

Even knowing he couldn't do anything, he still blindly charged onto a deadly battlefield.

Hidow knew that he was foolish enough to do such a thing. Harghent was definitely going to go, even if he had to be smeared with mud and crawl through the gutter to get there.

Steadying his breathing, intermingled with an exasperated chuckle, Hidow returned to the next radzio call and his next instructions.

Information on Harghent's movements was simply that inconsequential. However...

I'm going to kill hopeless utter fools like you, you hear me?

◆

"Alus the Star Runner's getting lured away by Shalk the Sound Slicer. Honestly don't know how long that'll last, though."

"...Is that so?"

The two were sitting down beside each other on debris of the city now turned to ruins.

Harghent the Still and Kuze the Passing Disaster.

He was a run-down and sullen man.

"Might be best...to fortify the airborne defenses in the Jikiegee

Mercantile District. If Horizon's Roar's air superiority is waning, then the easiest path for a wyvern to take to the royal palace is bound to pass through one spot in that district... Erm, so did Hidow say anything along those lines?"

"*Bweh-heh-heh.* Look, they only give me the bare minimum of what I need to know. Heck, I don't even know how to find Alus."

"......I see..."

The sky was blue.

The loud thunderclaps of Mele's arrows from a few moments ago had stopped, and the quiet made it seem like it had never happened at all.

However, somewhere in the second borough here, Alus was battling with Shalk, and the slightest tremor from the aftershocks would have been enough to blast away Harghent where he sat.

He could hear far off in the distance what sounded like an explosion and something collapsing.

Far away. Harghent unconsciously rose to his feet, but it was definitely not a distance he could hope to run on foot.

"W-well then."

Harghent asked, his voice cracking, "You're going...to kill me?"

"Pretty much. Also, there was something I had wanted to ask you once we met. See, I'm still technically a clergyman and all... I thought that if you had anything to confess, I'd hear you out."

"What do you want to ask?"

"About Curte of the Fair Skies."

Harghent gulped. The truth behind the sense of shame he felt toward Kuze was his guilt about his own actions during the Lithia War.

"R-right. I remember. That girl...she was a civilian. She shouldn't have been a casualty. If I was better put together...she could've come back from that tragedy and so much more..."

Curte had faced off against Harghent of her own volition.

She had formed a true bond with a wyvern, which was precisely why she tried fighting Harghent, who killed them. The white-haired young girl he saw that day seemed to be almost a mirror image of Harghent himself.

"I-if by any chance—"

"It's okay. Calm down."

"...Right. Excuse me. I've thought before that, if there had been some way to save her...then that would have been the right thing to do. She must have wanted to be happy. Curte, the citizens of Lithia, the Mage City soldiers...even all the wyvern fighters, too."

"I was the one at her side when she died... So you talked with the girl, did you?"

"Th-that's right. I...I killed her. That's what I've always...how I've always seen it..."

"Well, I...so this is just my own thinking here. But I think that girl chose her fate to go together with the wyverns. If she had chosen a path as a minia, then...she might've recovered and even still be alive, too. The thing is, no one's decided that's what happiness means or anything. Even the Wordmaker's never said anything about what's right between minia or wyverns."

Those who chose a minia's path didn't necessarily find happiness.

That was exactly it. Harghent had continued to battle as a minia, became a general, and yet this was how he had ended up.

"...I've always regretted it all. The whole time."

Was he talking about Curte's death or about the life he had led for himself? Likely both.

"I'm the same way, General Harghent."

Kuze's big hand touched Harghent's back.

"Hey. What d'ya think you're doing there?"

There came a voice from the opposite side of the collapsed alleyway.

Soujirou the Willow-Sword was looking their way, his sword hanging in one hand.

"Try anything stupid, and I'll slice that arm right off."

"...Sorry to say, but you're not able to kill me, Soujirou the Willow-Sword."

Harghent watched the exchange as if it didn't concern him in the slightest, but it took him a moment to recognize the hard, sharp sensation he felt on his back through his clothes.

A blade—most likely a kitchen knife he had picked up from the charred ruins—was being pressed into Harghent's back by Kuze.

This man had come to kill him.

"Let me go ahead and explain the situation. A little bit before I arrived, I got a notice from Hidow the Clamp."

"H-Hidow...?!"

"Told me, if Harghent managed to make it this far, to do him a favor and kill him."

"*Ha.* That's, well...*ha-ha.*"

Harghent couldn't help but laugh.

Too stunned even to fall to his knees, he cried as he laughed.

"I—I guess...*that makes sense.*"

An incompetent like him had been forsaken by Aureatia a long time ago.

Harghent's incompetence was so hopeless, it had driven the brilliant Hidow to hand down such an order. While driving the automobile here, he had continued to pointlessly ponder the meaning in coming to a place like this, but the problem was far more fundamental than that.

"R-right. *Ha-ha.* What a worthless life. I can't come up with anything to say back, even right before I'm killed. I—I never...had the right to find my resolve or choose my own path...from the very start..."

"...Cut the crap, you asshole," Soujirou said, irritated.

Even from this distance, he was likely capable of unleashing sword skills that could instantly end Kuze's life. However, they wouldn't reach him. Kuze the Passing Disaster's abilities were already common knowledge to a majority of the Twenty-Nine Officials.

The ability to immediately slay his enemy first, the instant he faced a risk of death.

Even Soujirou the Willow-Sword was sure to intuitively sense the threat Kuze posed.

Harghent, possessing nothing at all, had no way to avoid such a death.

"The fact you haven't come at me yet means that you can actually see your fate, can't you...Soujirou?"

Kuze placed his hand on his own left breast. He was terribly quiet, and ominous, like death itself.

"............"

"Harghent the Still. I know exactly how Curte of the Fair Skies died. There's one other thing I realized from that girl's final moments..."

"Alus..."

Harghent called his friend's name.

Kuze wasn't looking up at the sky. He hadn't noticed.

"That's right. There was no need to search. That's because Alus the Star Runner..."

Those wings, in the narrow patch of sky Harghent saw when he looked upward. A familiar three-armed silhouette.

The figure, tragically transformed entirely from who he once was, had his musket raised.

The mumble, as if whispered into the sky, rang loud and clear in Harghent's ears.

"...My friend..."

He went to pull the trigger.

Kuze the Passing Disaster looked up into the sky as if he understood how everything was going to end.

"...*will try to protect you.*"

A star fell.

I like to talk to minia.

That's why I made sure to talk to any of them I spotted who had strayed from their flock.

What sort of tools were being invented in minian towns? What sort of dungeon rumors were there, and what sort of people returned from them? What sort of magic items were used in recent wars and battles?

That was the sort of stuff I would ask them.

What I truly wanted to ask more than anything was what Harghent was currently up to, and how important he had gotten, but I didn't.

If my friendliness with Harghent got exposed, while it wouldn't bother me any, it would cause trouble for him. Since that wouldn't be fair, I tried not to do that as much as I could.

That was why when I first heard about Harghent after I began my journey, it made me really, really happy.

I think I heard his name come up as a commander of a wyvern subjugation squad somewhere along the border between the Northern Kingdom and the Central Kingdom. There were the names of three others, but I was so happy to hear Harghent's name pop up, I totally forgot about the other commanders' names.

Harghent was doing exactly what he told me he would do, after all.

Once I knew he was still giving it his all, I went out on more and more adventures of my own.

If Harghent was moving forward, then I had to grow, too, and catch up with him.

We didn't see each other for a long time, but I was always racing around to see new worlds to make sure I could boast about it all to him when we did.

The continent was far more vast than the map used by minia in the kingdoms I had seen.

I thought there was nothing beyond the four corners of the map, so this was like I was being told I could still fly out even farther, way beyond the horizon, with their own civilizations, dungeons, and treasures, too, and the excitement kept me awake for several days.

There were times I'd worry, too—since wyverns could be found anywhere, I thought Harghent might have been in these far-off places as well. And given that if he was, he'd be there to fight wyverns. It mean that Harghent might never show up to places where there weren't any of them at all.

My treasure stash grew more and more. I also defeated incredible enemies, whom I myself couldn't even believe I'd bested.

The occasions where I would skillfully use my treasure to obtain my next piece of treasure increased as well.

This was because I had trained in the seaside shack to grip pebbles in my hands.

It was thanks to Harghent that I became able to move my arms well.

...There were also occasionally years when I'd get really worried that Harghent might have died. In times like that, I'd often talk with minia who seemed to know a lot about anti-wyvern campaigns. I'd anxiously wait for his name to crop up, so that was probably when I most often brought up my own adventures to others.

But Harghent was always off fighting somewhere, even if it was unbeknownst to everyone else. He had been a kingdom soldier at one point, and there were other times he was fighting off in some land with a name I'd never heard of before.

Each time I heard this, it made me happy.

I was happy to hear that Harghent hadn't stopped his adventure.

I continued such adventures for several decades.

The treasure I had amassed to show off to Harghent had swelled to an innumerable amount.

Harghent really was an incredible guy, but he didn't do the sort of stuff I did, like defeating dragons, or conquering labyrinths and dungeons, which nearly proved fatal.

Harghent wasn't going to grow stronger than a dragon, and he even lost sometimes to other minia as well.

I had known all about that for a long time.

When I'd be talking and Harghent's name came up, there were some who would make fun of him for that sort of stuff, but I always wondered why they didn't praise him.

Harghent had continued advancing onward without stopping for several decades.

I had never heard about Harghent stopping his wyvern hunt while I was continuing my own journey, not even once.

The fact that he didn't stop his adventuring or fighting, become a normal minia whose name wasn't known to anyone, and give it all up for good was the most incredible thing of all.

So even when I met with Harghent again, I thought I'd try not to flaunt all the treasure I'd amassed on my adventures as much as possible.

Since I'm still a wyvern, I could never create anything on my own.

My treasure and my prestige were all stolen from someone else.

Someday when I met Harghent, I wanted to bring something I could really brag to him about.

Like how Horizon's Roar held Sine Riverstead so precious, something of my own.

It wasn't that Harghent started my adventure for me.

It wasn't that Harghent was my only friend.

No matter the terrible things someone may have said about him, I was always able to say it with total confidence—

Harghent was an incredible guy.

Unlike me, he never stole anything.

◆

Eastern Outer Ward, second borough.

Amid the bizarre stillness after the tempest of destruction halted, there were some who witnessed the conclusion.

Half of them were the Aureatia soldiers under Sabfom's command who had been engaged in rescuing civilians. The remaining half were the residents they had saved from the gaps between houses and canals.

Unlike the back-and-forth clash from earlier, Star Runner had appeared at lower altitudes, visible to many of the residents.

Then, without any warning, he crashed down.

The din of destruction, of battle, showed no signs of continuing.

"Alus, he's...," one of the Aureatia soldiers said.

"Who felled him?"

"A wyvern. That must've been Alus."

"It wasn't from that light attack that was flying around a few moments ago?"

Each one was a quiet murmur, but in the townscape, now silent after being entirely consumed in flames, their voices resounded far.

Harghent the Still and Kuze the Passing Disaster heard this commotion as well.

"Alus! Alus! Wait for me...!"

Escaping Kuze's grasp, Harghent ran with tottering steps.

Forward ahead. To where Alus fell to the ground.

"...There's no point in trying," Kuze murmured as he watched the small figure depart.

No matter how invincible Alus the Star Runner's body may

have become, there was only one fate for those stabbed by Death's Fang.

"He's going to die."

He hadn't any had intention of killing Harghent from the beginning.

The brief pantomime was a tactic dictated to him by Hidow.

He had made use of the most unnecessary piece on the battle-field, Harghent, to take down the strongest of all adventurers.

Kuze looked up to the heavens. A fair afternoon sky.

Both Curte and Alus had hearts that cared for someone of a completely different species.

Which was why they had lost.

"*Bweh-heh-heh.*"

Beginning to walk off toward where Alus had crash-landed, Kuze then turned back around to look at the other side of the road.

Soujirou was still lingering there.

"You're not gonna go after him?"

"Nah. From here…"

His sword was sheathed. There wasn't any life here that he was supposed to cut down.

"From here, the rest's up to Old Man Harghent."

◆

He nearly tripped over himself as he ran.

To the spot where Alus had fallen.

The place could no longer be described as a "building."

It was some mass of stacked debris, collapsing in the blaze, piled up in a heap.

The metal staircase leaning diagonally must have been a vestige of the construction that had once stood.

"I'm coming...!"

Harghent forcibly continued forward as he put his foot through the now brittle staircase.

Falling over so much that he wasn't even sure if he could stand again, he grabbed the rubble with his hand and crawled his way up the hill.

Blood seeped from the fresh wounds all over his body. He didn't even know where or how he had gotten any of them, so numerous were his awkward trips and falls.

It was as if they were representing Harghent's life itself.

Recklessly jumping forward, fighting haphazardly, he was beginning to lose sight of his goal; and by the time he saw his friend's back, he had used up absolutely everything, leaving himself completely exhausted.

"Alus...I, *haah*, I... Alus... We haven't settled..."

He had continued fighting for over forty years.

The child who told a deformed wyvern about his ambitions that fateful day was now an old man.

He lost his breath every time he ran, and his knee joints had hurt him from long before he even sortied from the hospital.

Each time he took a step up the rubble, it felt like his heart was going to give out.

He hadn't even been able to become the madman he was supposed to be.

Which was why he couldn't move on while ignoring the intense pain he was in.

He had never once been able to mentally maintain control over his physical body.

However.

He couldn't break. He couldn't stop.

Because he was sure it had been far more than this.

The journey the strongest rogue of all had raced through had included far more hardship than what he was experiencing now.

"Hah…hah… *Hargent io kouto.*" (From Harghent to Aureatia steel.)

He had gone on a long journey himself. A journey to catch up to his only wyvern friend whom he could never possibly reach.

The sixth wyvern cleanup campaign. The eighth wyvern cleanup campaign. The twenty-second wyvern cleanup campaign.

Like the champions who had been defeated throughout history, he had even challenged Vikeon the Smoldering.

He had confronted Lucnoca the Winter, whom no one had ever seen before, and made her acknowledge his proposal.

Praise me.

Someone, say that I did a good job.

"*Haml nanta. Sainmec.*" (Approaching waves. Tower of shadow.)

He incanted fragmented Craft Arts with breaths nearly lacking any oxygen.

Twisting the staircase iron, he began to create a colossal crossbow.

A weapon for battle. That was what he had come here for and nothing else.

"Meaoi nam tell! Laivoine!" (Revolving firmament! Nock this arrow!)

He was Aureatia's Sixth General. His second name was Harghent the Still.

His Craft Arts wove together a mounted mechanical bow, its mass on par with a carriage.

It had a name, as well.

The sort of name a child would come up with, shameless and far grander than it deserved.

Dragon Slayer.

"Alus. You... This time, I've come to kill you for good... Alus..."

"......"

Alus the Star Runner lay at the top of the rubble.

The strongest adventurer of all, who had traversed across all legends and grabbed all imaginable glory in his own hands.

A champion who'd carried out his sole selfhood to whatever lengths, even slaying dragons in the process.

He had lost all the treasure he had amassed.

His enchanted swords had been taken to hell.

Both Ground Runner and Rotting Soil Sun were lost.

He had dropped the musket he carried until the end, and the Greatshield of the Dead, and even Chiklorakk the Eternity Machine, now fused with his body, were unable to preserve his fading life.

Defeated, and lying nearly covered by rubble, that life was beginning to run out.

"You're..."

"Incredible" was what he wanted to say.

When Harghent had first met him, he wasn't even able to move his third arm.

He hadn't seemed capable of learning proper language, either.

Harghent had belittled him, thinking he probably wouldn't last long.

He hadn't thought that they'd be able to become friends.

That same three-armed wyvern had done all of this.

Alus the Star Runner had become a mighty champion known to everyone throughout the land.

The true story, much bigger than anything else he had accomplished, was known only to Harghent.

"...Harghent."

"D-don't die."

That wasn't it. That was unnecessary.

That wasn't what he had come all this way to say.

"I... Thinking back...about Toroa the Awful..."

Right now, Alus had nothing.

He was losing the memories of his glory and his very ego.

"Why didn't he finish me off...? Maybe he understood...what I wanted."

"Can you hear me? Alus...Alus!"

What had Alus the Star Runner wanted?

Harghent had known the answer from the start.

He desperately yelled to make sure Alus could hear him from the grips of death.

"Alus... You're...awesome! It's true! I've always thought so! There weren't any other wyverns like you! You were strong, faster than any one of them...stronger..."

These childish words were the only ones that came to Harghent.

He had thought Alus was incredible.

Just like Alus would always laud Harghent with praise no matter what, the truth was Harghent wanted to acknowledge Alus and praise him, too.

"You're...you're the most incredible guy in the world! Alus!"

"...Really?"

Alus tried to raise up his arm.

He didn't have any strength left. He didn't have a single weapon on him.

However, Harghent knew what he wanted to do.

Alus was trying to aim his gun.

Until the very end, the moment his life was exhausted.

He was trying to duel a foolish, stunted minia who had never seized any glory of his own.

"I...did nothing but...steal, however..."

It doesn't make me happy at all to get complimented by a wyvern like you!

That was all a lie.

It had made him the happiest of all.

"...Now I'm finally...able to give back..."

"Sniff... Hngaaaaaugh!"

Harghent loosed the projectile.

The massive arrow pierced through Alus's skull, and with it, Wing-Plucker killed the lone wyvern.

◆

His strength began to drain from him, but he couldn't let himself collapse.

He understood what he needed to do.

Harghent the Still staggered as he walked to Alus the Star Runner's carcass.

Then he looked down below him from atop the rubble.

There was ruined city. Residents menaced by fear.

The citizens who got left behind. The soldiers who went through the do-or-die battle. They were waiting for him to speak.

"Al...Alus. Alus the Star Runner! Has just been slain!"

A wave of whispers spread through the silence.

"W-we are—"

There wasn't a single person among them who was expecting Harghent the Still to achieve something.

He was an outdated, powerless military officer who never once paid any heed to the people, fully absorbed in his own self-preservation.

He had never once seized true glory for himself.

"We are victorious! N-no longer...will you all be threatened by this self-proclaimed demon king! The citizens who endured, the soldiers who supported them...have conquered this terror! Here is the proof! I, Sixth General, Harghent the Still! Proclaim that Alus the Star Runner has been put down!"

To ensure that everyone there could see—to convey a conclusion to a bitter struggle.

A new champion held aloft his friend's pitiful corpse.

"He's...he's dead!"

"It's over! General Harghent got him!"

"I saw it for myself, Harghent!"

"Lord Harghent!"

"Ahhh... I can finally go home!"

"Harghent!"

"Harghent!"

"General Harghent!"

"Sixth General Harghent!"

Among the cheers of the citizens extolling his grand achievement, Harghent crouched down.

I'll become a hero.

Praised and recognized by so many more people, not just the people of the village.

"Sniff... Nhauuugh...!"

Two hundred and nineteen dead or missing. Seven hundred and forty injured.

The second to fifth boroughs of the Eastern Outer Ward annihilated.

The battle Aureatia had dedicated all its efforts to, against a self-proclaimed demon king, was over.

Cheers could be heard in the city of rubble.

From the direction where Alus the Star Runner had fallen, on the opposite bank of the river.

"…If you've got something to say, make it quick."

Shouldering his white spear, Shalk spoke with a fed-up tone.

He spoke to the figure who had appeared behind him.

"I don't have time to hang around until Star Runner is finished off, see."

"Alus has already been killed. You know that, don't you? Aureatia…probably used Kuze the Passing Disaster to do him in."

It was man with a camera dangling from his neck. Yukiharu the Twilight Diver.

He was probably right, Shalk thought. Soujirou the Willow-Sword and Kuze the Passing Disaster were there on the scene.

To Shalk, it was a horribly bad joke. Now fighting on a combined front with them, Shalk wanted to avoid seeing them as much as possible.

"Coming out to a place like this must mean you've got something to talk about that you really don't want anyone else to hear."

"Oh, no, no. In fact, quickly arriving on a scene like this is, if anything, because of my main occupation. Aureatia cooperated with me, so I thought I'd try getting some interesting reporting done."

"Don't decide on what you cover based just on whether you find it interesting or not."

"Well, I can't help it if the truth ends up being interesting, now can I? Putting that aside, have you reconsidered the commission I spoke of before, Shalk?"

"Nope. Why don't you tell me how I stand to benefit from it."

The Gray-Haired Child was trying to utilize Shalk the Sound Slicer to undergo an investigation into the vampires that had infiltrated Aureatia. They were likely contriving a way that would ensure Shalk went down in the process, too, in case their enemy possessed fighting strength of their own.

Getting wrapped up in this sort of conflict between major players basically never ended well.

Moreover, Yukiharu had said he would provide information on the True Hero as collateral, but—

"The Hero is Uhak the Silent."

"What?"

Even Shalk couldn't help being taken aback by the unexpected statement.

Was that really the sort of information that should be blurted out like it was relaxed chitchat between friends?

"...No, seriously, what?"

"We've learned the identity of the True Hero. As you are aware,

Shalk, in the eighth match, Zigita Zogi was killed, and Uhak the Silent advanced. In other words…"

Yukiharu's eyes narrowed behind his round glasses when he spoke.

Shalk knew the times when an information broker readily gave away their information for free.

It was when, by learning something, their client would then *seek even more information*.

"In your next match, you're going to be fighting against the Hero."

◆

In front of the castle garden theater.

It was a vast empty space. The plaza that was always overflowing with people during the day, with all manner of street stalls lined up, was now, with all the citizens evacuated, controlled by a deathly silence.

There was a group going through the middle of it. Goblins.

The minia walking near the center looked like a child, but his almost-white gray hair left a mature impression at odds with his facial features.

"Zigita Zogi definitely doesn't do anything useless or unproductive," Hiroto the Paradox said to the bald man walking next to him.

Aureatia's Twenty-Fourth General, Dant the Heath Furrow. He had been the sponsor for the defeated Zigita Zogi.

"He must have thought that using the eighth match to *bring awareness* to the spread of corpses in Aureatia was an indispensable move to claim victory over Obsidian Eyes, and he enacted a plan. While I'm sure he didn't fight with the intention of losing, it would be reasonable to believe he thought, in the worst-case scenario…even if he lost and died, that itself would prove the vampire's existence."

"…That's true. From here on out, Okafu and Aureatia will now be able to cooperate in dealing with Obsidian Eyes. But what about after that? There isn't anyone in our camp with a mind that can equal Zigita Zogi's. No one who understood the operation he was advancing and can take it over, nor is there anyone capable of making new deals that will overturn the current power relationships. Now that my candidate's been defeated, I'll be in a difficult position politically, too."

"We'll deploy Morio the Sentinel."

"Wha—?!"

Dant was at a loss for words.

Morio the Sentinel. The visitor leading the Free City of Okafu who had long been in an adversarial relationship with Aureatia.

Deploying this man carried a far greater meaning behind it than getting Aureatia to allow goblins from the new continent and a selection of Okafu mercenaries into their borders.

…*No. He can't possibly be planning on starting an open war with Aureatia, can he?*

Not only that, but all of this while in their current situation, having just lost the world's strongest tactician.

Hiroto wouldn't do something that reckless. While it was certainly impossible to get a read on Hiroto the Paradox's real intentions, he was a levelheaded man who operated logically.

"It's okay. I've lost comrades before, but I've never broken a public promise," Hiroto said, a faint smile coming to his face. "I'm sure things will get *better*."

◆

Eastern Outer Ward, fifth borough.

In this area, submerged in a sea of mud after the conflagration, there were sixteen bodies pulled up from this hopeless state of affairs, yet unbelievably, ten of them had managed to escape death.

"...W-wow." Looking at the wounded's perfectly stitched-up scars, Qwell the Wax Flower muttered quietly.

Ozonezma the Capricious, rushing over to this area together with her and Flinsuda's medical squad, had pulled up individuals needing rescue one after another without any hesitation whatsoever. Establishing the treatment priority, in addition to his brilliant and precise surgical methods, he worked with a mercilessness to immediately adapt the skin and organs of the dead for the survivors and transfer them over, to save as many lives on the scene as he could.

His countless arms, which had concurrently dealt with processes numbering in the hundreds, were now all shut away inside the beast's body.

"THERE WILL BE AFTEREFFECTS IN THEIR RIGHT ARM. HOWEVER, I HAVE RECONSTRUCTED THE AREA WHERE THE BURNS REACHED THE TENDONS AS MUCH AS POSSIBLE. WHEN INCLUDING THE OTHER PATIENTS, I WILL

NEED A LARGE SUPPLY OF ANTIBIOTICS. WE CANNOT LET OUR GUARD DOWN."

"Wh-when…when this person was raised up, I thought, for sure that…that they couldn't be saved. Why did you know WHERE in the mud people were submerged?"

"I DO NOT HAVE ANY SUPERNATURAL ABILITIES OF PERCEPTION LIKE WILLOW-SWORD. I SIMPLY LISTENED FOR THE ECHOES INSIDE THE MUD—WITH TRAINING, THERE ARE EVEN MINIA WHO CAN DO THE SAME."

As he answered, Ozonezma was stepping into the deepest part of the mud sea, in the heart of the town around it.

It must have already been too deep for his legs to reach the bottom.

"Wh-where are you going? Um… They said this was the last person who needed rescue…"

"I KNOW. THERE IS ONE OTHER PERSON I *PUT OFF SAVING FOR LATER*."

"What…?! U-um! Th-there's no way anyone would survive in there! Wh-why…why couldn't you treat them immediately?!"

"YOU'LL UNDERSTAND SOON."

With his short reply, his wolflike head submerged down below the mud's surface.

The almost imperceptibly small air bubbles floated up in longer intervals. It was an operation they had repeated many times since they had arrived in the district. Freely swimming through the sea of mud, far more resistant than regular water, and with his sights obscured, Ozonezma had accurately reached where survivors were located and rescued them.

Ozonezma was a medic with not only atypical medical techniques but also first-rate search and rescue abilities.

At long last, Ozonezma's face surfaced.

He carried a young woman's naked body in his mouth. A beautiful and clean body, completely unlike the casualties Qwell had seen up until that point.

Ozonezma tossed the young girl a bit roughly on dry land before saying, "ESCAPE ON YOUR OWN NEXT TIME."

She was a beautiful girl. She had a long chestnut braid and lifted her eyelids to reveal green eyes beneath.

"*Tee-hee-hee.* It sorta took me a while to chat with *this thing.*"

The young girl—Tu the Magic—carried a sphere resembling a mass of mud close to her chest.

The name of the magic item previously belonging to Alus the Star Runner was Rotting Soil Sun.

"WAIT, DID YOU REALLY SUCCEED IN GAINING CONTROL OVER THAT MAGIC ITEM?"

"...Yup. It's fine now."

Ozonezma wasn't the only one in this district saving people's lives.

There was a champion who kept the overflowing mud in check and prevented the damage from spreading any further.

"I thought for sure that you'd come for me, Ozonezma."

"...I AM YOUR *BIG BROTHER*, AFTER ALL."

Far off to the west of Aureatia—Igania Ice Lake.

Naturally, for the inhabitant living here, there was no reason to know anything about the crisis facing Aureatia from Alus the Star Runner's attack.

However, this being, in a certain sense, was situated at the core of this series of disasters, more than any other.

...Normally, dreams were the only thing I had to enjoy.

There was a colossal mass that seemed to melt into the shining, mirrorlike ice field.

It was no mass of ice. It was a beautiful white dragon.

However, there was a spoiled section of this almost mythical perfection.

Her tail was severed halfway down, and her white dragon scales had been greatly gouged out from her neck area.

But another battle so much more wonderful than any dream is right around the corner.

With the immense fires of war Alus had wrought, there was likely none who would soon forget her name.

In this world remained a being who had battled against Alus the Star Runner on her own and had made him fall from the skies.

And she was anxiously looking forward to an even more tremendous battle.

Lucnoca the Winter.

The war against the enemies of peace, called shura, was not yet over.

◆

Ten days passed.

That day, the Aureatia Assembly had gathered citizens to the castle garden theater to make a public statement regarding Alus the Star Runner's invasion. Although the atrocity and breadth of the incident were well known among most of Aureatia's citizens, this would be the first proclamation regarding future policy based on the event.

More than anything else, the focus was on the continuation of the Sixways Exhibition.

Would this great enterprise, with the kingdom's dignity on the line, actually endure?

Perhaps because of the silence that accompanied this tension, there was a strained, solemn atmosphere across the arena.

On top of the altar set up in the center stood Aureatia's Third Minister, Jelky the Swift Ink.

"…We have been dealt a heavy blow."

His voice was clear and distinct, stiff but traveling far.

The castle garden theater was a place that symbolized Aureatia's history, continuing from its time as the Central Kingdom.

Proclamations made inside it were said to hold power equal to the words of the monarch.

"I express my condolences and sympathies to the citizens who fell victim to this series of disasters. I acknowledge that rebuilding our daily lives and compensating the families of the deceased are the duties of the entire Aureatia Assembly, and I swear that we will put forth every effort to do so."

A special budget to compensate for losses. As well as substitute homes for the destroyed city.

The various provisions, starting with these, had been already prepared from the opening of the Sixways Exhibition.

From the beginning, this battle wasn't one that would end without sacrifices. Jel had already established the finances needed for immediate compensation, as long as the sacrifices were within the projected scope.

If any cog in the process had gone awry in the slightest, even these estimations would have easily crumbled away. This time, they had merely managed to avoid it happening by some miracle and nothing more. Jel understood that.

The sixteen hero candidates who had gathered at this place. They were all heroes, and also demon kings.

The power to save Aureatia was simultaneously a power that could annihilate it.

"...Nevertheless, there is something I would like to declare to you all now. Despite suffering the largest-scale attack by a self-proclaimed demon king this country has ever known—we were able to secure victory against Alus the Star Runner. Every single one of us...including you, the people...put forth our best efforts to handle this calamity. You all are here, able to listen to me make this proclamation. That serves as the clearest evidence that we have come out of this triumphant."

An uncontrolled cheer rose up in the middle of the audience.

As if to send a cold breeze over the signs of wild enthusiasm, Jel spoke.

"There is one other thing—I want to shed light on a fact that you all may fear."

There was a considerable problem concerning the continuation of the Sixways Exhibition. Alus the Star Runner was *a hero candidate*.

Although he had already been defeated, if the perception spread that Alus had attacked Aureatia of his own volition, then there was the possibility that the Aureatia citizenry would start to regard the hero candidates themselves as latent threats.

That was, in fact, the truth. The Sixways Exhibition was to ensure that they were annihilated.

However, it was a truth that *couldn't be allowed to be recognized properly*.

"There are perhaps some among you who were examined en masse at the evacuation areas. These examinations were testing for corpse infections—directly following the end of the first round of matches, we were able to secure a large number of corpses in a severe state of infection. Additionally, from our autopsy of the body, we have determined that Alus the Star Runner's rampage was *caused by a vampire*. In order to identify and eradicate this vampire threat, I once again ask the citizens to unite together and cooperate. Just as the hero candidates exert themselves to their limits, I would like to ask each and every one of you to provide some of your own effort to this cause."

Jelky bowed his head low.

Through this series of disasters, a fear had surely been engraved in the hearts and minds of the citizens of Aureatia.

This wasn't the terror of the now-gone True Demon King. It was a terror right there in front of them.

That a *new something* could potentially threaten them once again.

That was exactly why they were necessary.

"Right now in Aureatia, there is a hero."

It may have been nothing more than a vague, undefined premonition.

Yet that was the very deeply felt motivation that made them continue to seek a hero.

The form of madness had been engrained in them by the True Demon King.

At this point, everyone was clearly cognizant of the fact.

Something would arrive next. Something to threaten the future.

And surely the hero was the only one capable of defeating that terror.

"I would like to make this clear. As a result of the hero candidate's brave struggle, Sixth General Harghent slew Alus the Star Runner. They were gathered here due to the Sixways Exhibition—if they hadn't been here in this moment, we would not have possessed any means to confront Alus the Star Runner or this vampire menace."

For that purpose, they would make as many sacrifices as they could.

For the sake of this goal, they would make as many sacrifices as they could afford.

There was enough value in finding them, even if it meant going to such lengths.

"I, Third Minister Jelky, once again make a promise to you here! The combined eight candidates, who won and advanced through the first round of this Sixways Exhibition! I guarantee that the hero exists among them! That they are the necessary light that will dispel the fear of this age and clear away a path into a new world!"

They all needed a hero.

Not only the citizens. The Twenty-Nine Officials leading the people, even Jel himself, wanted one as well.

They wanted to sweep away the terror that never cleared.

Whether it was real or fake, they wanted to believe there was one ultimate strength.

If they didn't entrust their wish to someone else, things would surely never be able to return to normal.

The path guiding their hearts, the courage to stand up again—

It was all to create a singular symbol.

They did indeed exist.

"Thus, I will declare here and now."

There existed a Grappler who had mastered the extensive martial arts of another world, reaching the farthest ends of infinity.

There existed a Silencer who embodied death and despair, strongest of all and standing apart.

There existed a Blade who commanded complete control over the destiny of his sword, abnormal in the land of the deviant.

There existed a Knight, perfect and almighty, the blessing and curse of absolute unconquerability focused onto himself.

There existed a Stabber arriving from the realm beyond perception, a singularity given authority over death.

There existed a Scout who laid out a web of unextractable schemes, overturning decided outcomes.

There existed a Spearhead, able to deliver a single attack that surpassed the speed of perception, from any possible location.

There existed an Oracle who eliminated all impossibilities in the realm and projected nihility over the present world.

"It will resume."

The true duel battle to decide a single winner.

"It will continue! We shall continue with the Sixways Exhibition!"

No matter how cruel and tragic the conclusion that may ultimately arrive...

The fate of all had begun to move, and no one was able to make it stop.

With it, a new battle was beginning.

Afterword

Hello again. Keiso here. Thank you very much for reading the latest volume of *Ishura*. I believe the fifth volume went on sale in September of last year, so there's been about a ten-month gap between volumes. I very much apologize for keeping you waiting so long. The story in Volume 6 is the climactic conclusion to the first round of the Sixways Exhibition, and with it being about a battle outside the arena, a lot of the main shura appeared at once, and I had too many things I wanted to add on…so with these various elements all mixed together, this volume turned into what is likely the longest volume I've written. In regard to this clumsiness on your author Keiso's part, I hope you'll see the wonderful job Kureta-sensei has done on the illustrations in this volume, as always, and forgive me.

Also, as of this volume, my editor, Nagahori, who has been looking after me from the very start of the *Ishura* series, was transferred to a different department and removed from managing this series. Nagahori has a mind for battle and scheming on par with me, the author, and was truly very well suited to working on *Ishura*, always making sure there were no contradictions in the characters' thinking or ensuring there were enough moments of battle to serve as ups and downs in the plot. I wanted to use this space to express my gratitude once again for the two and half years of help. Thank you.

There is a delicious pasta dish that I would absolutely love for Nagahori to try. Up until now, the menu options have all sought simplicity when it came to prep and cleanup, but for this special occasion, I'd like to outline a slightly better pasta recipe to bring out when it really counts. I call it the Nagahori Special.

This is an extremely important step, but before you begin your prep, make sure you have plenty of ice in your freezer. Once you begin cooking, you definitely won't be able to get this ice ready...

Once you begin boiling your pasta in a microwave pasta cooker, first, crush a single cube's worth of consommé. I imagine it'll be rigid and impossible to fully pulverize, but there's no real need to whittle it down with a grater. You'll just have more dishes to wash. Put the cube on a microwave-safe plate, and if you wet it with a tiny bit of water and microwave it for about thirty seconds, it'll make it easier to smash up. For those of you who already have powdered consommé, you just need to measure out five grams of it, making it much easier.

Next, heat up garlic in about a tablespoon's worth of olive oil. In my case, whenever I specify garlic, I am never referring to raw garlic, but the glass bottles of minced garlic. This is much more convenient than totally normal garlic, and not only is it possible to preserve, but there's also no need to mince or grate it yourself, and it's seasoned from the start to be compatible with pretty much any type of cooking, so unless you are quite picky about your garlic, it's much more convenient to have this on hand. Incidentally, you heat up this minced garlic until it's golden brown, but you could actually just take it from this point, toss however much you like over some raw veggies, and turn it into salad dressing. I encourage you to give it a try.

Now, once the garlic's cooked, turn off the heat, and thoroughly dissolve the broken-up consommé in the olive oil that cooked the garlic, and let it cool down. While that is happening, it's time to cut up the ingredients you'll be adding into it.

First, you'll use half of an apple. Cut this down even farther into a quarter, then cut one fragment into cubes and the other into thin slices. If that's a bit troublesome, though, you could thinly slice them both or dice them both; it doesn't matter. I also peel off the skin, but if that's a pain, feel free not to.

From there, cut the mozzarella that they sell in the supermarket into bite-size pieces. There's the other version of mozzarella that's already prepared to be put on pizza, but this time we'll be using fresh mozzarella, the type that's submerged in water. You can get away with just a third of the mozzarella you normally find on the shelves, but feel free to add as much as you like.

Then, take the cut-up apple and mozzarella, put them in a bowl along with the garlic oil you dissolved the consommé in, throw in three to four ice cubes, mix in a teaspoon of lemon juice, and it's finished.

I believe the pasta in the microwave will finish cooking while you're doing all of this, but rinse the boiled pasta in cold water to cool it, add in all the leftover ice you didn't put in the bowl, and basically get it as freezing cold as possible.

Add the pasta to the bowl, mix it well, and then sprinkle it with as many hand-torn leaves of arugula or basil as you would like, and the Nagahori Special is finished.

I imagine there might be some of you reading this who question if the flavor of apples goes well with consommé and garlic-seasoned cold pasta, but I am very proud of this tasty dish, as it allows you to savor the fragrance of the olive oil and garlic through the sweet and acidic taste of the apple, and it's a dish I'd like to make every week if my financial situation allowed me to buy fresh mozzarella whenever I wanted.

If the name of this pasta dish ends up being passed on through the ages, then I'm sure *Ishura*'s original editor, Nagahori, will be called the modern-day Earl of Sandwich! I would love it if my readers were to give this recipe a try in their own homes.

Furthermore, this volume of *Ishura*, like all the ones before it, is a product that has arrived in your hands thanks to the help of many people throughout the process, from proofreading and book binding to distribution, marketing, and more. Although my editor is the only person I interact with directly, every person across the entire process has done their absolute best, and I'm certain their contributions were just as extraordinary as my editor's. It wouldn't be too much of a stretch to say that the Nagahori Special, to all these individuals, may as well be called the [Insert Name Here] Special. Please do refer to it as such, and consider it a reward for your hard work.

Though I ended up saving this until the end, I already owe a great deal to Nagahori's successor and my new editor, Satou, for helping me with the cover illustration and the revision back and forth...! I believe the seventh volume onward will be when I begin giving them trouble in earnest (?), but they are another editor with strong feelings for the *Ishura* series, and at some point, I'd like to create a Satou Special for them, too. To all of you readers as well, I hope that you'll keep watch over *Ishura* and the great efforts of the editors overseeing it.